M000159758

SLAYING *the* FROST KING

CANDACE ROBINSON
ELLE BEAUMONT

This story is for the odd ones and the never fit in anywhere ones.
You were born to rule.

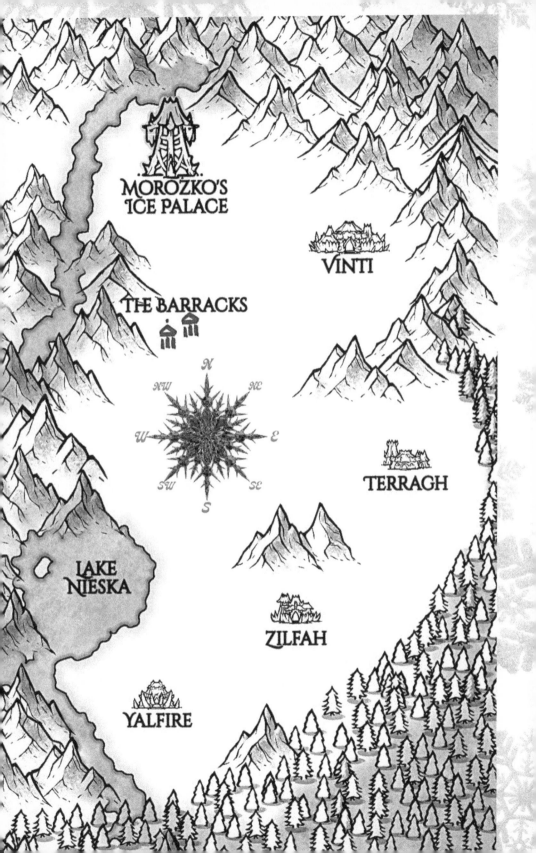

I

MOROZKO

S now fell onto the cobblestones in the castle's courtyard, painting the picture of serenity—or at least it would have—had it not been for the writhing body beneath Morozko's boot.

Whimpers escaped from the mortal, and he clawed at the ice, chipping away his nails in a futile attempt to escape the king.

The wind in the mountains whipped through Morozko's hair, catching on his nose. "Stop moving. You're sullying the ground with your blood." Morozko frowned, motioning to the flecks of red soaking through the snowdrifts. Soon enough, the mortal would cease moving—he was, after all, a treasonous wretch.

Not only had he been milling around the castle, which was forbidden unless summoned, but he—and the entire village of Vinti—had chosen not to hold a ceremony that had taken place for centuries. It was not only Morozko's honor at stake but so much more. Certainly, the villagers thought it wise to continue celebrating but somehow forgot the most significant part of the ceremony: the animal sacrifice.

Oh, but Vinti believed themselves clever by dancing around their bonfire, drinking, and partaking in food meant to celebrate the animal's spilled blood. They not only slighted and mocked him but Frosteria as well.

The Frost King would remedy that.

How fortunate Morozko was to send an emissary to witness it all, and said emissary was accompanied by the captain of the royal guard, Andras.

Andras had done well by capturing the flailing man, bringing the mortal to Morozko for him to question and, if he felt so inclined, torture.

Morozko increased the pressure of his boot, and the human's life spilled further from a gash on his side. The flesh peeled away, revealing muscle and bone. "I—I told the captain," the male coughed, "it was the chieftain's decision to pass on the sacrifice. Not all of us wanted to displease you so. But we lost a lot of our livestock in the past storm." His body convulsed. "Please, sire, please. We only thought—"

"That is just it, mortal. You didn't think at all. None of you did. You could have easily cast one of your own on the slab instead of an animal and have been done with it." Removing his foot from the man, Morozko turned away and stepped toward the captain of the guard. The frost demon's crimson hair danced in the wind, and Andras didn't so much as blink as Morozko pulled the captain's sword free.

"But Vinti couldn't even do that. The village will pay, starting with you." Morozko narrowed his eyes as fury rose within.

All Morozko had asked once they had slain his mother was to hold a ceremony—a ritual—where they would sacrifice an animal on an altar, allowing the blood to saturate the ground, and speak the words she demanded of them. *Let this blood sate you. Let this blood please you. It is freely given in remembrance of your life.* Leave it to Maranna to want praise even in death. He snorted.

Morozko's mother had been a cruel and unfair ruler, which was why she was overthrown and murdered by the mortals. If it hadn't been for her foresight to hide Morozko in an ice cavern, he likely would have been slain, too. But his guards took pity on him, protected him, and assured the masses Morozko was different, and in some ways, he was.

The mortal slapped his hand at the ground, pulling himself to his feet, and swayed. "Have mercy, Your Majesty, I beg of you."

Morozko looked into the eyes of the captain, who watched the futile attempt to escape. He shrugged one shoulder and sucked in his bottom lip, then spun on his heel, throwing the sword. It flew hilt over tip until it met its mark in the villager's back with a sickening squelch. The man fell to the ice at once, twitching until he moved no more.

"A pity your blood is a waste and couldn't save someone else." Alas, his body wasn't on an altar, nor were the sacrificial words spoken. Morozko's lip curled in disgust as he turned away. "Sever his hand. Make sure Vinti receives their gift of *gratitude,* with the explicit instructions that they're to hold a ceremony in a week's time. Oh... and clean up this damn mess." When Morozko stepped away from the captain, strands of his white hair fell into his view. Crimson marred his pristine tresses. He scowled, wiping at his face, which also had flecks of blood. What a mess the mortal had made. Sighing, he walked toward the entrance of the castle, and two guards opened the massive ebony doors.

"Missives have arrived and are in your study, Your Majesty." Ulva, one of his servants, bobbed a quick curtsy before disappearing down the long, winding hallway.

Letters from peasants in the villages, or perhaps noblemen trying to pawn their daughter off on him, swearing her hair was a fine shade of gold. He was not in want of a wife, but a plaything. He was always in need of one of *those*.

Morozko's boots fell heavily on the marble flooring, echoing off the walls. Even the promise of a warm body against his wasn't enough to distract him. The foolish mortals didn't have any knowledge as to *why* the sacrifices needed to continue.

He frowned. His steward, Xezu, was nowhere in sight. There were matters to address, a *celebration* to prepare for. Where was he?

Not having the mortal in his reach gave him time to consider the refusal. More than his pride was at stake. Unrest lapped at Morozko's patience, akin to a dam readying to burst. The mortals did not know what they'd done. Their world as they knew it could crumble with just this one minor misstep.

He gritted his teeth, scanning the foyer and the grand staircase. Xezu was still nowhere to be found. "Where is that mortal?" he growled, flinging his cape back lest it tangle in front of him.

Morozko didn't want to think of his mother or the curse she'd laid on the land. The queen had protected him from outside evils, but that didn't mean he was safe from *her*. There was a definite lack of maternal instinct.

Morozko never knew his father. In fact, his father hadn't lived long past Morozko's conception because Maranna had driven a blade of ice through his heart. It was something she'd gloated about.

To Maranna, her son was another subject, another pawn that was of use to her. A means to continue her line and ensure her rule.

Her death hadn't struck him in the heart, but it *had* made his blood boil because the humans had thought to rise against their superiors—their prince.

"Xezu!" he bellowed for his steward.

The middle-aged human male rounded a corner. His long, dark hair was neatly braided and fell over his shoulder as he bowed at the waist. Soft lines crinkled the corners of his eyes, but his sun-kissed face was otherwise smooth. "Your Majesty."

The steward of Frosteria sullied his hands, so Morozko didn't have to, but that didn't mean the king wouldn't. The proof of that was in his hair and on his fingers. But Xezu was his second in-command and when the king needed him, the mortal did whatever was asked of him.

"Unfortunately, the mortals have thought themselves clever and didn't perform the ritual." He sauntered toward Xezu, sneering. "And you know what that means." A flicker of surprise—and possibly fear—entered his steward's gaze. Morozko was anything but gleeful, but he didn't want to show the uptick of panic within. Of how the *others* would knock at the seal that his darling mother loosened. Morozko could almost hear the claws scraping at the magical seal, the high-pitched keening...

"But that means..."

His steward knew the truth. Once a villager himself, Xezu was oblivious to the reason behind it. Now, in Morozko's service, he knew and feared the dire consequences. Rightfully so.

"Precisely. Therefore, they will be forced to sacrifice one of their own. We don't want to ruffle mother dearest's feathers, dead or not. Her curse is alive and well." Morozko reached forward, his fingers taking hold of the popped collar on Xezu's leather uniform. "We will not risk being overrun by my mother's creatures, do you understand?" He gave a tug on the fabric, then smiled mirthlessly.

Xezu bowed his head. "Y-yes, Your Majesty."

Morozko started to walk away, then turned his head. "Find Andras before he leaves. Make certain Vinti puts their all into this ritual. They're to make it bolder. The bonfire, the feast, the music... They're to decorate their entire village." He paused, his smile widening into one of wicked delight. "This time, their sacrifice will be one of their own. And I will decide who it shall be because *I* will be there to ensure they're holding up their end of this age-old bargain." He'd take the one that would hurt the village most. The one the village sought to protect because he wanted the cut to sting.

Xezu blinked. "You mean to go there yourself?"

"Indeed. I don't trust them now, and if I'm not present, who is to say they won't try to spite me again?"

His steward seemed to understand the reasoning and nodded. "Very well. I will relay this to Andras, Your Majesty."

He'd better.

For now, a hot bath was a top priority.

The white marble flooring gave way to a black staircase. The balusters looked like willow branches, and their gnarled limbs twisted around one another, jutting toward the railing.

Morozko ascended the stairs and unbuttoned his doublet. By the time he reached his chamber, he'd slid the article of clothing off and tossed it.

A grand bed sat in the middle of the room, and four black walnut posts held up a silken canopy of white. The far wall was mostly a window that looked over the mountain range, and on most days, mist or snow clouds cloaked their massive forms. But on clear days, the sharp contours of the mountains and the snow-covered valleys were visible. And at night, the vibrant blue, green, and purple hues danced like a banner in the wind.

Sauntering into his washroom, he filled the bath. Steaming water hit the porcelain, and the heat rushed into his face. He removed the rest of his clothing, then stepped in, groaning as the heat lapped at his ankles and calves.

The warmth ate away at the tension in his form but did nothing to quell the fury bubbling within. Mortals always thought they knew better with their novel ideas and new ways to accomplish tasks. When in truth, the old ways were there for a reason...

"You wretched fools." Morozko swiped at the water, glowering as he cupped a handful and poured it over his head. "And yet, I'd be the one you'd blame after all that I've done for Frosteria."

After all the protection he offered.

The peace.

Now it was *they* who threatened to disrupt it. And the blame would rest on his head, like a crown of daggers.

No. He wouldn't allow it. The mortals would pay.

2

EIRAH

Mortality in a world of immortals was but a weakness. Even the animals outside Eirah's homeland lived forever. Frosteria, in a sense, was never meant for humans. The biting cold was endless, and only a fire in one's home provided true warmth. However, living for eternity could also be one's curse, especially in an existence destined for loneliness.

The harsh wind blew, sending shivers through Eirah. She drew her fur cloak tighter around her body. "Perhaps immortality would be lovely at this moment, then I could walk outside bare if I so chose," she murmured to herself. "I mean, not that I would. But there would at least be the opportunity."

Eirah's teeth chattered as she stared through the darkness, up into the branches of the snow-covered trees where the moon's light shone. As on most nights, she couldn't get a wink of sleep, so she'd ventured out from her cozy cottage to the edge of the forest behind her home.

"Where are you, Adair?" Eirah whispered toward the familiar branch where he usually rested. Over the years, owls came and went, except for one who had continued to return since she was a child.

The beat of wings sounded, followed by a loud hoot piercing through the wind. A wide smile crossed her heart-shaped face as she peered up toward the stars. Bright ivory stood out against the night, and she took a step closer to the tree as the owl's talons cradled his familiar branch.

"Ah, there you are, sweet prince." She beamed, no longer thinking about the freezing weather.

Adair cocked his snowy-white head at her and released another hoot before hopping to a lower limb.

As always, Eirah lifted her arm and motioned at it. "Come on, it's the same as resting on a branch, only softer."

The owl watched her silently, his eyes glowing a brilliant orange. He inched nearer, and she took another step toward him—the closest they had ever been to one another—when a high-pitched squeak radiated in the distance.

The owl jerked up his head and darted off into the distance to snatch up his nightly meal. "Perhaps tomorrow we'll meet again." She sighed.

Some demons in Frosteria had animals that were their familiars. Humans didn't have that luxury—an owl she endlessly tried to provoke to land on her arm was the closest she would ever get.

Eirah glanced once more at the stars painting the obsidian sky. The moon rested above, seeming to watch over them, its shape the thinnest of slits on this night. If only the stars were made from ice and she held magic, then she would have created a frozen rope from water, latching onto one of their forms. She would have pulled it down to her hands and gifted the star to her father. Perhaps then he would smile, knowing her mother's soul may not have been eternal here but possibly somewhere else.

She wondered if she achieved such things, would a star's flesh be soft or hard? Would its temperature be cold or warm? And once in her hand, did the way it shone mean it would pulse like a heart?

"Enough with the nonsense, Eirah. So many foolish questions that will never be answered. And stop talking to yourself —the villagers already look at you strangely enough." Unless they wanted to purchase items from her and her father. Even then, she felt their heavy stares as they studied some of her more grim music boxes and marionettes. Those were for herself and herself alone.

"Bah!" She threw her hands up in the air and whirled around. "I don't give a damn what anyone thinks."

The snow sloshed beneath her boots as she headed back toward her cottage. After she closed the door behind her, a rush of heat pricked her frozen hands. A new log rested in the fireplace, flames eating away at its wooden layers. Her father —Fedir—glanced up at her from the desk in the corner of the room, his spectacles sitting low on his nose while he worked on attaching an arm to a marionette. Ever since she could remember, the sitting room had been littered with parts for toys and music boxes. Her father used to make weapons before Eirah was born, but when her mother became with child, his craft had turned to toymaking for both mortals and demons.

"Couldn't sleep?" she asked, removing her cloak and hanging it on the wall hook.

"No, but it seems you couldn't, either." He smiled, patting the stool beside him. Under the room's low light, the wrinkles beside his gray eyes seemed to have deepened these past few months. Even his chestnut hair held more streaks of gray.

Eirah warmed her hands by the fire for a moment, regaining the feeling in them before sinking down on the wooden stool. Her father hadn't slept well ever since Eirah's mother passed away from a cough that had turned fatal. Eirah had only been five years old then, but she'd taken over assisting her father after that. She'd thought he would marry again, and Eirah wouldn't have minded, yet he remained content with his toy-making and daughter.

At twenty, Eirah didn't know when, or if, she would ever leave home. But for now, she had her marionettes, music boxes, and wind-up toys. Before starting on one of her creations, she quickly pulled her dark hair into a braid, then wound up one of her unfinished boxes and opened it. She watched as the dancer spun in a circle, elegantly holding out her hands while wearing a gown of blue ice and matching flowers in her hair.

The music drifted around her, its melody a little too crackly. She needed to work on that, but before she could think more about it, the music stopped.

Damn. If she *did* have magic, she knew precisely what she would have done with it, created a dancer of *real* ice, and let her rotate for eternity without the song ever having to end. There would be no constant need to keep winding the box, and the mechanics wouldn't need constant tweaking.

"Are you going to paint her face?" her father asked, his gaze meeting hers.

She studied the smooth brown face of the dancer, the onyx

curls falling to her waist. "No, I like that no one knows what she's thinking or feeling."

"Gloomy thoughts, daughter."

"Ah, Papa, but they are the best thoughts for creating, aren't they?" She laughed, adjusting a piece of metal at the bottom of the box. She wound it up once more, letting the soft tinkling fill the room, this time the melody perfect.

"You're so much like your mother. And me—but the second part might be a terrible thing." He chuckled. "How about I make us some tea since our heads want to stay busy?"

"Peppermint, please." Eirah scooped up one of the incomplete marionettes for a customer. This one did desire a face. Lifting a brush, she dipped it into pink paint to make the marionette cheeks.

For the remainder of the night, Eirah concentrated on painting, carving, and drinking tea until the sun rose through the window, lighting up the room. Her mind hadn't rested once, taking her from one project to another, leaving some unfinished, some completed, even sparing a bit of time to make a deceased marionette wearing a wedding gown of all black. Too "macabre."

Her stomach rumbled, and she glanced down. "Oh, you troublesome thing, always getting in the way of work."

"Would you like me to start breakfast?" her father asked, using a needle to move around a minuscule piece of metal on a toy sleigh.

"No, it's my turn." With a yawn, Eirah stood from the stool and padded toward the kitchen when a knock pounded at the door.

"Tell the customer we don't allow them here this early." Her father frowned.

Eirah rolled her eyes. "Now, now, we can't run them off."

Even though she would have rather snatched a piece of fruit first, she brushed her palms down the front of her deep sapphire dress before opening the door.

Desmond, the village chieftain's son, stood on the porch, his thin lips pursed. "Good morning, Eirah." He pushed a few dark braids behind his ear, his mahogany eyes appearing as unenthusiastic as his expression. "There's to be a village meeting."

She arched a brow. "When?" Eirah's stomach now roiled with unease instead of hunger. It was much too soon for the monthly meeting, seeing as how they'd just had one the week prior.

"Now. It involves the king." His fingers fidgeted with the edges of his cloak.

Morozko... Even thinking his name unsettled her, and she'd never once met the Frost King. "What is it?"

"Father hasn't told me, but I know it isn't going to be pretty. Hurry. I need to finish rounding up the other villagers." With that, he turned on his pristine booted heel, adjusting his fur cloak, and trudged to the cottage next door. Desmond knew something, but she could tell the chieftain had most likely told him not to say anything. She'd grown up with Desmond—they were the same age, yet they'd never been close as he was too focused on carrying on his father's legacy.

When she turned to grab an apple, her father was already fastening his cloak. "It must be important if it involves the king. We'll have to eat later."

"Grabbing an apple first won't hurt anyone," she mumbled.

"You can have two when we return." He tossed Eirah her cloak.

"More like three." She grinned and wrapped the thick

13

fabric around her shoulders as they walked out into the snow. No one lingered in front of their homes as they all headed toward the center of the village. Most of the people had already gathered around the dais, where the chieftain stood in front of his carved throne, chatting with one of the elders. His thick gray fur cloak was bundled around him, and his onyx braids were drawn back with a leather strap.

Someone stepped beside Eirah, and she glanced over to find her friend toying with the lace of her cloak. "His Righteousness demands we come here," Saren said in a low voice. "Why doesn't the king come himself?"

"Perhaps because he's an arrogant prick." Eirah rolled her eyes. "Most likely too busy relaxing in a bath while sipping on a goblet filled with blood."

Saren pressed a fist to her mouth to muffle her laughter. "Indeed." They'd been friends since they could walk, even though everyone in the village noticed Saren—her long, golden hair, and eyes the color of the sky. She shone like sunshine and twinkled like the stars. Eirah had always preferred the shadows, but even shadows needed the sun sometimes.

The chieftain cleared his throat, taking a scroll from inside his cloak. "The Frost King is quite disappointed in us. In a week's time, there is to be a village celebration. There, he will choose a maiden sacrifice, then we will return once more to providing him with an annual animal sacrifice. If we deny his request, the entire village will end in bloodshed."

Gasps echoed throughout the crowd. Eirah's eyes widened, the cold, dry air stinging her flesh. How could that self-righteous bastard do this? Couldn't he see that the village had stopped sacrificing their animals because there was no reason to? If they sacrificed more, there wouldn't be enough to feed their bellies.

Vinti had held the ceremony ever since Morozko was crowned king—a pointless ritual with no true purpose except to please him.

"A maiden, you say?" one of the young men spoke up.

Eirah rolled her eyes at the fool, who must have been proud to be a man, safe.

"Only... one of his choosing." The chieftain glanced toward his son. "And if we don't allow him this, he will decimate the village for disrespecting him. To prove his point, he sent Jonah's hand after he was found near the king's palace. Jonah knew it was forbidden to go there unless summoned."

The crowd gasped, and Eirah's throat grew dry... he'd given a *hand* as a threat. Even though Jonah was a fool and shouldn't have been there, he didn't deserve to have his hand removed from his dead body and sent to the village. A chill crawled through Eirah, not for herself, but for someone very dear to her. If the king was to choose a sacrifice, then he would most likely choose the most beautiful girl in the village... *Saren*. Beside her, Saren paled.

"At the celebration," Eirah whispered to her friend, "keep your head down and wear the ugliest dress you own. Untidy your hair as though birds slept through the night in it."

"You do the same," Saren whispered back. "I don't want to lose anyone here, but especially you."

That was incredibly sweet of her friend to say, but Eirah didn't need to work on doing that at the celebration. She always looked unkempt, and the Frost King, in all his arrogance, would never choose her.

This was precisely why immortality was a curse. It created

a blasé male who had nothing better to do than end an inno-cent's life because mortals chose not to be at his beck and call any longer. He and his wounded ego wouldn't even allow someone to choose to sacrifice themselves if they so wished.

The bastard.

3

MOROZKO

The wind blew hard, howling through the boughs of the trees. Snow piled higher than a cottage in some areas, and if one weren't careful, they'd fall through. Morozko, in his youth, had done as much. But he didn't have to worry about succumbing to the cold, nor did he fuss over it collapsing on top of him. He was a frost demon. Snow and ice would bend to his will.

The sleigh ride to Vinti had been uneventful, allowing Morozko to stew over what female he would select. Which one would burn a hole in the hearts of everyone with her absence?

He stepped from the small, black iron sleigh and surveyed the village before him. Lifeless. No songs ringing out, no scents of food tickling his senses. So, Vinti decided not to hold the ritual—even after he demanded the sacrifice of a villager?

Morozko's lip curled in a sneer. He shoved his cape behind him, and it waved like a battle standard.

He edged forward, and the road cracked beneath his boot. Morozko quirked a brow, then took a second step—another crack formed and spider-webbed across the ground.

"What the fuck?" he muttered, spinning around to take in the sight. His guards uselessly shifted back, their mouths in tight lines, as if afraid to continue.

The icy wind tore across his face, pulling his white hair into his eyes. Through the tendrils, the cracks grew as their groans echoed off the structures.

Against his better judgment, he moved in the village's direction, but this time, a shriek pierced the air, accompanied by the distinct sound of nails clawing at the frozen ground. As he peered down once more, a face peeked from the other side—pale, mouthless, and wide-eyed.

"Get ready to—" Before he could finish, the ground tilted and sent him careening forward. He didn't crash to the snow—he leaped onto a solid piece of ground and cast an accusatory glance toward the waxen figure slipping from its hole. The creature chittered at him, stretching out a long, gangly arm.

A blanket of snow dropped from the sky, and Morozko squinted, trying to see through the clouded air. Slowly, another figure took shape. This time, he didn't hesitate to pull his jagged ice blade free.

Morozko hissed, lifting the sword before charging. But at the last moment, before he struck the unknown foe down, a face came into view. Messy, obsidian hair, dark brown eyes that were almost black, and features that would never draw his attention like the females he brought to his bed. Her face softened, giving him pause. Not because he wouldn't strike a female down, but because she was saying something.

"Morozko," her voice came, disembodied, echoing from every corner of the village.

Who was this impudent female?

As the creature sprung to the side, she lifted her hand, and the bastard fell to the ground, writhing in pain. She was wielding *magic that no human ought to, and it rankled him to consider that she could be a danger to him—to Frosteria.*

"Who are you?" he growled, lifting his free hand to strike her, but when his palm should have connected with her flesh, it didn't. It passed through her. She was gone.

Morozko jolted from his slumber, his chest heaving. He didn't have to glance in a mirror to know he was coated in a slick sheen of sweat. It rolled down his back, forehead, and chest.

Sometimes, it was difficult to decipher what was a dream and what was a vision. But that female's face, the creatures in the ground... he shuddered. While he had never seen his mother's creations, she had certainly threatened to unleash them—her changelings, she called them— frequently. *Do as I say, or Frosteria as you know it will end.* He'd watched as she pulled the strings of the humans, using them as nothing more than a puppet to stir trouble in the villages and the city. She pinned brother and sister against one another. Morozko loathed it. They were subjects of the realm. And all he strove to do was keep the balance. Yet, the damnable village had refused to make an offering.

Pitiful humans.

He snarled and threw his fur blankets off, exposing the female he'd chosen to bed last night. The cool air licked at her bare ass, and even though she was a frost demon, she slapped her hand down in search of the warmth that had been there only moments ago.

"Fucking dreams," he whispered, pacing his room. The blazing fire had long since burned out, lending a numbing cold to the air. Although, he couldn't know because ice might as well have flowed through his veins.

"My king, come back to bed." The female sighed, rolling

over so her breasts teased him, her nipples pebbled, begging to be flicked and tasted by his tongue.

He had his fill of her, though—two evenings was far too much.

"Get dressed and leave. I'm done with you." Morozko didn't wait for her to stumble out of bed—he grabbed her discarded dress and coat, then threw them at her. "Now."

She opened her mouth, readying to argue, but as the muscles in his face tensed, she leaped from the bed and hurriedly dressed before storming out of his chambers. They always got attached after a night of fucking, as if they truly believed that would make him want them as his queen. Naïve things that they were.

Another one will replace her. Morozko combed his fingers through his hair and padded across the room.

A knock sounded on the door as he pulled on his trousers. He sighed, rolling his eyes, half expecting the female to sprint back into the room. "Come in." He opened his wardrobe doors and pulled out a navy-blue vest with silver brocade and snowflake embellished buttons.

"Your Majesty, if you'll be eating before departure, I can have it brought up to you now."

Morozko glanced over his shoulder, spying Xezu chewing on his cheek. "A light breakfast, in case we encounter any issues." Like what, he wasn't certain. The ungrateful village of Vinti could spring a trap, thinking of doing away with him in the same fashion they'd killed his mother—by ambushing, pushing the guards off, and piercing her heart with a spear.

"Sire, it is midday." Xezu's eyes darted to the side, perhaps regretting the correction.

Midday? He *had* spent the night rioting away with—what was her name again? Gita? Katlin? It didn't matter.

20

"Very well, bring up food befitting of a light breakfast."

He tapped his fingers against his bare chest, then pulled on the navy vest. His movements reflected at him in the floor-length mirror across the room, and he strode toward it, staring at himself.

Maranna's clone. From the ivory hair to the pale gray skin, lacking the pink undertones, even to his pointed ears and sharp canines. Harsh angles all around. He was every part his mother, not that he remembered anything about his father, and she certainly never told him.

"Are you happy, Maranna?" he cooed to his reflection and dragged a slender finger down the glass. "That your curse lives on while you rot and fester in the ground?" A slow, sinister smile spread across his face. "You wicked bi—"

Someone cleared their throat from the doorway—it wasn't Xezu but Ulva. She scuttled into the room, deposited the tray onto the small table, and fled as quickly as she came.

Morozko grunted and swept his hair back, pulling it into a messy top knot, but at least it wouldn't brush his neck or fall into his face. Once he was dressed, he made quick work of his breakfast. A honey cake, winterberries, and sweet custard.

He spent the rest of the day attending to trivial matters, but when the sun dipped on the horizon, Morozko was outside, waiting for the small party of frost demons to assemble. Behind him, Nuka paced back and forth. His white fur rippled in the breeze, and his clever yellow eyes watched on, waiting for what came next. He was the size of two war horses stacked on top of one another, and considering Nuka was a frost wolf, he was intimidating to most.

In his youth, the wolf had been Morozko's only companion, and because of that, their bond was unbreakable.

Nuka whined, agitated that they weren't moving yet.

Someone had already equipped him with his saddle, which usually meant patrolling, and, if the wolf was lucky, a battle.

"Settle. We'll be off soon enough." And as the words left Morozko's mouth, a team of frost demons approached, clad in their black attire.

Andras took a step forward. His crimson hair was pulled back into several rows of braids, and the sides of his head were shaved down to the skin.

"Your Majesty," Andras offered with a bow. "It's time we leave."

Morozko's red cape flapped behind him. "Very well."

Finally, they could venture to the wretched village and be done with it all. Morozko turned to Nuka, who laid down obediently and allowed him to climb onto his back. The wolf stood as Morozko gathered the reins. Instead of connecting to the wolf's mouth like a horse, they were attached to a leather collar, and when tugged, Nuka took the cue to turn.

Morozko lifted his hand and motioned forward. Nuka leaped into a smooth trot, padding softly on the tundra as the frost demons followed behind on their horses, elk, or reindeer. There was no need for a rallying speech. For one, it wasn't in his nature to build his following up. Two, they were harbingers of death.

Whoever he chose for the maiden sacrifice would die before the next day. What a waste it all was when it could've been avoided if the mortals had just obeyed. But the wretched humans didn't want to listen, and now they must pay the price for their betrayal.

When the party reached the village, the sun gave way to the full moon. Music hummed in the air, but it was neither joyful nor celebratory. Townsfolk bustled in the streets, but no cries of gaiety rang out, which was just as well with Morozko.

Small shops dotted the dirt road, and a few log homes stood in between. If he followed the main road through town, it'd lead to the farmlands, where they kept livestock and large frozen-over lakes used for ice-fishing. But this was the heart of Vinti. The very heart the changelings wanted to crush in their clawed grasp.

Morozko wouldn't dare let it happen, not if he could help it. Frosteria belonged to him—he was every part of the land as it was him.

Nuka halted, and Morozko dismounted. His fingers dove into the fur on his familiar's leg, then scratched roughly. "Stay alert," he commanded, not only to his guard but to the wolf as well.

Dregs of his vision entwined with reality, making it diffi-cult for him to decipher whether it was only a dream. But he'd seen the changelings before, the demons his mother created, writhing in his dreams, clawing at the seal. The maiden's face was unknown, and Morozko decided then, whoever she was, she belonged to him.

4

EIRAH

After the chieftain finished speaking, he left with Desmond to prepare for the king's arrival. Per the chieftain's command, Eirah and the other villagers helped decorate the outside of each shop and home over the next week. Making the village grander for *His Majesty*, even after he'd murdered one of their own. On sacrificial nights, they did nothing of this nature, but this was a way to cater to the king, to woo him.

They strung cascading garlands and bows across the village. Some elders entwined yellow camellias and other flowers into the decorations as if this was a celebration of happiness, not death. Even the poles of the torches were draped in blue and white ribbons, ready to be lit once night fell.

Eirah wiped the perspiration from her brow as she bid farewell to Saren and went inside her cottage. Her father was getting cleaned up for the evening, so she grabbed a few apples, then sat on her stool in front of their shared work desk. She knew she should bathe and dress in her finest, but she refused. Jonah hadn't been the kindest man, lived alone, and was generally a fool, but did the king have to send his hand back to the village as a token?

She took a wooden doll from a shelf behind her that fit perfectly in her palm. It was meant to be a future piece for a customer, but she had other plans for it now—she would make a representation of Frosteria's *gracious* king.

The prick, she thought as she bit into her apple.

Although Eirah had never seen Morozko, she'd heard tales of his ivory hair, pale gray skin, and elongated canines that could rip apart any throat. Or she imagined that was what he would do, followed by lapping up the victim's blood. Women swooned at tales of the immortal king, wishing for an opportunity to be in his bed for a single night, praying to be his queen. Even though the rumor was that he would toss any maiden aside once he'd had his fill. Yet none of the maidens spoke ill of him since he apparently had brought them to the utmost bliss, and besides that, he was their king. *Bah*, she didn't care how good of a lover he was. If he had done that to her, she would have slapped him across the face. Not that she would ever bed such a male, a *murderer*, when she finally decided to.

The doll's trousers were already painted a deep black, and after finishing her apple, she carved out a few areas of his white shirt to make it more pompous. She then colored the doll's hair white and dipped her brush into blue paint to make two dots for the eyes.

Once complete, she studied the Morozko figure and smiled. When the celebration ended tonight, Eirah would burn the wooden doll, and she swore to herself that Saren would be at her side to watch.

The door to her father's room creaked open, and he pushed his glasses up the bridge of his nose as he came out from the hallway. He wore his finest attire: a silken blue tunic, black trousers, and leather boots that didn't have a single scuff. His gaze fell on her, and his eyes widened. "Eirah, you aren't ready!" he hissed.

"Oh, Papa, I certainly am." She motioned at her dress speckled in paint. He couldn't see the hem or her dirt-covered boots just yet.

"Don't act like a child." He ran a hand down his face. "This is the king of Frosteria. I know what tonight is, and I know you're angered at what he did to Jonah. But the man never listened to anyone, and he shouldn't have been near the palace. Now please, for me, for your mother's respect, at least brush your hair and put on something that isn't covered in muck."

Her father's words rang true, but did it make it right? "For you, fine." She stood from the stool, taking the doll in her grasp. "I was only making a gift for the king."

Her father gripped the back of his neck but fought a smile. "You are as stubborn as your mother was. Just pick a clean dress, or you really will stand out."

He was right, but if anything, she would be banished by the king for her disgrace before she was chosen as his sacrifice. "I love you, Papa."

"I love you, daughter."

Eirah padded to her room and shut the door behind her. The bedroom was clean compared to her workspace. Her bed was pressed against the wall with a wardrobe opposite it. Hugging the two back corners were shelves filled with music boxes and dolls she'd made. Hidden beneath her bed were tales of romance she sometimes read when her father was out hunting or asleep.

Tossing the Morozko doll on the quilt, Eirah opened her wardrobe and sifted through the fabrics. She still had all her mother's dresses, which would've been too pretty for her to wear, even though she would have if the occasion had been different. "Mama, protect Saren tonight. I don't want to lose my only friend," she whispered as she took out a simple dress.

Eirah removed her clothing and inhaled beneath her arm —no putrid odors, so that would be good enough. She slipped on the lavender fabric—no lace, no fine embroidery, only two pockets on the sides. Her mother had always sewn pockets on Eirah's dresses so she could put things in them when they would walk through the forests. Pebbles, leaves, twigs... After her mother passed, Eirah continued to make pockets in her dresses, but they'd always remained empty.

Until now.

Eirah slipped the Morozko doll inside her left pocket. "Get comfortable in there, *King*."

She peered at herself in the oval mirror hanging on the wall, deciding to leave her hair in her mussed braid. Black circles rimmed her dark brown eyes, and she kept her face free of powders or added colors.

As she entered the sitting room, her father glanced up from eating one of the apples she'd left him and nodded in approval. "Thank you, daughter."

Eirah shrugged. "I'm going to Saren's, so I'll see you tonight at the celebration."

"Stay by her side."

"He's going to pick her." There were so many young maidens in the village, but in her gut, she knew—just knew—

he would choose Saren as his sacrifice. How was he planning to do it? A slit to the throat, a stab to the heart, burn her alive...

"Maybe not." Her father chewed on his lip, seeming to not believe his own answer.

"See you soon." Eirah drew on her cloak and stepped outside into the crisp air. The night would fall soon, so she hurried next door to Saren's. Snowdrops and yellow-berried bushes bloomed in the garden, and two white rocking chairs rested on the porch. It was only Saren and her younger brother, Petre, who lived there. Two years ago, their parents had been slaughtered by a snow lion when visiting a frost demon village.

Eirah knocked on the door, and Petre answered, dressed in a black tunic and matching trousers. His short blond hair, parted on the side, was the same shade as Saren's. He had another year before he reached maturity, but he'd been a head taller than the both of them since he was twelve years of age.

"Hello, Eirah." Petre motioned her inside. The familiar hint of citrus brushed her nose as she stepped into the neatly arranged sitting room. Not a single speck of dust coated the bookshelves or the furniture. "Saren's still primping in the other room."

"Primping?" Eirah's stomach sank. She walked past the snowflake wall decor to the short hall leading to Saren's room.

The door was shut, and Eirah knocked lightly on it. A few seconds later, Saren answered, and she looked... beautiful.

"You were supposed to make yourself *not* stand out." Eirah sighed, but she couldn't deny that she would be in awe of her on any other occasion.

"What?" Saren huffed. "I didn't!"

Eirah brushed a finger down the silken strands of hair that hung loose to her friend's waist. "You have the top of your hair in a braided crown like a queen! And you're wearing a red dress that is hugging your curves in all the perfect places! Any man would want to tumble you when seeing you like this!"

"Well, thankfully, no one is being tumbled by the king tonight." Saren rolled her eyes.

"That's right—someone is going to be *slaughtered* instead," Eirah hissed. Unless the king did want to tumble his chosen maiden first... A new sense of horror washed over her because that might be precisely what the bastard would do.

"I'm not finished getting ready yet." Saren pointed toward her bed. "I'm wearing a raggedy cloak, and I'm tucking my hair that's loose beneath it."

Her pulse calmed a fraction, and she sat on the mattress. "I'm sorry for overreacting—I'm just frightened."

"We'll be fine, and we'll both keep our heads down." Saren sank onto the bed beside her, grasping Eirah's hand and gently squeezing it. "I do feel dirty from not bathing, though." She wrinkled her nose and smiled.

"Good." Eirah laughed.

She glanced at Saren's night table and the shelves along her walls, filled with music boxes and marionettes that Eirah had made for her over the years.

"Once tonight's over, I have my own sacrifice to burn." Eirah drew out her Morozko doll from her pocket.

"Is that the king?" Saren snorted. "He looks positively arrogant."

"You can let me know if I made him accurate enough when we see him." Eirah grinned.

Bells rang outside, signaling the villagers, who hadn't already, to come out of their homes and meet for the celebration. Saren hurried to put on her cloak before tucking in her hair and slipping on a pair of black-furred boots.

Petre waited for them in the sitting room near the supper table. He kissed his sister on the cheek and pressed a silver dagger into her hand.

"Petre!" Saren gasped. "I'm not going to kill the king."

"I don't give a damn about Frosteria, just you. You're the only blood I have left. Pray you won't have to use it, but take it."

Saren slammed the blade on the table. "I will not be the cause of his warriors seeking vengeance."

Petre's brows pinched together, but he nodded.

The bells continued to ring, and Eirah led the way outside into the chilly breeze. A lovely aroma of pastries mingling with meat drifted through the air. The night had arrived, and the torches were lit, their orange glow casting a beautiful aura over the village. It truly was a celebration fit for a conceited king.

Smoke curled toward the moon and stars from the bonfire blazing in the village's center. Music floated around them, a combination of flutes and stringed instruments, the sound more melancholic than cheerful. Or at least that was how it seemed to Eirah.

Movement above caught her eye, and she stared up, catching sight of snowy-white wings flapping through the darkness. It was too far up for her to see clearly, but she knew it was Adair coming to watch over them this night. Even though a male wasn't to be chosen as a sacrifice, most of their expressions were tight and grim as they held their loved ones close.

The chieftain stood at the front, near the bonfire, dressed in his fur cloak. He sipped from an iron mug as he whispered into his son's ear. Desmond nodded and peered around at the villagers' faces, his usual smile nowhere in sight.

Eirah and Saren lingered at the edge of the crowd near the forest, the birds' caws the only loud sound besides the crackling of the fire.

"You could hide until it's over," Eirah whispered to her friend.

"I refuse to do that." Saren frowned. "Besides, the king threatened to kill us if we weren't all in attendance."

Eirah glanced behind her, finding a bright white spot high in a tree. It was Adair. *Thank you for coming.* He wouldn't hear her, but she was grateful for his presence nonetheless.

The instruments stopped, and Eirah whirled back around as the crowd parted for the newcomer. Eirah stepped in front of Saren to hide her friend as best she could without being too obvious.

The form became clearer, a crimson cape billowing behind him. She would have been a fool to not recognize Morozko. His lithe form sauntered across the snow like a god of frost. The king's ivory hair hung past his chin, one side swept neatly behind a pointed ear. His skin was pale gray, perfect, and smooth as ice. Not a single scar marred his flesh, letting her wonder if anything had ever come close to harming him. But the vicious smirk he held on his face made her want to get close enough to carve it away.

At that moment, she wished she'd taken Petre's blade for herself, ran through the crowd, and pierced his heart.

"Villagers of Vinti," Morozko said, his voice deep, arrogant, "you made a grave mistake by not providing an animal sacrifice. We could have avoided this, but now you'll pay with a human life, and *I'm* to be the giver of those repercussions. You have no one to blame but yourselves." He sneered, ugly and beautiful all at once.

"Prick," Eirah whispered under her breath.

Morozko's ice-blue gaze met hers and halted, holding. A scowl formed on his handsome face.

Eirah blinked, her shoulders squared, but no words escaped his shapely lips, only a strange game of him continuing to study her.

The crowd remained silent as he walked in her direction, coming to move her aside and claim Saren.

5

MOROZKO

Morozko strode forward, and the ground didn't crack as it had in his vision. There were no writhing changelings scraping at the ice, trying to break free. He pushed aside the crowd of villagers—none of them mattered at that moment. Only the female in front of him, the one from *his vision*. She was *here*. He paused in front of her, his brows pinching together as he frowned, considering her. She was pretty, in a plain sort of way. Delicate, doll-like features, full pouting lips, and thick ebony tresses escaped her raggedy braid, framing her heart-shaped face. *Pretty, but not a maiden I'd tumble.* Yet that wasn't why he was standing in front of her.

His lips tilted into a smirk as she glanced at a golden-haired female tucked behind her—someone he'd certainly bring to his bed for the evening. When the female shifted, her cloak slid to the side, showing Morozko the curve of her breasts. He didn't need her to shed the cumbersome layer to know she possessed curves that would tempt a saint. Unlike her friend from his vision. Not that she had even *tried*. Not with the plain dress. No, this golden-haired woman, he supposed, inspired mortals to write poetry of her beauty, but Morozko wasn't here for that, either. He was here to select a sacrifice. The lamb that the village would give him to slaughter.

Morozko lifted his hand and dragged a finger beneath the female from his vision's chin. The pretty mortal jolted as he did, muscles visibly coiling like she was readying to shove him away. *Go on, I dare you.* The king sneered.

"What is your name?" he cooed.

She didn't respond, only pulled her chin away.

The crowd murmured, but Morozko didn't pay them any mind. He grabbed the mortal by the chin, turning her head to look at him once more. "Your name. I won't ask again before I drag it out of you."

Her dark eyes hardened, hatred swirling within them. "Eirah."

Unfamiliar and infuriating.

Since he had a vision about her, he thought her name would stir something—another piece of what he saw sliding into place or familiarity. But there was nothing. He half expected her to unleash magic at him in that moment, yet all that flared was hatred in *Eirah's* eyes, with no simmering surge of power. *Interesting.*

Morozko dropped his hand and turned to the crowd, assessing them. The chieftain's weathered face was set in a grim expression.

"Your Majesty," the chieftain said, bowing. His long, braided hair fell forward, draping over his furs.

All around, torches lined the pathways, blazing to light the way. Spiced pastries and minced meat permeated the air, tempting Morozko to indulge, and perhaps he would.

"No need to hold your breath any longer. I have chosen a sacrifice." He inclined his head toward Eirah and smiled, his sharp canines grazing his bottom lip.

The beautiful mortal beside Eirah gasped, whispering, "Please, no."

"Eirah, no!" a male's voice carried over the din. "Not my daughter." He burst through the crowd and fell to his knees before Morozko. "Not Eirah, please, Your Majesty." His graying head bowed as he pleaded, but when Morozko didn't speak, he tilted it back. Wire-framed glasses slid into place as he peered up at him. Lines of worry or lack of sleep creased the mortal's face, inspiring disgust in Morozko. *Weak mortal.*

"Papa!" Eirah shouted. The other female held her back, preventing Eirah from going to her father.

Royal guards shifted behind Morozko as if readying to dispose of the man. He lifted a hand, halting them. The display was sincere and possibly even touching, but it was a waste of energy.

Morozko leaned forward, resting his palm on top of the man's head. "What is your name?"

"Fedir," the man proclaimed. "Your Majesty..."

"Fedir, had your simple-minded village done as they were asked, I wouldn't be here, and Eirah would still be yours. But she isn't." Morozko hissed as the man lifted his eyes. "She is *mine.*" He stepped backward and chuckled darkly, motioning for his guards to haul Fedir back.

"Don't hurt him!" Eirah rushed out.

Morozko flicked an invisible piece of dust from his

doublet. "He is safe. For now." Sighing, he cast a glance at Eirah. "I believe now is when I request a dance—your very last one." Morozko extended his hand, palm facing upward.

Eirah stared at him, then recoiled. "No."

No? Morozko bristled, straightening. "Pardon?" he asked flatly.

"I said *no.*" Eirah spat her words. "If I'm to be your sacrifice, then I would rather you take a blade across my throat."

The gall. She was a bold one, but if she thought her backbone would save her, she was wrong. He gritted his teeth, reeling in his self-control so he didn't wrap his fingers around her slender, pale throat and end her right there. "The point is, I requested a dance, and I can always select your father for the sacrifice instead... or maybe your beautiful friend who is clutching on your arm ever so tightly."

Eirah's dark eyes followed from the mortal beside her to her father through the crowd, the threat visibly sobering her. "As you wish, Your Majesty," she said coolly, offering her hand to him.

Morozko's fingers curled around the tips of her warm digits, and he lowered his head to brush his lips against them. Death's kiss caressed her knuckles in a mockery of affection, then he glanced up at her, smirking. "How lovely of you to acquiesce."

The bards had all but ceased their playing. Morozko frowned—this wouldn't do. He couldn't dance to the sound of torches blazing. He turned on his heel, snapping with his free hand. "Play music. Something lively."

There was a pause, then the mandolin players plucked their strings, a slow melody for the dance.

Morozko closed the distance between him and Eirah. His

arm slid around her slender waist, tugging her against him roughly. She scarcely hid her scowl. Hatred was easier to deal with than a simpering female.

Eirah placed her hand on his shoulder, and he led them in a slow dance as if this was merely a celebration in his ballroom and not a death sentence for the human gathered in his arms. Her lips pressed together so tightly they were nearly white.

"Do you wish to say something?" Morozko baited her, wanting nothing more than to give her a reason to fumble and infuriate him. Every glare, every mutter beneath her breath, was just another moment closer to her demise.

That's not true. It wasn't. He needed to know her part in all of this. If she was alive during the changelings breaking free, surely it meant he couldn't kill her. *Yet.*

She shook her head in response, refusing him the argument.

If he'd come to the village and selected another, everything would have been greatly different. Blood would have poured down the slate slab on the altar, coated his fingers, and dripped from his ice blade, but no. Eirah was the female in his vision, the one who vexed him, and tonight he wouldn't sacrifice her. He'd devise another plan to buy more time, but this was an infuriating complication he had to sort out prior to ending her life. And then, there would be a true cause to celebrate, for the sacrificial blood would rain down, and the seal would be sated again.

Morozko slid his hand down her spine until it was just above the dip of her backside. He smirked as she tripped over her feet and color rushed into her cheeks, having nothing to do with rage and everything to do with his *touch*.

He chuckled, spinning her when she hadn't recovered yet. If she were going to remain silent, so be it. But in turn, he scrutinized her features. If he closed his eyes, he'd be able to see her high cheekbones, sharp nose, and full lips. Since the morning, the vision of her had played in his mind. Her hand reached out to him, the changelings writhing on the ground. But one thing he hadn't noticed was the lack of malice she'd held. Now, with her in his arms, malice was the only expression on her face. Yet, in his vision, there had been... concern? Perhaps she was looking past him, at someone behind him, and he couldn't see.

His visions were never clear in the beginning, but one thing he knew for certain—she was the female. There was no mistaking that. But where was the damn magic?

When the music came to an end, he didn't withdraw right away, but Eirah inched backward like a bird cornered in a cage. He held onto her firmly. "Not so fast, little bird. We'll be leaving shortly, so say farewell to your loved ones, and then we leave."

"Leave?" Eirah jerked away from him, glowering. "The *sacrifice* is supposed to occur here."

"The sacrifice," he said slowly, "will take place when I say so. And for now, you are coming to my palace unless you want me to spill dear *Papa's* blood right now."

"You really are cold and heartless," she said softly, her nostrils flaring.

Morozko cocked his head, lifting a pale brow. "I doubt the rumors even touch how cold I am, little bird," he purred and turned on his heel. "Be quick, or I'll lose my patience." His gaze followed her as she ran into the crowd, hugging her father, then her friend. If she thought to escape, she wouldn't get very far.

He scoffed and approached his guard. "You haven't seen anything...? No cracks in the ground, nothing out of sorts?"

Andras shook his head. "No, Your Majesty. Nothing is out of the ordinary."

For now. Who knew how long it would remain that way? How long would it take for the changelings to fully break the seal? Never before had the demon created by Maranna been in Frosteria—a threat against the mortals, should they question her, should they cease swearing their allegiance.

"Keep an eye out," Morozko ordered, then, having lost his patience, he searched for Eirah. He homed in on her, embracing Fedir, who sobbed. Others nearby wept, too.

"Tch. Humans and their frail emotions," he said to no one in particular, but it was as if Eirah had heard him because she turned her head and glared in his direction.

Amusement blazed within him, twisting his lips into a broad grin. He strode forward, cutting through the throng of villagers until he was before Eirah. "Your loathing is like a beacon. I could find you anywhere with *that* kind of aura."

"You're a prick," Eirah hissed under her breath, trying so very hard to control the volume of her voice.

"What was that?" He leaned toward her simply to antagonize her. "Your *king* didn't quite hear that." Morozko raised his voice and glanced around.

Villagers ceased their riotous conversation and focused on Eirah and Morozko.

She said nothing at first, then, "Should we not be leaving, Your Majesty?" Eirah amended her tone.

"You're right, little bird. After all, we wouldn't want to keep the guillotine waiting." Morozko didn't wait to see her reaction as he led the way to Nuka, who sat not far from the villagers. His familiar's ears swiveled, listening to the chatter around them and beyond. The wolf's yellow gaze focused on Eirah as she approached.

"Where is your sleigh, Your Majesty?" Even as Eirah spoke, she looked around for a sleigh she would never find.

It existed, of course. All the way back in the palace courtyard.

"There is no sleigh." Morozko patted Nuka's foreleg, stroking his fingers through the silken fur. "We are riding Nuka."

"What?"

"Well, originally, your throat was to be slit on the altar, and there was no need for a sleigh."

Eirah drew in a breath and touched her throat.

"Don't worry. I'll be sure there is an audience when I spill your blood. You don't have to fret over it for the time being."

Morozko ushered her to Nuka's shoulder and motioned for the wolf to lie down. He complied, lowering himself so they could mount him.

"You first," he offered, not trusting that she wouldn't flee.

She clumsily climbed onto Nuka's saddle and sat tall and rigid. *Proud.* There was something he could do about such pride. Pick it apart piece by piece, strand by strand. She would break before the end and beg him to sacrifice her life.

But you need her alive.

For now, if only to figure out what her place in the visions meant.

He pulled himself up behind her, settling in closer than necessary. This close, he could smell woods, fresh air, and a hint of lavender. The combination reminded him of runs through the forest with Nuka, training in the courtyard, and hiding on his balcony in the early mornings. Perhaps he *would* allow her into his bed for a night—she could ride him until that scowl dissipated from her face while he waited on the precise moment for the blade to glide across her throat.

"Eirah of Vinti," he breathed in her ear. "Your life here is over."

6

EIRAH

The wind kicked up as the Frost King's wolf carried Morozko and Eirah across the snowy terrain. Morozko gripped the reins with one hand, bringing them down for Nuka to go faster. His other arm circled her waist, holding her like his prisoner. Her death had been delayed, and that gave her a reason not to shove his arm away. But, oh, how she wished she did take the blade Petre had offered Saren. She hadn't even been allowed to gather her things to sneak one in, yet she would find a way to put an end to him if he didn't sacrifice her first.

Eirah was riding on a *wolf*, a massive white one at that. One like she'd never seen, although she had heard the stories about Morozko's familiar. Heard how Morozko would pick his maidens, then after the Frost King was finished pleasuring them, the familiar would bring the females home without the king accompanying them.

On either side of Eirah, the frost guards rode on their ivory stags. Their black and red uniforms were all the same. Eirah wasn't angry at the guards—they were only doing their duty. Every word whispered and shouted about Morozko's cruelty was true—he could have given the village another chance and told them that if they didn't perform the ritual, he would take a maiden. Yet he hadn't.

Another gust of chilly wind licked across her—she hadn't even been given a pair of gloves. Her teeth chattered as she drew her cloak tighter, then leaned into Morozko's warmth, inhaling a spicy scent. She hated herself for it, but with the wolf's increased speed and the icy wind, her chest heaved, her lungs finding it difficult to drink in the air.

"Not too much longer, little bird," Morozko cooed in her ear.

Eirah kept her words locked inside her mouth—there wouldn't be a point in speaking them aloud. She was the sacrifice, *his* sacrifice. Back at the village, she hadn't cried—not a single tear spilled down her cheek. When Morozko had chosen her, relief overpowered the anger that had flooded her. Relief that her closest friend hadn't been chosen by this vicious king. But that hadn't meant Saren was relieved.

"Let me sacrifice myself to him instead," Saren begged, gripping Eirah's shoulders. "I can offer myself to the king in other ways to entice him..."

The thought horrified Eirah. As beautiful as Saren was, and with as many men that had tried to woo her, she hadn't tumbled one before. "You will do no such thing for me," Eirah said, her voice soft. "Your brother still needs you—you both have already lost so much."

"So have you and your father," Saren whispered, the words strangled.

"I've made my decision, and you will be safe." Eirah hugged her friend tightly.

"Find a way to survive," Saren sobbed as she hugged her back.

Eirah's father had wept, not wanting to let her go, but she'd told him to stay strong and that she loved him.

Nuka charged through the forest—darkness blanketed them, no beast daring to attack Morozko and his guards.

She couldn't see well in the dark like an immortal could—only the outlines of shadows and branches. Morozko's arm tightened around her waist as though she would leap from his familiar at this very instance.

Might as well, Eirah. Breaking your neck may disappoint the prick since it wouldn't be by his hand. The thought of his ire over it made the act tempting. But no, she wouldn't end her life—she would fight back until her last breath. If she killed the Frost King at the palace, the guards would most likely only kill her, not her village, and the sacrificial ceremonies could end. She also needed to make sure she succeeded—otherwise, she knew Morozko would pluck Saren to become his sacrifice next.

They broke through the forest, and the massive outline of the king's mountain rested just ahead with the moon illuminating Morozko's ice palace. Nuka hauled them up the slopes and curves of the mountain leading to the castle. Eirah had seen it from a distance when traveling to frost demon villages to deliver toys but never this close. The palace was sculpted from pure ice, its spiked towers brushing the starry sky. She couldn't see the smaller details in the night, only the icy drawbridge when they barreled across it.

Nuka slowed as they approached Morozko's home. Not a single garden in sight. Only the castle, trees, and snow.

Once the wolf halted, Morozko didn't hesitate to hop down, his boots crunching the snow. He held out his hand with a smirk on his irritatingly perfect face, his red cape billowing behind him. She ignored him and leaped from Nuka, her feet stumbling as she hit the ground, her body careening forward into the freezing snow.

Morozko tsked, hovering over her, a tendril of white hair falling over his eye. "Should've taken my hand, little bird," he purred, reaching out to her once more. "Or perhaps used magic."

"You know damn well humans don't have magic." Scowling, she pushed herself from the ground and brushed the snow from her dress with frozen fingers.

"Thank you for the ride, Nuka," Eirah said to the familiar, then turned and trudged past a frowning Morozko for the door. She didn't hate his wolf familiar—he'd been doing his duty like the guards.

Two guards stood at the entrance of the ornate double doors, swirling designs etched into the ice. They drew open the doors, and Eirah entered the large space, the spicy aroma of Morozko heavier here. It wasn't an awful scent, but rather something she would have longed to smell again if it didn't belong to *him*.

Morozko sauntered past her, glancing over his shoulder, his ice-blue eyes meeting hers. "Are you going to stand there and freeze all night?" He motioned for her with a finger to follow him before resuming his pace. She narrowed her gaze at his back but followed him down a hallway filled with sculpted wolf heads lining the walls.

They ascended two flights of ivory stairs, leading down another hallway—this one with carved wooden battles decorating the walls. One of the doors was open, and they entered the room where a fireplace was already lit, its orange flames eating away at two logs.

Eirah shivered as she stepped inside, her gaze roaming

across the red and black room. A scarlet velvet chaise was in the middle of the space, with two high-backed chairs across from it. A black fur rug sprawled in front of the fireplace, obscuring the onyx floor. Metal snowflakes, she noticed, hung from the walls. On the opposite side of the room, two glass doors with dark curving handles led to what looked to be a balcony.

"Welcome home," Morozko drawled, then spun on his boot to leave.

"Wait!" Eirah shouted, surprising herself, but confusion swirled within her. "Where are you going?"

He slowly faced her, a wicked smirk on his face. "I'm going to take a bath, but you can join me if you wish. My bath is rather large, the water *warm,* and I can show you that I am not entirely made of ice..."

Taking a deep swallow, Eirah took a step back, and she could feel the flush staining her cheeks crimson. "I'd rather not."

"Your loss." The infuriating smile remained, and her gaze hurried to shift away from his shapely lips. "For now, warm yourself in front of the fire, and a servant will bring you something to eat and drink."

"Are you trying to fatten me up before making me your sacrifice?" Her heart thundered in her chest, not truly knowing what he would do with her body afterward. Most likely throw it off the mountain.

"I'm not planning to *eat* you." Morozko chuckled. "I'm not *that* beastly. Now, do as you're told."

Do as I'm told? She wanted to curse him until she was blue in the face but contained herself. "Why do you have us continue performing sacrifices when we need the animals?"

"I need their blood much more than you need the *one* animal a year to fill your bellies."

"And why is that? Why not just kill me now if it's so important?" If he had a good reason, he would have slit her throat in Vinti or told the village long ago.

"Perhaps I prefer toying with you." Morozko grinned wolfishly as he unclasped his cape. "*Warm* yourself." He tossed it to her, and she struck the heavy red fabric to the side. "A pity you did that." He chuckled again, turning on his heel as he left her standing there and closed the door behind him.

Eirah clenched her jaw, searching the room for anything she could use as a weapon. Nothing. The metal snowflakes wouldn't even rip from the walls. She drew open the door, only to find a tall guard, his light blue hair swept back into a low ponytail and a scar marring the left side of his lips, lingering in the hallway. Closing it without speaking a word, she kicked Morozko's cape to the side, then stomped on it for good measure. Drawing her cloak tight, she nestled in front of the fire atop the fur rug, her body shivering, gooseflesh pebbling her arms and legs. She held out her hands, her fingers prickling as the flames took away the cold, the feeling starting to come back into them. Thoughts of her father and Saren spun inside her mind, and she wondered what they were doing at that very moment. Were they able to sleep or were they wide awake?

After a little while, footsteps echoed down the hall, and Eirah glanced over her shoulder as a human woman entered. She wore a deep red tunic and dark leather skirt, carrying a wicker basket in one hand and a porcelain tea cup in the other. The woman was middle-aged, gray streaked her dark bun, and fine lines creased her forehead and around her deep brown eyes. "Xezu informed me that you were in need of food and drink." Her gaze fell to the cape on the floor. "Interesting."

"Xezu?" Eirah wrinkled her nose, not that she knew anyone's names besides Morozko and his familiar.

"My husband and the king's steward."

Eirah wondered how long the woman had been a servant in the palace as she handed her the cup of steaming tea, along with the basket. She peeled back the white cloth to find the wicker basket filled with fruit, bread, and sugared pastries.

"Thank you. I'm Eirah," she said.

The servant arched a brow. "The women the king brings here usually don't bother speaking to me."

Even though Eirah didn't bother speaking to many people, she had manners that her father instilled in her since she was a babe. "They must be foolish then."

The woman smiled. "I'm Ulva."

"Has the king ever had a sacrifice here or only me?" Her question came out steady, but nervousness coursed through her veins. The unknowing of what a steel blade would feel like pressed against her throat and gliding across gnawed at her.

"Oh my." Ulva blinked, wringing her hands over her apron. "I was not informed he was bringing the sacrifice here. I thought you were being prepared for His Majesty's bed."

"I would never!" Eirah spat, pushing away the horrifying image of Morozko's shapely lips on hers, his strong hands lifting her onto his bed, his lithe body settling between her legs. She would *never*.

Ulva pursed her lips, seeming to fight a smile. "That would be a first, then. No female has ever denied the king." It couldn't have been his *lovely* attitude that drew them in...

"Not even when asked to be a sacrifice, it seems." Eirah bit the inside of her cheek, drawing her knees to her chest.

Ulva's expression turned grim, and she nodded briefly before exiting the room, leaving Eirah alone once more.

Eirah lingered in front of the fire, sipping the peppermint tea until the cup was empty. She couldn't stomach the food, even though she'd always been fond of eating at any time of day. But she knew if she tried to force anything down, it would come back up.

Taking the cup, she slammed it against the floor to break it into sharp shards, the sound echoing. But the cup remained whole as if the king was prepared for anything. *Bastard.*

The guard threw the door wide, his hand held out as if prepared to release magic. "Is everything all right in here?"

"Perfect." Eirah sighed.

As the guard pursed his lips and closed the door, Eirah remembered something she still had with her. She drew out the Morozko wooden doll from inside her cloak and tossed it into the fire without looking at it. "I hope you feel the burn, King."

Morozko still hadn't returned, and she didn't know when he would either. Perhaps the burning of the doll had worked, and he was truly gone, but she knew she wasn't that lucky. An antsy feeling washed over her as the reality of her confinement settled in. She stared at the glass doors leading out to the balcony.

Eirah pushed up from the floor and held her cloak tight as she opened one of the doors. She hadn't been inside the palace walls long, but she already needed the fresh air, the escape.

The balcony was empty save for a rail of ice and icicles dangling from it. If she lived here, she would've at least decorated it with ivy.

Down below, frost guards circled the palace in the snow. Even if she planned on escaping, she would have failed and easily been caught. But she wouldn't try—she wouldn't put another's life at risk from her village. Hadn't that been what she would've done, though? If Saren had taken her offer and let them run and hide from the celebration? Hadn't she wished someone other than Saren would be chosen?

The wind ruffled the ends of Eirah's braid, and she peered up at the night sky, her gaze catching on an alabaster form. She squinted as it dipped in the air, drawing closer.

It can't be, can it?

Adair flapped his snowy wings, swooping down to the balcony rail. "I'm sorry I didn't get to say goodbye to you," she said.

He studied her for a long moment, letting out a low hoot before taking off, flying wild and free through the night while she was here. She had made the choice to come and not run, though, so it was what it was.

Eirah padded back inside, shutting the door behind her. She settled on the chaise, staring at the crackling fire until her eyelids grew heavy, waiting for Morozko to return, and possibly strangle him with his own cloak. But as time passed, he never walked through the door.

Her wish was that he would sacrifice himself, yet she knew it wouldn't come true.

7

MOROZKO

None of this had been part of Morozko's plan. He had fully intended to storm into the mortal village, select a sacrifice, and slice a swift gash across the maiden's throat before the villagers of Vinti. They needed to remember their place, and more importantly, the damnable seal needed to remain closed.

But here he was, with a stubborn maiden in *his* home. The sooner his vision came together, the sooner he could learn about her magic and dispose of her, rectifying the bloody seal.

The fire crackled in the bathing room's hearth, and Morozko was grateful for the reprieve. Neither realm matters nor those pertaining to Eirah chattered in his ears. Holed away in the room adjacent to his quarters, he closed his eyes and sank deeper into the water. The heat lapped at his flesh, but it wouldn't be long until the water chilled.

Crimson stained the ground, and Eirah lifted a bloodied hand. Her eyes widened as she looked at him, her lips forming his name.

Morozko curled his lip and slashed his hand through the

steaming water of his bath. The water rippled, reflecting the scowl on his face. *Another piece to the same moment.* A fleeting part of him wished Eirah had taken him up on the offer of bathing with him, mostly so he could have fucked the frustration out of his system. Perhaps being with her would clarify the wretched vision.

Still, it wasn't too late to send for another maiden. He'd never been denied by any female until Eirah. The image of her tossing his cloak to the floor should have made his blood boil, but it only intrigued him. What a feisty little bird.

But why was she screaming his name in the vision? And the blood... that was new. His heart roared in his ears, making the room spin.

He stood from the bath, water cascading down his slender figure. A musky scent of cinnamon and clove clung to him, wafting in the air. Just as he grabbed a towel, the door opened, and a throat cleared.

I can't even bathe in peace.

"Your Majesty," Xezu murmured from the doorway, bowing before he entered the oversized room. "The maiden has fallen asleep... shouldn't you—"

"What?" he snapped. "Carry her off to bed? No." Morozko patted his face dry, followed by the rest of his body. He glanced at his steward and wrapped the towel around his lower half.

Xezu folded his hands behind his back. "What are your plans for her?"

Morozko pressed his lips together. He didn't know how long it would take for everything to piece together, nor if he could wait that long. The longer he put off spilling her blood, the weaker the seal. The more the balance in the realm would suffer, and who knew what would become of

Frosteria? His sharp canines bit into his lower lip, pricking the skin.

"I don't know." He stared at the blazing hearth in the washroom and shrugged. "Draw out her death, I suppose."

"Have... you seen something, Your Majesty?" Xezu's brows pinched together as he met Morozko's gaze.

His steward was privy to what he saw because Morozko trusted him despite the fact he was a human. Perhaps it was because he could threaten Xezu's wife on a whim, or maybe it was because there was mutual respect between them. Morozko couldn't say, nor would he.

"More than just the changelings gnawing at the ice. It was... it was the village this time, and *she* was there. There was blood on the ground, too." Morozko was rambling, even he knew that, but the images in his mind were so unclear, save for the changelings and Eirah's face.

Xezu tried to hide his grimace but wasn't successful. "I am certain you'll have another vision to bring clarity soon enough. And whatever you decide will be just, Your Majesty."

Was he certain? Morozko strode up to his steward, towering over him as he leaned forward. "Is that so, or do you just say that to stroke my ego?"

Xezu's eyes lowered, but he didn't balk. "After all these years in your service, Your Majesty, would I ever deceive you in such a way?"

The answer was no. His current steward would never deign to do such a thing. His last one? He had. And he was dead.

Morozko motioned for him to leave, and his steward nodded. "And Xezu, don't get attached to the maiden. She is but a wisp drifting through the halls. Do you understand?"

Xezu met his gaze, throat bobbing. "Of course."

"Nevertheless, ensure the birdcage room is warmed for her in the east wing. Look through the trunks for a change of clothing. I'm certain something will fit her."

A hint of surprise flickered in Xezu's eyes, but he averted his gaze and nodded before leaving the room.

"And Xezu, she isn't to drink a thing before supper, understand?"

His steward's brows drew together as if trying to figure out what Morozko had up his sleeve, but then thought better of it. Xezu tsked and disappeared down the hall.

Alone again, Morozko growled and stormed toward the privacy screen where his clothing awaited. He tugged on his black trousers, lacing them up, then pulled the white linen shirt on. His long digits methodically rolled the sleeves to his biceps. When he was dressed, he gathered a leather tie in his hand and strapped his hair into a top knot.

There was no sense in leaving Eirah to rot in a sitting room. Besides, it was already morning. The first light of the sun peeked over the horizon, casting a purple glow over the land. Morozko assumed Eirah's mood would only fester like an open wound, growing more and more poisonous as the minutes ticked by—asleep or not. He didn't care how dour she became, but if she posed a problem to him, if she threatened *his* mood, he'd start caring rather promptly.

He walked down the hall, muscles tensing in frustration with every stride he took. When he reached where he had left Eirah, Morozko nodded to the guard, Kusav.

"I checked on her once, Your Majesty."

"Only once?" Morozko's lips twitched, and he wondered if there was anything left of the room. He pushed open the door, glancing around the room until he spotted Eirah sleeping on the chaise. Between the physical exhaustion of prepping for the celebration, the stress of fretting over his arrival, and the ride back to the palace, he was certain she *was* tired.

Morozko could leave her there until she roused, or he could wake her and show her to the room Xezu readied for her. Deciding on the latter, he strode into the room, taking care not to make a sound. He approached the chaise and took a moment to appraise her softened features that had been warped into a scowl before. This close, he could see the woman in his vision. *Who are you?* He mused, hovering over her. He considered kicking over the chaise, rattling her again, but opted to reach for her shoulder. Before he could shake her, her eyelids flew open, horror written across her face, and she swung at him. Morozko caught her delicate wrist and squeezed lightly.

"What are you doing?" Eirah gasped, her chest heaving.

He clucked his tongue and shook his head. "Now, now. I wouldn't advise striking your gracious host, little bird," he said through gritted teeth and hauled her against his chest, forcing Eirah to her feet.

Sleep vanished from her eyes instantly. She was bright, alert, and ready to fight him.

He chuckled at her and loosened his hold but didn't release her. "A room has been prepared for you."

"A room? Don't you mean a prison cell?" Her lips twisted into a thin line.

Morozko arched a brow. "I considered a cell, but you wouldn't last long in the belly of the castle. You'd freeze, and spilling your blood would be a task." He rolled his eyes. Eirah's disregard for what he was offering her was tiresome. How many sacrifices could boast about staying in a palace, in the same wing as the king? He released her wrist and motioned toward the door. "Shall I escort you?"

Eirah lifted her chin, and in the faint tremble he saw in her lips, he knew she fought back a torrent of hatred. What would she say if he gave her permission to spew her emotions freely?

He brushed past her and led her down the hallway toward the east wing—where his quarters were. Perhaps it was foolish on his behalf, keeping her so close to where he slept at night. But with guards standing post outside his and her chambers, he didn't think much of the little bird.

Three-quarters of the way down the length of the wall, Morozko stopped and opened a door. "This is where you'll be staying." He stepped through the door and assessed the room quickly. Just as instructed, the hearth was blazing, and hungry flames lapped at fresh logs. The walls, which resembled the northern lights, were green and blue except for fine lines of gold, lending it the illusion of a cage.

"Welcome to your cage, little bird." He extended a hand, waving to her amenities. A luxurious bed sat in the middle of the room, and on the far wall, an oversized wardrobe.

"It may as well be one," she huffed.

Morozko nodded in agreement. "Yes, it may as well, but this room *is* called the birdcage." He caught himself marveling at the room, remembering how he'd hide in here when he was a youngling. Just him and his wolf pup, hunkering down in the corner of the birdcage. Back then, dozens of wire cages filled with birds had lined the space. But when his mother was slain, Morozko had run into this very room and set them free because no beast deserved to be caged. Most flew out the balcony door, but some remained behind. There would be no unpacking the thoughts of *why* he chose one of his favored rooms for her.

"You should change into something of better quality." He

didn't bother glancing at her as he spoke, instead eyeing the bed where the clothes awaited her.

Eirah wouldn't freeze in the fur-lined dress Xezu had fetched for her. She was human and couldn't endure the cold like him—his steward knew that all too well.

"I don't want your stolen dresses," Eirah hissed, snapping his attention to her.

His face heated with indignation, and he charged forward. "Let me rephrase, in case I gave you the notion I cared as to what you want. You *will* change into that dress, make yourself look presentable, and meet me tonight for supper." Morozko walked away but halted at the door. "Oh, and I don't steal dresses. I keep spare clothes on hand in case any are destroyed in the process of fucking. However, that one was left for me as a *gift*."

Eirah spat near his boot and spun away from him, her ratty braid swinging like a pendulum.

"You missed." He lifted his brows, smirking. "I'll ensure a bath is drawn for you and instruct the servants. If you prefer my assistance, I can gladly pin you down and wash you myself."

She scowled over her shoulder at him. "I would rather be washed by an animal."

With a chuckle, he exited the room, closed the door behind him, and leaned against the wall. While riling Eirah was entertaining, it was only a distraction from the more important matter of deciphering who she was in all the madness.

What's the matter, my son? You can't figure it out? It was as though his mother had never left. Her voice, so full of derision, filled his head, goading him.

"I will. Somehow, I fucking will," he seethed. But unlike

his earlier tauntings with Eirah, it couldn't take months or years. With the seal weakening and his visions increasing, time was of the essence. He couldn't predict how long it would be before a sacrifice had to be made, but he knew it was soon. His visions always bombarded him before the event took place.

Morozko couldn't let the seal crumble.

Eirah had to die.

8

EIRAH

Morning light spilled through the glass doors leading out to the balcony as Eirah stood in the middle of the room. The birdcage room. She gritted her teeth, thinking about Morozko, wishing she had spat on his face instead of the marble floor beside his pristine boot. Why hadn't he just murdered her? Was this his plan all along? To keep her as his plaything? To taunt her before he came in for the kill? He certainly hadn't tried to woo her. And if wooing was inviting her to bathe with him, he needed to work on his skills or, better yet, use his hand to pleasure himself.

The Frost King had only left moments ago, but the door remained unlocked. Eirah still wasn't planning on escaping—however, she wanted to see if he'd put a guard outside her room as he had the other. She drew the door open to find the same tall, blue-haired frost demon who'd guarded her outside the previous room.

"Do you need me to escort you somewhere?" the guard asked, his voice deep but not unkind.

"No, thank you." She shut the door behind her and peered around the room where she would remain for however long Morozko deemed it necessary.

Pushed up against the far right side of a cream wall was a large bed fit for a queen, covered in black furs, blue silken sheets, and the maiden's fur-lined yellow gown the king had left her to wear. On the opposite wall, a tall ivory wardrobe stood with ornate engravings and golden handles. Two velvet chairs tucked into a small circular desk lingered near the corner of the room. Across from it, a fire crackled in a wide hearth, giving off warmth. She searched the drawers of the desk, hoping to find a letter opener or something else sharp that she could use. But the spaces were empty.

Taking off her cloak, she rested it on the chair in front of the desk. Eirah hated to admit it to herself, but the room was lovely, cozy even. She warmed her hands in front of the flames for a few moments before walking to the wardrobe and opening both doors, her eyes widening at what rested inside.

So many beautiful dresses of various sizes and fabrics. Lace. Silks. Furs. Velvets. Leathers. She brushed her hands across each one, wishing she could show them all to Saren. Her friend would've been in love, begging to try them on. Her heart sank as she thought about not only Saren, but also her father. He was most likely sitting at their shared workspace, chipping away at anything he could to distract himself, the way he had with her mother.

The door opened, and Eirah whirled around to find Ulva entering the room, wearing a different crimson tunic and a black leather skirt. She carried two towels and a basket of soaps, her gaze drifting to the open wardrobe. "Per the king's request, I make those for the maidens who come here before they leave. A gift or token of sorts."

No wonder the mortals spread miraculous tales of the Frost King. They relished a fine gift after being pleasured by the king himself, then gossiped about it. After being kicked out of the palace, a pretty dress wouldn't be sufficient enough to satisfy Eirah. But the part of her that loved creating focused on another matter.

"You made these?" Eirah asked, trailing her finger across a lacy-capped sleeve.

"I did." Ulva smiled, inching closer, her hand skimming over a leather bodice before stepping back. "I make the uniforms for everyone here as well."

"You're talented," Eirah said, shutting the doors of the wardrobe. "I make things with my father... or did. But I could never create clothing like this. We make toys and other pieces for the nearby villages."

"Did you bring any with you?" Ulva asked, her interest piqued.

"I wasn't allowed to bring anything." Eirah pursed her lips, then remembered the Morozko doll she'd watched turn to ash in the fireplace of the sitting room and couldn't help but smile a little.

Ulva bit her lip and nodded as if remembering that she wasn't talking to a maiden who would leave the palace, but instead to one who was meant to be sacrificed. "I should prepare your bath."

"Thank you." Even though she wanted to fight against taking a bath to frustrate Morozko, Eirah was in dire need of one. Dirt and perspiration clung to her. And if she was going to find any pleasure while here, she might as well let herself find it in a warm bath.

Once Ulva filled the tub, she loosened the tie from Eirah's braid and unraveled her hair. Her long, dark locks cascaded over her shoulders and down her back, falling to her waist.

Ulva studied Eirah's face, squinting as she scanned her over. "You should wear your hair down—it accentuates your heart-shaped face."

Eirah didn't know if that was a good or bad thing—villagers never said anything about her face or noticed her unless they wanted a custom piece made.

Ulva unfastened the buttons of Eirah's dress. No one had undressed her since she'd been a child, making this the first time she'd ever been pampered.

Once Ulva reached the last button, Eirah said, "I can take care of the rest."

"Are you sure you don't need assistance getting dressed after?" Ulva asked, picking up the basket.

"No, but thank you."

Eirah removed her boots and walked into the bathing chamber, which was larger than any of the rooms in her cottage. A porcelain clawfoot tub was filled practically to the brim, light steam wafting from the water. At the back of the room stood a massive ivory vanity and a rectangular mirror decorated with golden snowflakes. Blue and white curving patterns were etched into the walls, looping and swirling. In front of the tub rested a spotted fur rug and the two fluffy towels that Ulva had left.

Shutting the door, Eirah peeled out of her clothing, and an unpleasant stench struck her nostrils. She was surprised Ulva hadn't mentioned anything, but the servant seemed incredibly polite. Far from what Morozko was...

Eirah stepped into the bath and released a low moan as she lowered herself into the warm water. She sank beneath the liquid, holding her breath as she thought about home, wishing she had gotten to say more before leaving. Spend a little extra time with her father and Saren.

She broke through the water's surface and sighed while grabbing a juniper soap bar. As she washed, she tried not to think about the king or the fact that she was only making herself luxurious before her impending death if she couldn't get her hands on a weapon. *Lovely.*

"I wonder what the village is saying about you now, Eirah?" she said to herself. "Most likely, why did the king choose the girl who speaks to herself and not someone of true beauty? *Bah.*" Rolling her eyes, she slammed down the soap.

Once she was clean and no longer smelling as though she rolled around in the hay with livestock, she pushed out of the bath and draped a fluffy towel around herself. She stared at her dirty dress on the floor, wanting to put it back on to irritate Morozko, but she also didn't want to smell like an animal again. However, she wouldn't put on the rumpled dress he'd left her... one that had been left behind from a pleasurable night.

Ulva didn't say Eirah couldn't take something from the wardrobe, and she was staying in the *birdcage* room after all.

She opened the door, whistling to herself as she padded into the bedroom to collect a dress, when her gaze drifted to the bed and settled on a lithe form sitting on it, his back leaning against the headboard.

"What are you doing in here?" she shrieked, snatching her cloak from the chair and wrapping it around herself. "I thought you didn't demand my presence until supper!"

"Decided I would bring you breakfast." Morozko smirked, motioning at the basket of rolls beside him.

"I'm surprised you didn't bring me someone's hand,"

Eirah said through gritted teeth. "You could have said you were here through the bathing chamber door, you prick."

His features tightened, the only indication that he was annoyed. "If you had allowed Ulva to stay and dress you, or brought the gown I gifted you, we wouldn't be in this predicament. As for the hand, the mortal knew the rules."

She furrowed her brow. "Why are you lingering? Is it time for you to put your blade to my throat?"

"I won't be sneaky about that. You'll know when, little bird." His gaze swept over her, lingering on her mouth for a moment. "I'll see you tonight at supper." He looked at the dress on the bed before scanning her over once more. "But if you prefer to wear the towel instead, I won't mind at all."

The king quirked a brow, and she narrowed her eyes.

"I look forward to dining with you," he said. An unpleasant smile tugged at his lips that she wanted to rip away. He then turned on his heel and sauntered out of the room.

She clenched her jaw and picked up the basket of rolls before throwing them at the door as it shut.

"I heard that, little bird," Morozko cooed from the other side of the door.

Tightening her fists, Eirah grabbed a simple blue cotton gown from the wardrobe and slid it on. She then shoved the used dress off the bed and drew back the covers, slipping beneath them. There was nothing else she could do in the room besides sleep or stare at the fire and wall.

For most of the day, Eirah remained in bed until a clink against the glass of the balcony door sounded. She sat up, squinting at the glass. When the sound came again, she stood and hurried to the door.

Eirah drew it open, finding nothing at first until her gaze

fell on a snowy-white owl perched in the corner of the balcony rail. "Adair," she gasped. "You're back? It's not even nightfall."

The owl cocked his head and studied her. He then held up a foot where something green and black rested in his talons. An olive branch.

"A gift?" she asked, carefully taking it from him, hoping not to scare him off. "Can I pet you?"

He lifted a wing and her eyes widened—he'd always kept his distance before. Yet this was twice now that he hadn't. With a smile, she stroked her fingers across his pale feathers. They were the softest thing she'd ever felt, more so than even silk.

"Eirah?" a voice called from inside her room.

Adair bolted from the balcony, flying up into the sky. Taking a deep swallow, she opened the door to find a tall, middle-aged man there, his dark hair drawn back into a braid. The mortal wasn't as tall as Morozko, but his body was broader, his arms thick with muscle.

"Who are you?" she asked.

"Xezu, His Majesty's steward."

Xezu... she remembered the name. "Ulva's husband?"

"She's my better half." He smiled, then sobered. "The king awaits you for supper. I'm here to escort you."

Eirah's throat was parched, and her stomach tightened with hunger. She wanted to go just to eat and drink everything in sight, but she wasn't there to please Morozko and play whatever game this was. "Tell him I'm not coming."

"Y-you're what?" Xezu stuttered.

"I'm not going to his supper."

Xezu's throat bobbed. "You need to come."

"No. If he wants my presence, then he'll have to drag me out of here."

"Give me a moment," the steward mumbled before turning to leave the room, quietly shutting the door behind him. Eirah knew Morozko wasn't going to be happy and she most likely wouldn't get food and drink brought to her room, either. So she would make do. Lifting a roll from the floor, she wiped the specks of dust away and bit into it. Even though it wasn't soft any longer, the buttery flavoring still ignited her taste buds. It may have been a mistake to eat it because her throat became drier, yearning for a sip of *anything*. She set the rest of the roll on the night table when the door to her room burst open.

Morozko stormed in, his nostrils flaring. "Didn't I say to meet me in the dining hall, little bird?"

"I never said I would go." She folded her arms over her chest, meeting his icy gaze. "This charade is getting ridiculous. Why are you asking me to dine with you instead of sacrificing me?"

He gestured at the air, continuing to glare at her. "I treat you fairly. Brought you to my palace, gave you a nice room, got you a warm bath, invited you to my table, provided you an elegant dress that you refused to wear—"

"I told you I wasn't wearing *that*, and there is a whole wardrobe of freshly-laundered dresses, you prick. I'm staying *here*."

Morozko scoffed, and a slow, mirthless smile formed as his tongue swiped along his plump lower lip. "No, I don't think so, little bird." Before she realized what he was doing, Morozko wrapped his arms around her waist and hoisted her over his shoulder. "You told Xezu you wouldn't dine with me unless I dragged you down there, so here we are."

"Put me down, you bastard!" She kicked and writhed like wildfire, yet he managed to keep a firm hold on her.

"You had the opportunity to walk, and you chose not to. This is the consequence of your poor decision." He chuckled as he carried her down a few hallways, then descended the stairs while she cursed him over and over. But all her screaming did was allow her to inhale his spicy scent further, and she hated that she took pleasure in that smell, the only thing decent about him.

Eirah's gaze connected with a blade at his waist, and hope filled her. As she reached down, she grabbed the dagger from its sheath, and he knocked it from her hand. "That was a test," he purred. "And it seems I can't trust you."

"It's what anyone would do who was being carried against their will!" she screamed.

"If circumstances were different, I may consider bringing you to my court to play the part of a fool. Your dramatics are astounding," he drawled as he brought her into a circular room decorated with golden wolf sculptures and a glass dining table that could fit at least twenty people. As he sat her in one of the glass chairs, Eirah stood, intending to flee, but he was too fast, placing her back in the seat like a naughty child.

Morozko tutted. "Again, you had your chance." Glistening blue magic swirled in the air, a wintry scent folding around her, and as she jerked, her wrists remained bound to the arms of the chair.

"Release me," she seethed.

Morozko ran his hand across his strong jaw, his blue irises locked on hers. "Not yet." He pulled up a chair so he was directly across from her. "How about we get to know one another?"

Eirah scowled. "You want me dead."

"*I* don't want you dead," he said slowly. "Blame your

village for this outcome. Also, yourself. You could have sacrificed one of the animals."

"You—"

"Prick? Surely you're more creative than that." He chuckled, relaxing against the back of his chair.

Eirah wanted to tear him apart, thrust a blade through his icy heart, as she'd planned the entire time. But even so, she couldn't help but stare at the lines of his face, admire how he was sculpted, then be angry at herself because she could never create a carved face so perfectly.

"Untie me," she demanded again.

"So impatient. We are here to acquaint ourselves better," he purred.

Why would she want to acquaint herself with someone who had her bound by magic to a damn *chair*? "How long will I be here?"

"However long I say. Days? Months? Years? Who knows, really?" he said flippantly, flicking his hand in the air.

Her breath caught. Years in a room with nothing? Even days sounded horrific. She would go mad just sitting in there with her hands not working on something—she'd rather be dead. "If I'm to stay until the sacrifice, to get to *know* you, then you'll have to do something for me." This would also give her time to prepare for a way to end him once and for all.

Morozko smirked, and a pale brow lifted. "And what is that, little bird?"

"Tools and supplies."

He scratched at his chin, leaning closer, enough so his spicy scent caressed her nose. "You'll have to do something for me first."

9

MOROZKO

Eirah's eyes widened at his words, and her brow furrowed. If she wanted to be released from his magic, she would have to do precisely what he wanted. Morozko didn't trust her as far as he could throw her, and the feeling was mutual, of that he was certain. She was to die by his hand—what about that screamed *trustworthy?* Still, he hadn't believed Eirah would be so bold as to actually grab his blade.

Morozko didn't think she'd speak for a moment, then she sighed, her shoulders dropping a fraction.

"What do you want from me?" she asked, her voice low.

He motioned to Ludo, a servant, who stood in the corner of the dining hall, and he ducked out through the back door. "It's a small thing really..." Morozko raised his hand, indicating with his fingers how little it was.

"That isn't an answer."

"Would you rather see what else I can do with my

69

fingers?" He arched a brow, leaning closer. A pleasant lavender fragrance struck his senses.

Eirah scowled, her gaze narrowing.

Footsteps broke through their growing tension as the servant returned. He placed a clear goblet on the table, then turned Eirah's chair to face it, the golden rim sparkling in the late afternoon light.

Ludo lifted a golden pitcher with holly leaves engraved on it. He poured the contents into the awaiting container, and the rich, ruby liquid filled the goblet.

Morozko tilted his head, his smile spreading wide as he studied Eirah. "Drink this, little bird, and I'll fetch the supplies you need."

As soon as the words left his lips, Eirah's jaw tightened, and her hands clenched the arms of her chair.

"No, I will not," she said. "You've poisoned it. Why else would the ultimatum be for me to drink a *mystery* liquid?" Eirah's dark eyes flicked to the ruby contents, and she shook her head.

Morozko settled against his chair, his lips thinning as she denied his request. Poison was a coward's way of killing someone, and he was no coward. "Don't be absurd, Eirah. I have never been fond of poisons. For one, I prefer my target to know I am about to kill them. And two, I don't require your sacrifice just yet."

"That isn't reassuring at all," she murmured and eyed the goblet again. The muscles in her jaw flexed before she caught his gaze. "Unbind me, and I'll drink it."

Morozko chuckled, drumming his fingers along his chest. "Pardon? You want me to release you so you can flee or try to impale me with one of these knives? I'm afraid not." He motioned to the set dinner table.

There may not have been any poison in the wine, but there was *something*. His blood. By drinking it, he would form a link with her and hopefully decipher just who she was, including how she was to inherit magic. If Eirah was a foe in the making, he would end her life before she got the chance to oppose him. But if she wasn't, if she could perhaps be an ally...

He curled his fingers into his palms and ground his knuckles into the wooden arm of his chair. An ally was always welcome, but it still didn't resolve the matter with the seal or the changelings. If she could be of use, then, perhaps she wasn't intended for a sacrifice. Which meant he needed to consider someone else. And he—Frosteria—desperately needed a resolution.

"I have no way of drinking it."

Morozko stood, pushing back his chair, the legs groaning as they scraped against the floor. "Do you think so little of me?" he asked softly, stepping by her side. His fingers slid beneath her chin, but she didn't jerk away, even with that pretty pouty mouth of hers set in a thin line. "I will raise the cup to your lips." He dipped his head toward her ear, grinning. "Open up for me, will you?"

He reached for the goblet, grabbing it before he brought it to her mouth. She, of course, wouldn't part her lips for him.

Morozko sighed. His patience grew thin, and while he wasn't opposed to blocking her nose or forcing her mouth open, he wanted her to make this move.

He pulled his head back a fraction, but the cup still lingered in front of Eirah. "I promise to fulfill your wish and bring you tools immediately. Otherwise, we can continue sitting here until you decide to."

Eirah licked her chapped lips. The hours in a warm room

no doubt had driven her thirst up. She finally nodded, the only hint of compliance she showed him.

Morozko slid behind her, stroking her slender shoulder with a hand. Tension rippled through her—though warm, she was as unyielding as the mountain. He brought the cup to her full lips, and to his surprise, she opened her lovely mouth and drank.

His free hand lightly touched the crown of her head. "There, there, little bird..." he cooed. Eirah sputtered on the wine, and he drew the cup away. He shifted to stand beside her. "Our bargain is sealed, and as such, you can relay your list of needs to Xezu or Ulva." Morozko collected a napkin from the table and dabbed away the trail of wine from the corner of her lips in slow, lingering strokes.

"Oh, I shall have plenty on the list, *Your Majesty*."

Morozko shook his head. He flicked his hand, making the bindings disappear. At the same instant, the servant returned with plates of roasted quail, boar sausage, cheese, and a cup of winterberries. "By all means, eat until you're content." He circled the table, sat down, and drew up a fork and knife. Whether she ate was of no consequence to him because he had what he wanted for now. It was only a matter of time until everything became clear, and he discovered just who and what Eirah of Vinti was.

THE FOLLOWING MORNING, Morozko spent breakfast by himself, poring over the events of his vision in the journal he kept. It was the best way to decipher them—he'd learned this when he was a boy. A secret he'd kept from his mother until just before the end, and it was why she thought nothing of plaguing Frosteria—her son—with a curse. He had seen her demise a thousand times over. Perhaps if his mother had been kinder, he would have relinquished the knowledge to her, but he'd witnessed, and even experienced her cruelties enough to know better.

She'd cast him aside, locked him in rooms, and belittled him in front of guests. Over time, fondness for his mother festered into hatred.

Morozko never uttered a word about the uprising. He had allowed the frost demons and mortals to turn on her. Maranna had earned such a fate in the end. Hiding him had been self-preservation, and she wanted to save Frosteria by saving her flesh and blood.

His only regret was not silencing her before she uttered the spell, summoning her creations to live behind the seal. Maranna was no fool. She knew Morozko would have to balance the loyalty of the mortals and frost demons. Without it, the seal would weaken... as it was now, the human village had lost its way. And he shouldn't have had to remind Vinti of how important the ritual was, shouldn't need to tend to the sheep-like mortals and their soft, forgetful minds.

Xezu entered the study just as the candle on Morozko's desk snuffed out. He'd been at his notes for the better part of the evening, and it seemed efficient to start where he had left off. Smoke billowed from the sliver of a wick, and he reached into a drawer to pull out a new candlestick.

"Your Majesty." Xezu bowed his head. "I've retrieved Eirah's tools and supplies."

Morozko swapped out the candles. "Bring them here." He wondered how Eirah felt after consuming a portion of his blood. He didn't sense anything on his end yet, but that didn't mean she wasn't beginning to show signs. Some grew ill, while others, if their innate abilities sparked to life, would exhibit small indications of their particular gift.

"Of course." Xezu bowed again, then left the room. It wasn't long until he returned with four large black sacks.

Curiosity got the better of Morozko, so he stood from his chair and crossed the room. "What's inside them?"

His steward shifted his weight, and an uneasy expression formed on his face. Like he didn't want to say. Why, Morozko had no idea. "Her tools, Your Majesty." Xezu grimaced when Morozko curled his lip, sneering. "For making toys."

Morozko's eyes narrowed in confusion. "Toys?" He had never considered what her role in the village had been prior to him selecting her. But the notion she was a toymaker surprised him. Someone as venomous as her ought to be the village crone. Still, he crouched down and opened one of the bags, finding a block of wood that had the makings of a shape. What would it become? A doll? A toy soldier? Morozko shifted a few other things around, noting all the sharp tools. One that could take out his eye, another to pierce his heart, and perhaps one that could clip his finger clean off. He supposed if Eirah wanted to try at his life again, she'd have to go through his guard and his magic as well. Morozko studied the four velvet bags. "I'll bring them to her."

Xezu's eyes widened. "Surely not, Your Majesty... You need to focus on your visions."

While it may be true, nothing was coming to him while he sat in his chair. He may as well make himself useful, or at the very least, pester Eirah with his presence. "I'll decide what suits me better at the moment, and I say that I'm taking the sacks to Eirah." This time, there was no argument. He scooped

SLAYING THE FROST KING

the bags up, grunting at their weight, and strode out the door, heading down the hall to Eirah's room.

Morozko slanted a glance at Kusav, who stood outside the room. The guard bowed his head but remained quiet.

He didn't knock. For one, his guests were usually in his bed, and for two, this was his home. Eirah wouldn't be the first—nor the last—female he would see naked. It wasn't as if she possessed any appendage he hadn't seen or dragged his fingers across before. While he hadn't done such things to Eirah *yet*, he wasn't an inept lover. Still, a pity she'd denied him. He had it on good authority that tumbling someone with such strong feelings, be it hate or otherwise, only heightened the experience.

Surprisingly, Eirah didn't spring across the room or snarl at him. Although, judging by the early hour—she could have been asleep. However, she sat on the edge of her bed, twisting her fingers into the sheets. Out of all the behaviors he'd seen thus far, this wasn't like her.

With a half-hearted sigh, he hurled the sacks down, motioning to them. "As I promised, your *things* are here. Let it be said that I am a gracious host. Because you are fed, and have your tools," he said all of this by way of greeting. "You can try attacking Kusav, but I'm afraid you won't get very far. He'll have magic coiled around your throat before you can pierce his flesh."

When she said nothing, he glanced down at the sacks. Morozko smirked, toeing the overstuffed bags with his boot. "I can always burn them if you're not pleased."

"Stop," she stated, turning her gaze to him finally. Dark circles lined beneath her eyes. She didn't look particularly well. "Don't you knock?"

"Not in my home. My guests are for pleasure, and if they

CANDACE ROBINSON & ELLE BEAUMONT

are an enemy, well, they don't get to come in and play." He cocked his head, running a finger across his lower lip. "Are you wondering where you fall, little bird?"

"No," she croaked and stood, slowly crossing the room.

Whether he was heartless or not, he couldn't help but notice she looked as though she were about to keel over. Morozko inched closer, scrutinizing her appearance. Sweat beaded her brow, her lips were drained of color, and her tan skin was now as pale as his. "Eirah, are you well—"

"You lied to me," she hissed, moving a hand to her stomach. "You *did* poison me."

"I did not!" Morozko spat. He was tired of her insolence. Did he blame her for not believing him? No, but one glimpse of all he'd done over the years, and one could discern when he was telling the truth. "I should never have brought you these useless things."

"They are not useless. They are *mine,* and they are part of our bargain." She stepped forward, swaying, but still holding her chin higher as if she were a match for him.

Indeed, little bird.

What went on in her head? What was she thinking when she approached him and spoke to him in such a manner? "Yes, I suppose you're right. And I wouldn't want to go back on our deal, considering the predicament we're in."

"What do you mean?" Eirah whispered.

"It isn't as though I can retract my blood from you once you've consumed it." Eirah's body was currently in the throes of battling his blood off, and in the process, if there was any latent magic or some other ability, his blood would bring it forth. And through this connection, he hoped, his vision would become clear.

Eirah's eyes saucered, and she clutched her stomach as if

76

she wanted to heave the contents onto his boots. Perhaps he'd have deserved that. "Your *what?*"

"At least it wasn't poison." He chuckled, dragging the tip of his tongue along a sharp canine. She wouldn't die from his blood, and she was just being overly dramatic. He was amused, but Eirah was on the verge of fainting or spewing, and he wasn't certain which to be more concerned over.

IO

EIRAH

"Why would you give me your blood to drink?" Eirah asked, her nostrils flaring. The nausea bubbling up her throat was lessening, and she seemed to be feeling a little better even though her sleep had been anything but pleasant. Perhaps Morozko's *deceitful* blood had finished traveling through her. "Better yet, why didn't you just tell me what it was before I consumed it?"

When she'd sipped from the red wine, she wouldn't admit it aloud, not to him, but she'd almost moaned from how good it tasted. The thought now crossed her mind that it was *his* blood which had tasted so sweet, so *lush*. And she was horrified by the thought.

"Would you have still drank it, little bird? Knowing you were putting a piece of me *inside* you," Morozko purred, stepping closer as he peered down at her beneath thick lashes.

She hated how everything that rolled off his tongue seemed as though it was intended to seduce her. As if he wanted to elicit pleasure from her so he could mock her afterward.

"For tools? Yes," she said, not backing away from his hooded stare. "If you promised a mountain of tools next, I just might consume your blood again."

"They're that important to you?" he asked, his brow arching.

"They're my life." Eirah walked around him and knelt in front of the four velvet bags he'd brought. She emptied them on the floor and spread the objects around so she could see everything properly. A smile spread across her face as she took in the wonderful gifts. When Ulva had come to collect the list, Eirah didn't think everything on it would be brought to her, even though the woman had promised to tell Xezu to make sure everything was there. And it all was.

Various fabrics, assorted woods, paints, gears, nails, strings, scissors, chisels, gouges, and more tools.

And a carving *knife*.

Heart pounding with excitement, she lifted the knife. The blade would cut cleanly while working fast and efficiently on her craft. But that wasn't the only thing she would use it for— the moment she'd been waiting for had arrived. Without another thought, she whirled around as she stood, then lunged for the king. She thrust the blade forward, but he was quicker than expected, grasping her arm and spinning around so her back was pressed to his chest.

"You should have been thanking me for the tools instead of trying to *kill* me," he cooed near her ear as if he was intrigued by her actions. "This is the second time you've attempted to use a blade on me. Both times I was being gracious. Providing you supper. Providing you with your *tools.*

And look how you treat me? If you were anyone else, you'd be dead."

Eirah scoffed, unable to believe the audacity of this arrogant male. "Then either let go of me or sacrifice me now," she seethed, wriggling to escape his hold.

"In due time, little bird." He sighed, tightening his hold on her. "It seems I still can't trust you, but I'll give you one more chance." Morozko's warm breath tickled her throat as he spoke to her. "Now, drop the knife." His voice came out soft as silk, as if he was attempting to calm a wild animal.

Eirah didn't—she only clutched the blade harder.

"Come now. Let me tell you *why* you don't want to end my life." Morozko's fingers trailed down her arm, and beneath the anger boiling in her, another sensation rose, warming within her as his hand folded around hers. She didn't want to release the weapon, but there wasn't a chance of her winning against him now.

Morozko gently took the knife from her, and she slowly turned around, her fists clenched at her sides. Eirah narrowed her eyes as he grinned at her.

"You care about Frosteria just as much as I do," Morozko started. "And although you couldn't care less if I ceased breathing right now, if I die, so does Frosteria. My life is tied to the land, just as my mother's was. When her life ended, the ties to this world were passed to me, but I have no heir and so if I die, the ones you care about most will, too." He paused for a moment, his full lips twisting in frustration before continuing on, "I tell you this because I don't take you for the type to whisk me away to some hidden prison, holding me hostage to ensure I remain alive." Morozko cocked his head, his shrewd blue eyes squinting as he looked down at her. "If you don't believe me, ask anyone in the palace. *Ask them* what happens if I die." He held the blade out to her.

Eirah's hands shook, her eyes widening in horror. If she had ended his life... It would've destroyed not only her father and Saren, but the entire realm. The plan to get a tool to murder him was for naught. There had to be another way... "I won't try to stab you again," she said between clenched teeth.

"Good. I'm glad we're on the same page. But perhaps you would try to draw my blood for another reason..." Morozko brought the blade to the tip of his index finger and pierced his flesh. Deep crimson bloomed to the surface of his skin, then he held his finger out to her. "Would you like to have a taste of my magic without the wine?"

"You're a true prick." Yet she couldn't deny the wintry smell of his blood was enticing, and a part of her wanted to run her tongue across the ruby pearl. "And disgusting."

"Oh, you haven't seen me at my worst." He chuckled, twisting his lips as he swept his gaze over her. "Your hesitation on the latter part speaks volumes. So, when you're ready to explore how *disgusting* I am, I'll be ready." He dropped the knife beside her supplies on the floor, then motioned at them. "Now, play with your trinkets. I have important matters to attend to."

Eirah cursed him as he shut the door. But for some reason, he hadn't put the dagger in her own heart for treason. Considering this and not understanding why he was prolonging her death, she sat on the floor and separated the items she'd been given into neat piles. If she couldn't trap the king in something, like a block of ice, then perhaps the only thing left she could do for Saren's safety, for her father's, would be to let him sacrifice her. No. She couldn't give up just yet.

After she set the last paintbrush in a small group, Eirah

plucked up a block of wood and settled against the baseboard of the bed when a knock came at the door before it opened. Ulva walked in, carrying a glass of water and a basket of fruits and rolls, her hair in a low braided bun. "The king said you might need some water."

Now he would give her something to drink... She hadn't wondered why he'd only brought her rolls to eat the day before, not until after she'd had his wine.

"Thank you for this and the supplies as well," Eirah said, taking the glass. She managed a few sips before she set it beside her. "He put blood in my wine last night. Did you know that?"

Ulva gazed down at her hands, not meeting Eirah's eyes. "His Majesty tends to do that when searching for answers, but it will do you no harm."

Eirah frowned. "I'm just a toymaker from Vinti. What answers could he possibly find with me?"

Ulva shook her head. "I'm not certain."

"The king told me he's tied to the land. Is that true?" Eirah ran the knife across the block of wood, slicing away thin slivers.

"He is, but I will not discuss more than that."

"What about the sacrifices? Why does the king choose to make Vinti perform them every year when we're struggling with animals as it is?"

"He has a good reason, one that everyone benefits from, and that's all I will say." Ulva sighed, then changed the subject. "What are you making?"

If it was such a good reason, then why wouldn't anyone speak of why it needed to be done? "A doll," Eirah finally answered.

"You'll have to show me when you finish." Ulva stood, her

knees popping. "If you need anything, Kusav will take you wherever you need."

Eirah nodded. She didn't want to go anywhere in the castle, just stay in this room, alone with her tools, tools she wouldn't be able to use against the king, only to make things. If she couldn't see her father or Saren, then this was the next best option.

Over the next few hours, Eirah cut into the wood, carving out chunks, shaping a head, and forming a sphere. As she worked on the other body parts, her stomach churned once more, and she drank a few more sips of water, hoping it would make the nausea disappear again.

A clinking noise sounded against the glass door, and Eirah jerked her head up, excitement swirling in her chest. She ventured outside to find Adair resting in the middle of the balcony rail, a twig with berries in his beak.

"Another gift?" She grinned, taking it from him. "You're too kind."

He cocked his head, studying her with his orange eyes. A strange feeling pulsed within her, not her heart or her blood, but something else, something hidden as she looked at him in return. A tugging of sorts, yet before she could unravel what was happening, he darted off into the air, flapping his snowy-white wings across the light blue sky.

"Strange," she whispered and shrugged it off.

Eirah went back into the room and sat on the floor, resuming her task on the doll while trying to figure out how to trap the Frost King. At the moment, she was too weak to over-power him, and even if she could get him on his back, Kusav was still outside the door.

As she made progress on the doll, she ate one of the apples and drank a little more water. She then cut, carved,

83

and chipped away until the small figure was ready to be painted.

Picking up a long brush with a thin tip, she dipped it into blue paint when the door opened. She didn't have to look up to know it was the king sauntering into her room.

"Yes, Your Majesty?" Eirah painted a blue eye on the doll's face.

"I brought you a peace offering," he drawled. "Since it looks like you don't want to come downstairs to eat."

"More blood?" she asked as she glanced up, noticing a glass in one hand and a steaming bowl of soup in the other. Morozko wore a simple white tunic paired with tight black trousers that accentuated his lean and muscular form a bit too well.

"We're done with that, little bird." He chuckled, kneeling beside her. "What are you fiddling with?"

Eirah looked at him from the corner of her eye, not knowing why he was sitting beside her and watching what she was doing. "I'm making another Morozko doll." Her lips tilted upward as she dipped the brush into the black paint.

"Another?" he drawled. "Well, I suppose I am a fine specimen. Show me the other."

Her gaze met his bright blue eyes, and she ignored the fact that they were the most beautiful, otherworldly ones she'd ever seen. Like every other blasted feature on him. "I made it back at the village, then burned it when I first arrived here since I was unable to do it at the bonfire." She grinned, baring all her teeth.

He blinked, studying her for a long moment before he chuckled and shifted closer to her, his spicy scent caressing her nose. Lovely and intoxicating. But a warm smell and a sculpted face wouldn't hide a dark and brutal heart.

Morozko took the doll from her hands, his fingers brushing hers *intentionally*, and she narrowed her eyes.

"You can't just take things from me," she grumbled. "Haven't you done that enough?"

Ignoring her, he grunted as he rolled it over. "It looks nothing like me."

"I'm not finished yet." Eirah ripped it back from him, then grabbed another brush to paint the doll's hair white. But her hand stalled when she could feel him watching her again. "Yes?" she said without looking at him.

"Why do you make these... toys?"

Eirah halted her movements and faced him as he relaxed against the bed, his arm propped on his knee while the other leg was straightened. "Why do we do anything?" she started. "My father is a toymaker, and ever since I was small, I helped him make things not only for our village, but for the frost demon villages as well. I specialize in music boxes, but I like creating darker dolls for myself when I'm not doing tasks for customers."

Morozko cocked his head, seeming to mull something over. "You're the toymaker they talk about? The one who makes the music boxes?"

"You've heard about them?"

"A maiden I took to bed brought one as a gift. It played the loveliest tune as we pleasured one another through the night." His predator's gaze remained on her, even as a slow, wicked smile tugged at his lips.

"Bah!" She waved a hand in the air. "I don't want to hear about your dalliances."

"Envious?" he cooed.

"I'd rather kiss a sheep." She'd rather keep her maidenhead until she was dead, too, but he didn't need to know she

85

hadn't ever taken a lover, or she would never hear the end of it from him.

"Would you now?" Morozko inched closer, and she held her ground, not backing down. "You have a beautiful neck," he whispered in her ear.

She rolled her eyes. "Is that how you get maidens in bed? By telling them how their *neck* looks?"

"So, it's poetry you seek." He ran the tip of his warm finger up the curve of her neck. A delicious shiver ran up her spine, and dare she say, she *liked* it. "Sleek and silken to the touch. I could glide my tongue up it, see what you taste like."

Her eyes fluttered, and she stood, crossing her arms over her chest as he chuckled. Laughed at the game he knew he was playing. The bastard.

"Just leave me alone until you decide my time here is done. I'm getting sick of these games. They aren't amusing. They're cruel." A sick feeling crept through her again, as though her blood was heating inside her veins like it had earlier. The room started to spin, and she needed fresh air, to get away from him.

His expression remained neutral, and he didn't say anything when she turned away from him to go outside.

The breeze blew against her skin as she tightened her grip on the rail. Even though she was out in the cold, her skin felt on fire. The longer she stood, the more she weakened and needed to lie down. She backed away from the rail to go inside, her body swaying. The white world grew hazy, and her knees buckled before she collapsed to the ground.

The door burst open, and Morozko was there, lifting her into his arms. She didn't have the strength to break free of him.

"What are you doing?" he spat. "Trying to get yourself killed?"

"I *fell*. I thought it would be a wonderful day to hit the ground, don't you agree?" she rasped.

"You're not well, are you?"

Was he a fool? Of course she wasn't. "It's because of your *blood*."

He frowned. "You shouldn't still be having symptoms."

"I suppose they come and go," she said, wiggling in his grasp. "Put me down. I can stand."

Morozko lowered her to her feet, and as soon as his fingertips left her waist, she collided with his chest. In an instant, she was off the floor once more, her body nestled into him.

"Put me down!" she hissed as exhaustion coursed through her.

"So you can fall *again*?" He pursed his lips, incredulous.

Eirah couldn't hear what else he complained about because her eyes fell shut, and everything became quiet.

NINE DAYS HAD GONE by of Eirah slipping in and out of consciousness. Ulva had come in and washed her as best she could, and the king had been at her bedside frequently, watching her contemplatively as if she were a puzzle to solve. Ulva had recently left, refusing to let her bathe just yet.

Eirah didn't care anymore, regardless if she was ill or not. She'd taken a bath by herself for years—she wasn't a newborn babe. Pushing herself from the bed, she stumbled as she walked into the bathing chamber, but she didn't collapse onto the floor. It was progress.

She turned on the water, letting the tub fill while peeling the sweat-soaked nightgown from her body. Ulva had helped change her nightly, so, thankfully, she hadn't worn the same clothing for days.

But her body smelled like the stables.

Eirah swayed as she stepped into the warm water, lowering herself into its depths. Grabbing the bar of soap, she ran it up her body and through her hair.

"This is good, Eirah. Just what you needed," she whispered as she settled against the back of the tub to relax before she attempted to walk to the bed.

And as fast as lightning striking the earth, sickness washed over her once more. Her chest heaved, and her breathing grew ragged. This was all Morozko's fault. He'd done this to her, and she didn't know why his blood was still clinging inside of her after all this time. It was like a pesky insect that wouldn't go away. What if it never vanished?

A new sensation brewed within her, tingling at first before a sharp pain traveled up her arms and down her legs. Eirah's eyes rolled to the back of her head, her body drifting downward, slipping beneath the water until she was completely covered. She tried to push herself up, but she was unable, just as she was unable to breathe.

Her heart thrummed inside her chest, crashing against her rib cage. She needed air and she couldn't do anything, even though she yelled at herself to thrash, to scream.

And then she stopped, knowing this was to be her sacrifice.

II

MOROZKO

Nine days were too long for this. The effects of Morozko's blood should've tapered off by day two, if not the same day. The reaction Eirah's body was having was extreme, and he'd witnessed nothing like it. It should have only brought to the surface what lingered in the depths of her being. The magic he'd seen in his visions... But what was wrong with the mortal? Morozko frowned, pinching the bridge of his nose as he stood in the hallway outside of his chambers. Xezu came to report about an area of interest—a part of the forest at the base of the mountain—which Morozko believed was the location from his visions. What the spot had to do in the grand scheme of things, he hadn't a clue, but it kept flickering in his mind.

"I don't understand why she's ill," Morozko ground out. He'd given a few humans his blood before, but not so many that he could predict what would happen. This was all a guessing game, and he was relying on what he saw in flashes to help him.

"She is human, Your Majesty. We... are unlike demons and don't recover as swiftly," Xezu replied, casting a glance down the hall. "As for her disposition, try having a care about her predicament, Your Majesty. It is a lot to take in."

"I told her how I'm tied to the land." Morozko glanced down at his hand, picking beneath his thumbnail.

Xezu didn't stammer, but he did begin to speak several times only to stop, then offered, "May I inquire as to *why*?"

He flexed his fingers, chuckling darkly. "She tried to stab me."

"Again, Your Majesty?" Xezu sighed tiredly.

Morozko's brows furrowed, and he shrugged. "I seem to have that effect on her."

The king pushed off the wall. Sometimes, he nearly forgot his steward was human. They weren't as close as kin, yet he did trust the man. But his differing complexion and shorter stature always reminded Morozko of what he was. Still, he appreciated Xezu reminding him of a mortal's frailties.

Morozko hissed. "That does not change the reason she is here." Besides, her emotional turmoil wasn't his responsibility. It wasn't his duty to ensure she was comfortable outside of the luxuries he gave her. His jaw muscles leaped as he clenched his teeth. The recent vision brewed a steady unease within him.

He closed his eyes, allowing the image to play within his mind again.

Eirah's lips pressed into a thin line as she faced him, her dark hair caked with dirt. Blood trickled from the corner of her mouth, and tears beaded her lashes. Morozko knelt on the ground, holding his throbbing side. Liquid seeped through his fingers, warm and sticky.

"Morozko. Please," she rasped.

It was clear, at that moment, that her sorrow and horror were directed at him. But why did she care if he succumbed to his injuries, if the entire legion of changelings swarmed him, taking him under?

"Morozko!"

"I should just kill her and be done with it. This sussing through things is only delaying the inevitable. It's either Eirah or Frosteria. One light isn't more important than the kingdom."

Still, his visions never lied. They bore the truth, and while the future changed depending on the decisions made, the outcome never strayed too far from what he saw. So, why did the little bird weep for him and utter his name in a way that cracked the ice surrounding his bloody heart? The same mortal he swore could breathe fire if she so willed it. He'd seen a spot of tenderness in her while she painted her dolls and spoke of why she did it, but toward him? It wasn't as if he deserved it.

Morozko's eyes snapped open when his name was uttered. It echoed until it was like a knife driving into his skull. *Morozko. Morozko. Morozko.* Without a word, he strode away from Xezu. The sharp staccato of his boots falling on the floor bounced off the walls, sounding more like running than walking. He gritted his teeth against the gnawing of his name rolling around in his head, but it was pulling him along to Eirah's room. He approached Eirah's door and threw it open, bolting inside, but she wasn't in her bed nor on the balcony. His muscles coiled as his icy heart pounded.

The smell of juniper soap lingered in the air, and his eyes widened. He charged toward the bathing chamber and rushed to the tub, where the water swirled within its depths. His limbs moved before he could process the fact she wasn't thrashing. Morozko scooped Eirah up, holding her like one would a child.

Her head rested against his bicep at an unnatural angle, her entire body limp and lifeless, cooling against him quickly.

Not like this, Eirah. Not like this!

"You will not die like this, Eirah of Vinti!" His voice took on a shrill note as he carried her out of the bathing chamber and to her bed. He laid her down, assessing her quickly. Her chest didn't rise, and her skin was gray and cold to the touch. How long had she been like this? The bath water was still warm.

"Fuck," he whispered. "Come on, Eirah." He cupped her cheeks, his brows furrowing. Morozko would've preferred to see the scowl on her face over the look of death she wore at the moment. But that was who he was. The bringer of death.

He hissed, torn between what he must do and what should be done. Without another thought, he brought his lips to Eirah's. Her mouth was slack, but this wasn't about a kiss or tasting the hint of cinnamon lingering on her lips. It was about not letting her die. His terms. Her death was supposed to be on *his* terms.

With one exhale, a chilled breath passed from him and into her. He drew to her side and whispered an incantation into her ear, commanding death's grip to cease and for his blood to work with hers. Not against her.

He peeled himself away from Eirah long enough to fetch a towel to dry her, then he pulled the covers back to slip her beneath them. By the time she was under the furred blankets, her back arched. Her eyes, normally dark and luminous, opened to reveal an icy blue to rival his. She sucked in a greedy breath, and he did the same.

Morozko brushed the dark strands of hair from her face.

"Do not forget you are a fighter, Eirah. So, fight your way back," he whispered.

Eirah's hand darted up as if she were reaching for something. Morozko dragged his palm down her forearm, and an electric pulse met him. He shivered at the foreign feeling brushing his own power. Both heady and alarming.

"Eirah, wake up!" he bellowed, and when her eyes opened, their usual deep brown locked on him for a moment. She choked once, twice, and he aided her to her side, where she spewed a mouthful of water.

Morozko pounded her back until the fits ceased. He frowned and drew back, assessing her again. Red painted her cheeks from the force of vomiting, and her brows pinched together as she looked at him, clearly dazed.

"Why do you look so ruffled?" she croaked, grimacing after.

Did he look ruffled? There was no mirror for him to glance at to confirm or deny her accusation, but judging by the ordeal they'd both faced, he wouldn't be surprised if it were true.

He chuckled, looking her over once more, and turned to the door. It hadn't been long since he'd entered the room and made a fuss, but Xezu and Kusav gaped at him—*them*. "Xezu, go have Ulva make some fresh tea for Eirah and perhaps some broth, too," Morozko instructed.

"Of course, Your Majesty." Xezu, wide-eyed, bowed and fled the room briskly.

"As for you, Kusav, go back to your post and shut the door. This isn't a public showing, am I clear?" Morozko shot the guard a pointed look.

Kusav pounded his fist against his chest. "Yes, Your Majesty." He clicked his heels together and returned to his position outside the room, but not before closing the door behind him.

With the other males gone, Morozko turned his attention to Eirah, who pulled herself into a sitting position. The blanket cascaded down her skin, pooling at her waist. He couldn't stop his eyes from following the motion, and as he dragged his gaze upward, he paused on the gentle slope of her breasts—her nipples hardened from the brush of cool air against them.

Eirah's senses seemed to crash down on her because she yanked the blankets up and scowled at him. "What did you do?"

Morozko snorted and brushed his hair out of his face. "Me?" Morozko stood, crossing the room to fetch her robe. He spun on his heel and pinned her with a hard look. "I saved your life, is what I did."

"What?" Her lips twisted as a look of confusion passed over her face.

He sauntered forward and laid her robe across the bed. "Let me refresh your memory. The bath and the inability to draw water into your lungs..." Morozko watched as the realization dawned on her, and he wasn't certain if she was more horrified by the notion she nearly drowned or that he had handled her while she was bare.

"I'll spare you the lecture on why you shouldn't have been bathing without a servant's help because I think you understand how foolish that was." He lifted a brow, waiting for some sign she realized just that. A rush of color painted her cheeks, perhaps from frustration or embarrassment. Either way, it was pleasing to see life blossoming in her face once again.

He crossed his arms and turned around, waiting for her to

don the robe. Fabric rustled, and when it ceased, Morozko faced Eirah, then a knock on the door cut through the moment.

"Come in," Morozko ordered.

The door opened, revealing Ulva with a tray. On it was a bowl of steaming broth and a crystal pot. At once, the salty fragrance of broth tickled Morozko's nose, accompanied by the minty scent of winterberry tea. Ulva bustled toward the bedside and set down the tray, then went about pouring a cup for Eirah. The woman paused for a moment as if she were on the verge of saying something, but Morozko sent her a sharp look that sent her fleeing toward the threshold.

"Thank you, Ulva," Eirah rushed out before the woman left the room and shut the door.

As soon as they were alone again, Morozko studied Eirah. Tension rippled in her newly alert body, and he knew if he riled her enough, she would tire easily. But he wasn't here to taunt or tease. He was here because—why?

The vision. The sound of his name threatening to crack his skull open?

"Why are you looking at me like that?" Eirah mumbled as she reached for the tray, but her hand shook enough that if she *did* lift her drink or bowl, it would spill over her.

Morozko stepped forward and took the tray up, only to rest it on the bed beside Eirah. "Don't be foolish. You can barely sit right now, let alone feed yourself." He took up a spoon and skimmed the surface of the broth and lifted it. Morozko thought he'd witness an argument, but only a hint of resignation was there. He brought the spoon to her lips, and she took delicate sips.

"I came to check on you, and it's a good thing I did because you were unconscious in the tub when I arrived." He brought another spoonful to her lips, shaking his head. Morozko wouldn't divulge the entire truth. He was still trying to piece together what his visions even meant. His fingers tingled where he'd felt a foreign pulse.

"You're not telling me everything." Eirah pushed away the spoon, but she didn't set her jaw in a hard line. It was those damnable dark eyes that roved along his features, assessing him too closely.

Morozko didn't like that she was studying him. Eirah had no place here, and as long as both maintained that understanding, everything would run smoothly. "You know nothing about me."

"Then tell me, savior of mine, tell me." Her tone dripped with sarcasm, and it was enough to bring forth cool laughter from him. "You wanted me as a sacrifice. That could have been it. Our *lovely* tale coming to an end."

Morozko set down the spoon, and he noticed Eirah's complexion was returning to her sun-kissed coloring. Even her lips were back to their rosy pink. He considered her words for a moment, of what Vinti might still know and what they had lost along the way. The humans forgot so easily, and if they didn't pass stories on or craft cautionary tales, everything was forgotten.

But a frost demon's curse was to remember.

"What else is there to know about me? I am a cold and ruthless king." He ran his tongue along the tip of his sharp canine. Morozko didn't want to dredge up his past, but what, pray tell, would she think of his truth? Would sorrow creep into her gaze or only pity? "One of my earliest memories is of a male who was my father's comrade." His eyes homed in on hers—he wanted to see every subtle shift in her demeanor.

"I know this because the male, Laku, told me so. It was the

eve of the blizzarding season, and Laku let it slip that he knew my father. He said, 'You may look the part of your mother, but you have the heart of your father.' Which prompted me to ask him, where did he go? I never knew him and never heard stories.

"The palace bustled with life for my sixth-year celebration the following day, but my attention was on Laku. He told me my father was the captain of my mother's royal guard, and she used him for pleasure. She also used him to secure her position in Frosteria by ensuring she had an heir. Before I was born, he was slain after he had served his purpose. And those who were closest to my father were also killed. Except for Laku."

The room was quiet enough that Morozko could almost hear the thrumming of Eirah's heart. While her gaze softened, her eyes held no pity, and he was grateful for that. "Laku's death came later once she discovered his betrayal. During my birthday feast, she brought him before me, only to behead him. A *wonderful* gift for a child, is it not?"

On the one hand, Morozko could see why his mother would do such a thing. Maranna's control had slipped, and she needed to assert herself to show the courtiers that *this* was what happened when they crossed the Frost Queen. But there was a fine line to tread, and she crossed it time and time again.

Eirah frowned. "I have heard stories of how wicked she was but never thorough details." She sucked her bottom lip into her mouth, possibly warring with what to say. But what *could* she say after that?

"And that, little bird, is enough bedtime horrors for you." He sighed. Eirah's eyelids fluttered as if she were readying to fall asleep. If luck was on his side, she'd forget the wretched story the way he wished he could. "You need rest, like it or not." He went to retrieve the tray, but she grabbed his wrist, stopping him. He eyed where her fingers circled around the linen shirt but didn't move to extricate her.

"I've had enough sleep to last a lifetime. I just... feel off. It's been coming in waves—it's strange."

Morozko reached out, and Eirah allowed him to brush his knuckles against her cheek. The same pulse as earlier met his skin, and he gritted his teeth together. Not knowing what he was doing, but he didn't care. He was only relieved she was warm and not feverish.

He shouldn't press her, but something niggled at the back of his mind. The vision, his questions, and the need to know *why this mortal was important.*

12

EIRAH

"I need to meet with Xezu. Can I trust that you won't get yourself killed?" Morozko arched a brow, his ice-blue eyes locked on Eirah's.

"I wouldn't have almost died if you hadn't given me your blood." She folded her arms across her chest. The memory of slipping beneath the water's surface—unable to move, unable to breathe, *helpless*—washed over her. She'd been content that it was her sacrifice while under the water, but she truly didn't want to die, didn't want to stop breathing. And even though she was meant to die by his hand, even though she'd tried to stab him, Morozko had saved her, brought her back from the brink of the unknown.

"My blood doesn't kill those who drink it. This is something else." Morozko stood from the edge of the bed. "If you need to get cleaned up again, I'll help you next time." And as though he couldn't help himself, he added, "We can finally bathe together in my chambers, if you wish."

Eirah rolled her eyes, though a small fire ignited within her at the thought. "Don't go back to being a prick."

"Back to one? I've fallen from grace so quickly." He smirked.

Her lips twitched and she fought a smile. Perhaps she was getting used to his vexing remarks. But then she thought about the events in his past that he'd confessed to her. How he'd been only a boy—on the day of his birthday, no less—when someone he cared about was decapitated in front of him by his own mother. A queen of true darkness. Morozko never knew his father and Eirah had heard the tales of his cruel mother, but she hadn't known that she was just as awful to her own son. Her stomach sank at the image of a helpless young prince being harmed by his mother. As she unraveled a little more about the king, she started to wonder if she should even be wanting to find another way to rid Frosteria of him. She remembered Ulva's words about him having a good reason for the sacrifice. Now, she believed that maybe there could be...

"I'll come to check on you later. For now, remain in bed," Morozko said, his tone leaving no room for argument.

"I won't leave this bed, but *only* if you bring a few of my things to me." Eirah tilted her head to the side and smiled.

"The Morozko doll?" he purred.

Eirah couldn't deny how she liked the way his deep voice sounded, the way his words rolled off his tongue. She had to remember *who* she was talking to and *why* she was in this bed in the first place. "No, he's waiting his turn," she drawled. "I just need a few pieces of wood and the carving tools to work on a music box."

Morozko knelt on the floor, shuffling through the items

before finally handing her several tools and a small stack of wood. "I'd like to hear it when you're finished."

She was ready to retort with a snarky reply, thinking he meant to tease her with the sound of maidens he pleasured. But the expression on his face looked serious, melancholic, as though he were deep in thought. Perhaps he was still reminiscing about his past, what he'd told her about his mother.

"Then I shall play it for you," she said softly.

His brows rose in surprise, and he gave her a brief nod before turning on his heel. He glanced over his shoulder at her one more time before leaving her alone.

Eirah lifted her tools, her strength slowly returning. She peered down at her robe and sighed, remembering how the king had seen her bare, how he'd carried her in his arms while she was dead to the world, how the blankets had dropped from her chest for mere moments, exposing her breasts.

No man had ever seen her in that manner—heat crawled up her neck and into her cheeks. "It's fine, Eirah. The king has seen hundreds of maidens without clothing. No, no, *thousands*. Your body wouldn't be special to him. It wouldn't be to anyone." Was it *thousands*?

She pinched the bridge of her nose to stop imagining how he would peel off a maiden's dress or lower the robe from *her own* shoulders. But there was something she couldn't stop mulling over—when he'd brushed her skin with his, an electric sensation hummed inside her. That had certainly not happened before from any of his touches.

Shaking off the thought, Eirah leaned forward and stared out the glass door as flakes of snow fell. A strange sensation had tugged at her with Adair, not as potent as with the king, but something different... Too many odd feelings that she didn't have answers for.

There wasn't any sign of the snowy white owl—she was tempted to disobey Morozko and go out on the balcony, but she didn't want to collapse again. If she fainted outside, she would most certainly freeze to death and, in this instance, the king might not find her in time.

Eirah took a few sips of tea from her glass before starting on the music box. She spent most of the day cutting the rectangular pieces to create the outer shell, then worked on carving designs into the wood.

The door opened to Ulva carrying a supper plate displaying steaming meat and vegetables, along with a glass of water. "This is my fault," she said. "I should've stayed to help you bathe."

"It wasn't your fault. I'm stubborn." Eirah set down the chisel, her expression growing serious as a horrid thought crossed her mind. "The king didn't hurt you, did he?"

Ulva shook her head, then straightened after she placed the plate and glass on the bedside table. "No, His Majesty is nothing of that nature to us. Raising his voice if we were to do wrong, yes, but he would never lay a hand on his servants unless they betrayed him."

Eirah let out a breath, her shoulders relaxing. "That eases me a bit."

"I'm sewing a few dresses today. Is there anything specific you would like?"

Ulva's words surprised her—she'd never had anyone make something specifically for her besides her parents or Saren. Then a dark thought crossed her mind, not knowing if the garments would be ready before she was to be sacrificed. But she forced a smile. "Something different. Maybe not even a dress but trousers and a tunic. I'll make you a gift in return."

"A bargain I won't deny." Ulva paused as she started to

turn. "And if you need a bath or anything else, let Kusav know and someone will fetch me."

"I promise." Eirah didn't want anything for the rest of the day, only to work on the music box. Perhaps to still go outside, but she would save that for another time.

As soon as Ulva left the room, Eirah lifted a piece of wood and carved deep grooves within its mahogany surface. Her focused pace continued for a long while until her fingers tingled. She flexed them, believing it was from her nonstop movements, yet when the prickling spread up her arms, a new sensation palpitated beneath her flesh. Along her hands, white feathers sprouted and unfurled.

Eirah's eyes widened, and she screamed so loud she thought the glass inside the room would shatter. The door flew open and Kusav burst in, staring at her in horror as his gaze fell to her hands, his mouth wide open.

"Get Morozko!" she shouted.

The room spun and the world around her seemed to get larger as she became smaller. When she looked down at herself, no longer were her legs human but thin and deep orange with curving talons along the edges of her feet. Her arms were now wings, ivory feathers cloaking her entire body, and as she tried to speak, a loud hoot echoed off the walls.

Her heart pounded, her body shaking. Eirah didn't know what to *do*—she was a *bird*.

A moment later, Morozko bolted into the room, his hair in disarray.

"Where is she?" he seethed, his gaze brushing past her.

Kusav came in and stopped beside the king. "I think that's her," he said, pointing in Eirah's direction.

She went to speak, but only hoots filled the room. *Why is this happening?* she thought.

"Eirah?" Morozko whispered, stepping toward her.

I don't know what your blood did to me now. But look *at me. Turn me back!*

"I heard you," Morozko said in awe, lowering himself to the mattress. He motioned to Kusav. "Stand guard unless I call for you."

Kusav nodded and left them alone together in the room.

Eirah's eyes met the king's, her breaths uneven. *I don't understand how you can hear me.*

"I don't know, either, but tell me. Explain what happened."

She then told him how she'd been working on the music box and how the tingling sensation had come out of nowhere, how earlier she'd felt something stir when he'd touched her.

"I felt that, too." He bit his lip.

Bring me a mirror. She needed to see herself, see what she'd become.

"Such a vain little bird." He chuckled.

Morozko must have heard the growl she made toward him inside her head because he grabbed one from inside the drawer by her bed and held the silver oval mirror up to her.

Eirah blinked at her reflection, fighting back a scream that threatened to escape her beak as she studied herself. She wasn't just any bird—she was a barn owl, similar to Adair— she could almost pass as his twin despite her smaller and narrower form.

This wouldn't have happened if it wasn't for Morozko's blood. *Change me back.*

"Don't look at me as though this is my fault. My magic doesn't turn maidens into animals."

Do something! Fear coursed through her. What if she remained a bird for the rest of her life? However short that life may be. She wouldn't even be able to lift her carving tools to finish the music box. Instead, she would sit here and wait to die while doing nothing. If she could, she would shrink the king and trap him in the music box!

A swirl of blue left Morozko's fingertips, tickling her flesh, caressing, but nothing happened besides her remaining an owl.

"You're coming with me." As always, he didn't wait for a reply while lifting her into his arms and striding out the door. "Inform Xezu to come to me immediately," he instructed Kusav.

Eirah remained quiet as the king carried her down the hallway. Various wood carvings stood out on the walls, and as Morozko turned to toe a door open, she could only assume it was his room. Glass animals hung across his walls, a large pale blue wardrobe rested in the corner, and deep blue fur blankets lay on his massive bed. A writing desk, neatly kept, was pressed against another wall beside a lit fireplace.

Heavy footsteps sounded, and Xezu rushed in, running a hand through his dark hair.

"She's an owl," Morozko said, a deep line settled between his brows.

Xezu studied Eirah as he stroked his chin. "I assume your magic didn't work to change her back?"

"I tried, but no, it didn't."

Perhaps you should try harder, Eirah thought bitterly.

"I know my magic." He frowned.

"You can hear her?" Xezu asked.

"Yes, and be grateful you can't." Eirah went to peck him at his irritating response, but he easily moved his hand away from her.

Xezu shook his head, daring to roll his eyes at the latter

comment. "With frost shifters, they generally change on their own. Perhaps she needs to will it."

"She's not a frost shifter, though. She's *human*." Morozko rested Eirah on the bed and she continued to listen to their conversation as her heart knocked against her rib cage.

"It had to be your blood that triggered something."

Just as I said, Eirah sang.

Morozko motioned for him to leave. "Let me think on it and see if I can figure something out. I'll see you in the morning."

Xezu nodded and shut the door behind him.

"Looks like tonight you will be sleeping in my bed after all," he teased, but this time it didn't meet his eyes.

I will do no such thing.

Morozko cocked his head. "Shall I bring you a cage to set at my bedside, then? I'm certain I can find one in the cellar."

Her blood boiled. *Stop being a prick. I'll stay in bed for now.*

He folded a fur blanket and set it in front of one of the silk pillows, then placed her on top of it. "Try shifting. Focus on what you want to become and let your body do the work."

Eirah shut her eyes, her body trembling as she concentrated, begging for it to respond. When she opened her lids, she remained in the same position, covered in feathers.

"You're trying *too* hard, little bird." He slipped in beside her and trailed a hand over her head, cupping her face. "Go to sleep for now. You've had a long day. Get your strength up and we'll work together tomorrow to correct this."

Eirah wouldn't deny the exhaustion flowing through her, and as his thumb stroked her face, her eyes fell shut. She couldn't help but wonder what it would be like to lie in his bed while in human form. Then she shoved away the horrid thought, knowing she would only ever be another maiden he would toss away... or sacrifice.

Sᴏᴍᴇᴛʜɪɴɢ soft stroked Eirah's face, and she peeled open her eyes, gazing into bright blue irises. But she wasn't afraid or ill at ease until she went to lift her arm... Not an arm but a *wing*.

"You're still an owl." Morozko pursed his lips.

Panic sewed its way through her, harping on her that she may remain a bird. *Will you try your magic again?*

He closed his eyes and the pale blue light seeped out of him, penetrating beneath her flesh, caressing her blood. *Something* pulsed in tune with it.

Morozko furrowed his brow. "Try shifting with me."

Her body tightened as she focused on getting out of this blasted form.

"You're not trying," he cooed.

I am, you fool!

"You're not." He ran his index finger across his lower lip. "I feel something inside you. It's as though magic has touched you. There is a fine line between forcing and willing your form to change."

Magic? She couldn't have magic tainting her unless it belonged to him from his blood. Yet she closed her eyes, reaching for a power she couldn't touch.

When nothing happened, Morozko sighed. "Let me take you outside. I have an idea." Before she could speak, he placed her on his shoulder, and she dug her talons into his flesh. But he didn't wince, only sauntered as though he was the most relaxed he'd ever been.

Prick.

"I heard that," he purred.

Eirah clenched her beak and narrowed her eyes as he strode them outside. A heavy breeze tore through the air, but she couldn't feel much of the cold.

What are we doing out here? she asked as he took her toward a wooded area, the thin trees spread far apart.

"You should try to fly."

I'm not doing that! Do you want me to break my neck?

As she cursed him, he took her from his shoulder and tossed her into the air. On instinct, she flapped her wings, going up, up. But then she fell down, down, into the soft snow.

You bastard! she shouted, shaking, her skin tingling as the feathers disappeared back into her skin. Her body stretched without pain, the robe she'd worn previously still cloaking her human form.

"Ah, there's the little bird I know." He scooped her up, walking back toward the palace as if none of this had just occurred. "We have much to discuss, and you need to get out of the cold."

As the breeze drifted past her once more, it didn't send a single chill through her. "I-I don't feel cold."

He halted, his gaze boring into hers as if he was trying to read something. "You don't feel cold at all?"

She shook her head. "No, it's as though there's a warm blanket inside of me."

His throat bobbed, and he set her on her bare feet in the snow, the coldness still not bothering her. "Nothing now?" he asked.

"No." She took a deep swallow, studying her feet.

He held up his arm, lifting snow from the ground until a

dagger of ice formed in his palm. "Let me see your hand. It will only be a prick."

Eirah's eyes widened, and she took a step back, wondering if this was the moment.

"I'm not sacrificing you right now, and I know you don't want to trust me, but trust this." The hard edges of his face seemed to soften.

Eirah hesitated, observing his expression, believing his words—he looked as disturbed as she felt. She then nodded, stretching out her arm toward him. Morozko cradled her hand, his warm fingers brushing her flesh, and that pull came to her once more.

He pressed the blade's tip into her finger, a sharp pain burning for only a second. She watched blood bloom to the surface, but also as her skin closed up. Fast. Too fast. *Healed.*

Her heart thudded while Morozko pursed his lips, releasing her hand. "It looks as though you're not human... That you do, indeed, have magic."

"Change me back to human," she rasped.

The tingling sensation tore through her again, the feathers sprouting, and she shifted back into an owl.

"I'm unable to do that, little bird." He lifted her from the snow, and a look of triumph washed over his features. "I think I'm getting closer to finding out what I need to, though."

OVER THE NEXT FEW DAYS, Eirah was able to control her shifting for the most part, yet occasionally it would come at the most inopportune times, pulling a chuckle from Morozko. He would take her outside to practice flying, yet he didn't seem worried that she would drift away from the castle.

Besides that, she was there to stay to protect her loved ones, and with how he could feel the magic pumping inside of her, he would know if she abandoned the castle. Just as she was starting to feel *him*.

Morozko didn't explain what he knew, as he should have, in her opinion. "Soon," he would say. And "prick" was always her response.

Today, the magic had grown stronger, begging to be a part of him. His blood wouldn't leave her—as if it owned her.

Eirah circled above him, ruffling his hair with her talons to irk him before landing in her human form. But she turned too soon, her feet stumbling in the snow, and she toppled forward, knocking the king to the ground.

"I knew you would get on top of me eventually." He chuckled, his hands falling to her hips.

"If I had a blade, I would cut you with it," she breathed, her comment half-hearted.

"By the way your heart is beating, I don't think you would." He rolled her onto her back, hovering above her. "How do you like being in this cage, little bird?"

Part of her still wanted to slice him open, while the other part wanted to discover what his shapely lips tasted like. As if he could read her thoughts, his nose skimmed up her throat, and her breath caught.

"You like this," he whispered in her ear, his finger brushing across her lips.

"No," she lied. And he knew it when her body naturally arched into his.

His warm mouth came to the tender spot just below her ear, followed by a flick of the tongue before he trailed his perfect lips along her jaw, making her eyelids flutter. Her hands drifted to his hips, pulling him closer, wanting him even *nearer*. As he settled between her thighs, he hardened against her, and she froze, remembering *what* she was doing, *who* she was with. And she hated herself for liking it too much, for acting like all the other maidens. She wouldn't be. She would be. No, she *wouldn't* be.

She rolled from beneath him and pushed up from the ground, trying not to focus on how good his warm lips had felt on her skin or wonder how good they would feel in other places. "Have you decided when I'm to be sacrificed yet?"

"No." He scowled, studying her hard. "Continue practicing your shifting."

"Tell me the truth. I deserve to know why we have done this for several days now?"

"Come to my bedchamber tonight." He waved her off, lifting his brows. "Now fly, little bird."

Eirah tightened her fists as blue magic poured out of her.

13

MOROZKO

Blue magic blasted from Eirah's fingertips. Morozko's brows furrowed, and he wondered just *what* she was capable of. Producing magic hadn't surprised him, he'd seen it, and now Morozko knew *he* had a part in it. For it was his blood that stirred her abilities to life. Yet, shifting into an owl... he hadn't seen that. He could have deemed her a shifter—one created and not born—but this was no shifter ability.

Morozko didn't know what she was. There had been a woman, long ago, when he was a boy, who'd served in his mother's court. She was a so-called witch. He'd witnessed her perform parlor tricks in the throne room, pleasing the noble frost demons, but she was no more than a trickster. She'd been his mother's confidant until Maranna felt threatened and dragged her out into the snow, thrust her onto the ground, and summoned an ice spear.

In our court, we slay traitors because we cannot risk having snakes slithering about.

And with one careless thrust, Maranna impaled Klinta.

Of course, his mother would force him to endure such a spectacle. It was a lesson, a warning that whoever rose against her would suffer. But Morozko always wondered if the *witch* truly had been guilty? He never knew.

Still, Klinta had never exhibited actual magic, nor had she ever shifted. Which posed the question *again*: what was Eirah? Witch? Shifter? Both?

Morozko kept pushing Eirah to see the extent of her abilities, hoping to find familiarity in her power, but there was none. Even as magic leaped within her, there wasn't a hint of recognition.

He dragged his tongue along a sharp canine and chuckled with a confidence he didn't feel. For all the time he spent in Eirah's company, taunting and demanding more from her, there was little Morozko knew about her. She was as unknown to him as her budding abilities.

The initial panic he experienced in the vision of when he first saw the magic bursting from her toward him hit Morozko at that moment. She could slay him if she so wished. He was certain of that. Or, at the very least, hold him captive since now she knew he was tied to the land. Whether her magic was tested or not, she had the strength within her, for he'd seen it himself in his visions.

"We should return inside. I think you've had enough fluttering about." His voice was cool, but his gaze didn't venture far from her glowing digits.

Eirah's frustration with his continuous sidestepping grew visible. "You will answer me." A plea melded with her tone, barely detectable, but Morozko was listening.

Tension stiffened her shoulders, and Morozko recalled the way her body had responded to his, as if it yearned for his lips to do more than trail kisses along her flesh. More than his tongue dragging along her sweet skin and the pressure of his hardened length pressing against her center. He despised the notion he *wanted* to do more, too. To nip along the slope of her breast and watch her come undone as he pleasured her.

"Will I?" He glanced toward the sky, needing a moment to reel himself in. "I don't believe I *have* to do anything." He dropped his gaze to her again. This time, he homed in on her pulse and the way it thrummed wildly. Morozko had seen her bare, held her in his arms as he carried her from the bath to her bed, but he hadn't lingered on each detail, hadn't committed them to memory, either. He couldn't afford another complication in the tangled web of his vision and the matters of Frosteria. However, here she was, standing before him with her hand stretched out, gawking at her fingertips.

Eirah glanced up at him, a hint of panic in her eyes. "Don't come any closer until you tell me the truth. Why have we been doing this? Why do you keep having me fly out here? Why won't you just sacrifice me?" Her full lips pressed into a thin line as he stepped forward.

Every time she pried, he sidestepped, and to her, Morozko supposed he came across as unwilling, which was just as well. But he kept pushing her to discover what she was capable of, and his vision wouldn't allow him to sacrifice her. Not yet. *I have to know what you are.* "Would you prefer careening into a chandelier or the dull air rather than the lively wind whispering through your wings?" His voice rumbled across the frozen cobblestone courtyard as he carefully approached.

Eirah studied her hand, a look of horror on her face as blue sparks crackled from her digits. She then shakily held her palm out toward him as if she was going to strike him down. "Are you really willing to find out? Because of you, I can somehow change into a bird, you can hear my thoughts in that form, and now, and now... what kind of magic is this, you *prick*? I should use whatever this is on you to bind you in a box. You've taken everything from me." Tears beaded her lashes, her body racking with sobs.

He frowned as she wept but didn't move forward to embrace her. She had every right to cry—none of this was her fault. It was because of the villagers who had thought they were wiser than he, that he needed a sacrifice. And, himself, for tricking her into drinking his blood.

Morozko pushed his hair from his face and sighed. "I am more than willing to find out, Eirah." He shrugged a shoulder, extending a hand in welcome. "You may try to use it against me, yet I must warn you, I don't advise it."

Eirah exhaled, but it sounded more like a growl. She scarcely moved her arm when a blast of blue energy careened Morozko's way.

Before it struck him, he raised his hands, forming a shield of ice. The blast ricocheted off the surface, struck a stone gargoyle, and it shattered.

Eirah turned her head, staring at what she'd done.

Morozko crossed the distance between them, mindful she could suddenly unleash her power again. What if the blast *had* struck him? He reached for her hand, and she yanked away from him.

Eirah's eyes widened. "I at least need to know why this is happening? Don't I deserve that?" she whispered.

"Come to my room this evening as I asked." His jaw shifted, and he attempted to grasp her hand again. This time, Eirah allowed it, though her body continued to tremble. Her dark eyes met his, hesitant and perhaps even still a bit suspicious.

Magic hummed beneath her skin as Morozko caressed between her thumb and forefinger, and a dizzying warmth spread through him. A gentle, intoxicating brushing against his subconscious that longed to dive deeper. Before whatever *that* feeling was sunk its barbs into his mind, Morozko lurched backward, dropping her hand as if it burned him.

He ran his fingers through his hair and turned away from her. Mostly so she couldn't see how ruffled the near connection had him. If Eirah said anything else, he didn't hear it as he strode across the courtyard and back into the palace. At that moment, he wasn't sure what bothered him most: the possibility Eirah was the end of Frosteria—or the notion that she was only the beginning.

Whatever it was, Morozko needed to decipher it quickly.

Or he and the realm would cease to function.

MOROZKO HAD WAITED, for how long he wasn't certain. An hour? Two? Nevertheless, Eirah never knocked on his door. He had half a mind to charge down the hall and drag her to his quarters, but the desire to bark at her, and cut her with his silver tongue, didn't appeal to him. Perhaps it was the fact he didn't want to test what her flighty abilities could do to him, or maybe it was that he preferred to wallow in his misery of *not knowing what the fuck was going on.*

He paced his room for a time, but when the novelty wore off and it was clear Eirah wasn't planning on arriving, Morozko opted to retire for the evening.

With the flick of his hand, the candles extinguished in the

room, casting it in utter darkness. He climbed into bed, willing sleep to overtake him.

Moonlight splashed onto the freshly fallen snow, illuminating the ice road in the village. It was the only light he and his party of twelve had. Fear gripped him, squeezing his chest, making it difficult to breathe. What would they find in the center of town?

No candles illuminated the windows of the homes. No chimneys smoked, and even the perched owls remained quiet, unwilling to announce their hiding place.

Eirah stood at his side, muttering under her breath. "We cannot stand by and do nothing." Her gaze flicked to the night sky as an owl flew overhead. "No!" she hissed, then ran forward, her cloak billowing behind her.

"Eirah!" Morozko growled and raced after her.

The royal guard flocked behind them, boots pounding far too loud.

"Eirah, stop at once." Morozko grabbed her by the arm as she approached the center of town. Bodies by the dozen littered the ground. Chests were torn open, and several pools of blood circled them, frozen like macabre art.

Morozko had seen death. Both by his hands and by those he had no control over. Death didn't make him flinch or give pause. This was more than death. This was butchery. The victims' organs had been consumed, save for the heart, which lay in a frozen, bloodied heap.

Eirah shuddered, and Morozko turned her away from the sight, holding her against his chest.

"We shouldn't be here," he whispered. His skin pricked with anxiety. Even the trees seemed to still, as if waiting for what was about to happen. "We need to get back to the sleigh—" The ground cracked beneath his feet, and Eirah jumped back. He was too slow reaching for his sword, and mid-grab, something struck him on his

vulnerable side. Sharp pain burned up his ribcage, sending him stumbling forward. "Get out of here!" When he pulled his hand away from his side, blood coated his fingers. His attention wasn't on the wound for long, because a waxlike figure leaped at him, and he whirled his blade around, slicing the creature's head clean off.

The changeling's skin looked crafted of a melted-down candle, yellowed and malnourished. A tuft of hair on the top of its head flopped in the breeze, and a mouth, nearly sewn together, hid most of its razor-sharp teeth.

"You know what we have to do!" Eirah shouted.

She shouldn't be here. Why did he think she would listen?

An ear-splitting shriek filled the air, accompanied by several more groans as the land cracked. Panic seized Morozko and rooted him in place.

"Morozko! We have to do it!" Eirah raced up to him, placing her forehead against his. "It's the only way." She grabbed his free hand, and with her other, she held a knife.

He jolted from sleep, sucking in a ragged breath. It took him a moment to settle into reality, the dregs of the vision slowly leaving him far more exhausted than he was before. "Why are the visions never enough at once?" Morozko peeled back his blankets, his chest rising and falling quickly. "And do what, Eirah? What are we supposed to do?" Morozko's voice raised, his fingers curling into his palms.

Someone knocked on his door, then Xezu entered. "Your Majesty, I have terrible news."

Morozko's limbs longed to tremble from the strain of the vision, but he steeled himself and slid toward the edge of the bed. "What could it possibly be at—" He glanced toward the window, the drape still open to let the moonlight in. "Not even dawn?"

Xezu shook his head, lips thinning into a grim expression.

"There has been an attack on Vinti. Something has... slaughtered many villagers."

Morozko didn't miss the way his steward emphasized the word *slaughtered*. His skin prickled with apprehension, and the image of the slain villagers in his vision came to mind.

He sprung to his feet, halfway across his room, when he finally spoke again. "Any more details? Any reports on what the assailants looked like?"

Vinti may have been a village of humans, but they were still his subjects, and it was *his* realm. An unwarranted attack was a punishable offense.

Fury boiled within Morozko, fusing with his mounting trepidation.

"I don't know how trustworthy it is, but it was said they were yellow-skinned, with slitted eyes, and the mouth—"

Changelings. "Fuck!" Morozko roared, pulling his linen shirt on, then his doublet. The seal had already broken, or at the very least, weakened enough to let a few slip out. In the past few days, when he wasn't with Eirah, he'd tried sacrificing a lamb, a calf, and a bloody cow, yet nothing worked. His visions were growing more vivid, indicating they were about to come to fruition.

Xezu grimaced. "I take it you know what I speak of?"

He shot an icy glare his way. Of course he did! He'd only seen it over and over... "Frosteria is about to change, and I don't know what that means, Xezu. If it's for the better or worse." Morozko yanked his trousers on, then shoved his feet into his boots.

"What of Eirah?" his steward ventured to ask and grabbed the red cape hanging on the coat rack. Xezu then stepped behind Morozko and draped it over his shoulders.

He recalled his vision, played it over in his mind, and

homed in on the moment she leaned her forehead against his. Morozko's heart galloped wildly, and it had little to do with the news. No, it was the fluttering in his chest, the terror he experienced knowing that *she* was in danger. The troubling thought was he wasn't sure why he cared. Perhaps it was only the visions confusing him and having him reconsider reality.

"Your Majesty..." Xezu prompted him.

Morozko squeezed his eyes shut. "All I know is that she's at the center of this madness. Savior or undoing, I don't know." When he turned to look at Xezu, the man was already backing out of the room. "Alert Captain Andras. Have him ready a small party—we'll be heading to Vinti."

Xezu rapped his fingers against his chest. "Now, Your Majesty?"

He lifted a brow, brushing past him. "Yes, now." Now, because he wanted to see the destruction himself. Right now, because Eirah would bear witness to what happened when the ritual didn't take place. But why did the notion of her being punished grate on him? It hadn't when she'd first arrived.

Morozko all but ran down the hall. He didn't greet Kusav or knock, only flung the door open and crossed the threshold to Eirah's room. He snapped his fingers, and flames leaped from the candles, offering a warm light. When he approached the bed, Eirah was fast asleep on her stomach, cheek pressed against her pillow and hand dipped beneath it.

He sat on the edge of the bed, contemplating leaving her behind, far away from what awaited them in Vinti. Yet, would that only be delaying what was to come? She already possessed the magic he'd seen in his visions. How much longer would it be before what he saw came to pass? Morozko clenched his teeth, reeling his frustrations in.

Asleep, Eirah appeared to be at peace. At that moment, he could see hints of the female in his visions, the softness and worry *for him.*

Wake and bring her. You're only delaying the inevitable.

"I know," he murmured. "But I'm not ready for what's coming yet." And he wasn't. Not for what awaited them, not for what Eirah could mean to Frosteria—to him.

Morozko leaned over, his hand brushing Eirah's shoulder. "Wake up, little bird," he said, dragging his knuckles down her arm. "We need to—"

"What hour is it?" She blinked, her eyes like daggers piercing into him.

Morozko's hand stilled on her. His lips twitched but didn't form his typical smirk. "There are pressing events in Vinti that require our presence."

"Vinti..." She sat up, clarity touching her eyes. "What is going on?"

He stood from the bed, motioning to her wardrobe. "Dress quickly, and I'll tell you about it on our journey." Morozko crossed the room and paused at the door. "Unless you choose not to come." A part of him hoped she wouldn't join him because he knew that by the time he returned to the castle, he and Frosteria would never be the same.

14

EIRAH

Something had happened in Vinti, and by Morozko's expression it wasn't pleasant in the least. Eirah's village, her *home,* was in trouble. How could this be? Her village had always been safe, except for the night Morozko had come to claim a maiden. Eirah's mind whirled in every direction imaginable, every possibility. Had her village caught fire? Were her father and Saren all right? *Please, please, let them be safe.*

Eirah's hands trembled as she changed out of her nightgown into a simple pair of trousers and a tunic. She shoved on her boots and fastened her cloak as she headed out of her bedroom.

Morozko wasn't outside her door as she'd expected—only Kusav stood waiting, his muscular arm outstretched for her to grasp.

"What happened in Vinti, Kusav?" she asked, taking his arm and guiding him toward the stairs.

"I know as much as you do on this matter," he said, his

expression neutral. "Word hasn't traveled this far into the castle yet."

Eirah's chest tightened—that wasn't the answer she was hoping for. Not at all. At the moment, she truly felt like a bird in a cage, except not physically. Morozko kept so many secrets from her, yet wouldn't confess any. *Why?* She hadn't given him a reason to trust her, but he made it difficult. Eirah could have ventured to his room like he'd said, demanded answers, even though there would be a taunt first that she'd wandered to him. She didn't want to come at his beck and call, didn't want to play any more games with her shifting magic.

But underneath it all, the true reason she hadn't gone to his room that night was because of what had happened earlier outside the palace, his firm and taut body atop hers, caging her in. The delicious way he'd flicked his tongue beneath her ear, how he'd hardened against her. The way he had looked at her with hunger, the way no male ever had. If she'd gone to his room, she feared she might have given into temptation— the feeling that continued to bloom within her day after day. She couldn't decide if that aching desire was a thorn or a rose. *Bah!* She needed to stop thinking about this.

Once Eirah and Kusav reached the end of the staircase, Morozko stood in the center of the room, instructing Xezu to watch over the palace and to keep the doors sealed until he returned.

"Yes, Your Majesty." Fist to his chest, Xezu bowed his head and turned to Eirah. "My condolences about your village."

At a loss for words, she only nodded, her heart thrumming, sinking. *Condolences?* She needed to get to her father and Saren *now*.

Ulva entered the room, giving her a look of sympathy as she drew open the front door. "Stay safe, Eirah."

Morozko adjusted his crimson cape before grasping Eirah's hand a little too tightly, the only telltale sign that something bothered him as he drew them toward the door. "The world will be dark when we arrive, but we need to leave now, little bird."

"What is happening in Vinti? What did Xezu mean by condolences?" she asked as they stepped outside. Nuka stood at the front in the snow, the saddle already on his back, the breath from his nostrils creating what looked to be a light fog. A small party of frost demons sat atop their stags, alert and ready.

"There's been an attack," Morozko said as he helped her mount Nuka, who dutifully laid down and waited. The king climbed up after her, settling in front.

"An attack?" she gasped. "Is everyone all right?"

"This is an answer I truly cannot give you because I, indeed, do not know." His voice came out softer than usual, perhaps even compassionate. "Now, hold on tight. We'll be traveling faster than when we rode together last."

She wrapped her trembling arms around him, tightening her grip, needing something to anchor her down, hold her together, and that was precisely what he was doing at that moment. Nuka took off in a sprint down the mountain with the stags' pounding hooves behind them.

The cool wind blew against her flesh, yet she was becoming used to not feeling the heavy chill of the breeze, to not have to shiver, to not have her teeth chatter. She couldn't deny she liked the new advantage, along with how her eyes adjusted to the dark. The foliage around her remained clearer, and she didn't even need a lantern to see through the night.

A tugging sensation pulled at her, as if magic demanded her to focus toward the sky. Eirah tilted her chin up, her gaze not meeting only the starry night but a white speck that glided downward, closer to them.

Adair. As he inched nearer, his snowy wings were easily recognizable, and a thought rose within her as the force of magic between them grew stronger. She'd heard tales of how frost demons gained a familiar. At birth, later on in life, or even once they inherited their magic. Eirah had magic now, and that possibly meant that Adair was—

Eirah tightened her grip on Morozko and shouted over the wind. "What does it feel like to have a familiar?"

Morozko glanced back at her, a scowl on his face. "I don't believe this is the time for that sort of discussion."

"I think it is," she bit back. "I believe I have one. His name's Adair, and he's been around practically my whole life. He's been visiting me at the palace."

Morozko laughed coolly. "Is he a *shifter*? He may require an arrow in the heart." His tone didn't make it clear whether that was a jest or not.

"No!" she shouted. "He's an *owl*. But I recently started feeling this bond with him, and since I now know what I have is magic, I believe it's like what I've heard in the tales."

He frowned, then peered up at the sky. "Is that him?"

"If you dare try to hurt him, I'll hurt you in return," she seethed.

"Out in the open, with my guards in firing range?" Morozko smirked, then it fell from his lips as fast as it had come. "We will discuss it later. We have more important matters to attend to now." He turned back around, but every so often, his gaze drifted up to the sky, where Adair continued to follow them toward Vinti.

Eirah tried to think of happier times to keep herself from unraveling. She and Saren when they were younger, playing with dolls in the forest while sipping tea. Then Eirah's father teaching her how to make her first music box. The thoughts kept her mind at ease, as did the comfort of having Adair above her, and even though she hated to admit it, so did Morozko's body against hers.

After a little while longer, Vinti came into view. No screams tore through the village as she'd expected, but something far worse. Smoke curled up from inside, and the burning smell invaded her senses when they drew closer.

Morozko tugged on Nuka's reins and the wolf halted, the other warriors behind mirroring his movements. The king lifted a hand, signaling the warriors to enter the village.

Eirah didn't wait for Morozko to hop to the ground first—she climbed down Nuka's shoulder, then leaped the remainder of the way. Before she could bolt toward the village, Morozko grabbed her by the wrist. "You may have magic, but you don't know how to use it properly. Always, *always*, protect yourself with a weapon when venturing into the unknown. The threat is gone for now, but it matters not." He held out his hand and snow lifted from the ground, shaping into a dagger made of ice. "It won't melt."

"Thank you," she whispered as he pressed it into her hand. "How do you know the threat is gone?"

"From my guards." He released his grip on her. "But that doesn't mean it can't return, little bird."

Eirah didn't ask any more questions, not when she needed to find her father. As they walked inside the village, the bonfire burned, its flames crackling, even though there wasn't a celebration or sacrifice—but something far worse. A small crowd of people stood near it, thick fur blankets wrapped around them.

The chieftain broke away from the crowd, his eyes

widening as he approached Morozko. "Your Majesty," he rasped. "We were attacked by creatures. Creatures like we've never seen. Where did they come from?"

Creatures? Some sort of creature had done this? Her gaze fell across the snow. Dead bodies lay strewn beside one another. Limbs were severed, others had torn-out chests, and their blood stained the snow in haphazard spatters. It looked as if they'd been set there, and then she knew why as she studied the cottages.

Eirah couldn't focus on what the chieftain and Morozko were discussing as she continued to peer at the destroyed homes. Most of the doors had been ripped off—on some, the windows were shattered. Smoke wafted from others, embers burning on the remains.

Chest heaving, Eirah surveyed the crowd, searching for her father and Saren. A pit formed in her stomach when she didn't find them. Not thinking clearly, she took off toward her home, skirting around cottages—several of the windows were lit by candles while the rest were dark with no sign of life.

A body rested on the porch of a cottage, the woman's chest torn open, blood pooling around her. Bile rose up Eirah's throat.

Almost every single home looked as though it had been rampaged or completely destroyed by fire, and a gut feeling told her more dead bodies lingered inside them. What sort of creatures could have done this? Snow lions wouldn't attack villages.

And then she discovered where the smoke in front of her was coming from. A choked sob escaped her throat as she stared at where her cottage had once stood. But now it was burned to the ground, nothing but broken pieces and ash.

"Papa," Eirah whispered. Her words grew louder as she

screamed, "Papa!" There was nothing to search through because she could see everything. Nothing was there to salvage, not even her father's body if he'd gone down in flames with their home.

Holding onto hope, she raced next door to Saren's. She prayed her father was with them, but dread filled her as she stared at the door thrown open.

"Saren!" Eirah called. "Petre!" Gripping the ice dagger, she slipped inside the cottage. The furniture was cracked and broken. Sewing items were slung about. Mattresses slashed.

No one answered as she screamed their names again in the empty rooms.

Eirah stumbled out of Saren's home, scanning the surrounding cottages. Tears pricked her eyes as her body shook. She wasn't certain what to do. As she took a step forward to knock on every single door in the village, Adair swooped down from above, circling her.

He flew toward the trees beside the remains of her house, then back to her, before heading in that direction once more. He seemed to want her to follow him.

Eirah held her breath while letting him lead her into the forest. As she stepped around a large trunk, a bright orange flame caught her attention. A *torch*.

She breathed a sigh of relief when she discovered her father was the one holding the torch. "Papa!" she cried.

He turned around, straining to look at her beneath his broken glasses. "Daughter, is that you?" His voice cracked on the last word.

She hurried toward him, finding him not alone, but with Saren and— Eirah ceased movement. The world stopped— everything stopped. Resting in Saren's arms as she sobbed was Petre. He lay still, his throat torn out, blood staining his chest.

"These creatures came," Saren cried, her teeth chattering, her lips blue. "They broke into the cottage and we ran, hid in the forest. We thought we were safe, but one must have followed us and tried to attack me. But Petre, foolish Petre, risked himself. Fedir came and scared the creature away. But it was too late. Why did Petre do this? Why? I would've rather it had been me."

"No." Eirah tucked the dagger at her waist and lowered herself beside her friend, wrapping her arms around her. "You're alive, and you'll stay that way." She then looked at her father, his face drained of any color. "What happened, Papa? What were these things?"

"I-I don't know. I've never seen them before. They were gangly and pale yellow with sharp teeth. One crashed through the window and attacked me. As I put up a fight, I knocked over a few candles, flames started licking across the floor, and it fled, afraid of the fire. I warned the village to light torches, and that helped to drive them out. Then I found Saren here, and I can't get her to return to the village."

"Saren," Eirah said softly. "We need to get you home for now. We can come back in the morning. You'll freeze out here."

"I'm not leaving Petre here!" she snapped.

"Then I'll help you take him home, and in the morning, we'll bury him," Eirah whispered.

It took Saren a long moment to respond before she slowly nodded. Eirah then helped her carry Petre to the cottage while her father hobbled beside them.

"Are you all right?" Eirah asked.

"I'm fine. Let's just get them home."

Once they entered Saren's cottage, they took Petre to his bedroom, where glass was shattered on the floor from the broken window. They laid him atop the ripped mattress, and Saren drew the blankets up to his chin, covering the wound on his neck.

"I'm going to stay with him a while," Saren said, leaving no room for argument.

"I'm truly sorry about this." A flood of memories washed over her of Petre. How he would tag along when they were younger, always bringing Eirah flowers he'd picked.

"It isn't your fault. I'm just glad you're here." Saren wiped her tears, then sank down in a chair beside her brother's bed and wrapped herself in a fur blanket.

Eirah went back into the sitting room, where flames were already lit inside the fireplace. Her father removed his cloak and she gasped. Wounds covered his arms, and claw marks slashed his chest and back.

"You said you were fine! This isn't fine!" she hissed, guiding her father to the settee. "Stay here while I find a healer."

"You're alive," he murmured, his breaths ragged.

"Do not leave this spot—do you hear me?" Eirah rushed out of the cottage, finding Morozko standing outside next door, peering at the remains of her home.

"Why are you just standing there?" she shouted, running her hands through her hair, making it more disheveled. "You're the king! Why did you let this happen? Saren's brother is dead. My father needs a healer. Will one of your guards heal him?"

"Many people suffered tonight," he said, a hint of melancholy in his tone.

"Did you not hear me?" she seethed. "My father is wounded and losing blood."

He inched closer, jaw clenching as he hovered over her. "Your village should've performed the sacrifice." Morozko's eyes hardened as they dropped to her hand.

Eirah drew the ice blade from her waist and held it up to his throat, teeth clenched. His pale blue gaze flicked back to hers, staring deep into her. "Why are you talking about sacrifices at a time like this? Help my father *now*."

He swallowed roughly, though a hint of a smirk touched his lips. But gone was his ever-present confidence. *Good.* "Are we back to you threatening me with blades so soon?"

"Your Majesty?" a deep voice boomed from behind her, and she turned to see the captain of the guard pointing a sword at her.

"Leave us be, Andras. I was waiting for you to return, so you could heal her father," Morozko said, motioning toward Saren's cabin. "If he dies, you die."

Andras nodded and ventured inside.

Eirah dropped the dagger to her side as she whirled around to follow Andras. Morozko's strong arms grabbed her, hauling her to his chest. "You will stay here. I will not have your emotions get in the way of him saving your father."

I hate you. I hate you mostly, but sometimes... Sometimes I don't hate you at all.

"Perhaps it's better if you hate me all the time."

Eirah wriggled out of his grip, balling one hand into a fist, the other gripping the dagger at her side as she faced him. "You can hear my thoughts in this form too?" Could she not even have privacy in her own mind?

"Only when you project yourself rather loudly. I don't hear everything. But earlier in the snow"—he leaned in, his fingers

131

tilting up her chin—"when you landed on top of me, when I was on top of you, I heard every one of your lust-filled thoughts, little bird."

Her nostrils flared as she backed him into a nearby tree. "Why are you saying these things? Why are you saying this when there is so much death around? When my father is in pain?"

A voice growled from the back of her mind that wasn't her own. *Perhaps to distract you, so I don't have to see you hurt.* "Why not? Death is a part of mortal life, is it not? Frosteria is the land of death and snow." His tone was sharp, but hints of sorrow broke through his eyes.

Eirah wrinkled her nose, stewing at what he'd said, but not the first part, not the part that had made her heart lurch. His mouth hadn't *moved*. "I heard you! You don't want to see me hurt!"

Morozko scowled. "If you plan on ending my life, grant me the mercy of a swift one." *It's as if she* is *a witch...*

Why wouldn't he admit such a simple thing? "You didn't answer me! And I'm not a witch, you fool! Those are a myth!"

His nostrils flared as he gazed down at her, a dark intensity brewing in the depths of his eyes. "Suppose I didn't answer," he whispered. "But here and now, you could end my life, Eirah. Just do it."

"Is that truly what you want from me?" she spat, her hand shaking as she squeezed the dagger. "For me to end you so it can destroy the whole world?"

"No, right now, I would rather take something from you." He leaned forward, cutting her off with his mouth before she could speak.

Eirah gave in to the kiss, surprising herself when she was the one who deepened it. She kissed him harder as he pulled her closer. He nipped her lower lip, then slipped his tongue between the seam of her mouth, letting it dance with hers. She mirrored his movements as if she'd done this a thousand times when she never had before. The kiss was taking her away from the pain of Petre, from her destroyed village, from seeing Saren suffering, from her father currently being healed...

Her eyes widened, and she drew back when she realized she was kissing the king in the middle of a destroyed village.

"A first of many things, little bird." *Why do I want nothing but to kiss her and never stop?*

"So it was." Eirah sighed. "And it will be our last." The words rang false—selfishly, she wanted nothing but to kiss him again and not only to take away the pain.

15

MOROZKO

Morozko's lips still tingled from the kiss. Despite the death and decay around them, he wanted to draw Eirah in for another. The loss of her body pinning him against the tree struck him harder than he cared to admit.

Eirah may not have verbally confessed it was her first kiss, but he'd heard the thrum of her thoughts in his mind. Her first with him, and the last, if she had anything to do about it. In truth, he was pleased that it was his lips that had claimed hers first. And knowing it could be the last ignited a wicked fury that blazed violently inside his chest.

Eirah could lie to herself and say it wouldn't happen again or that she didn't want his mouth on hers because he did the same. Every time he thought it was only a harmless taunt, kiss, or touch. It was a lie.

And now she saw that, much to Morozko's dismay. He'd have to be careful about guarding his thoughts better in her presence.

He swallowed roughly and wiped the corner of his mouth with his thumb. "You want answers, and I think it's time I give you some. But you have to show up this time." Not only did she deserve the truth, but with the horror the villagers now faced and his visions growing clearer, Eirah *had* to know.

"I will. I truly need to know," Eirah whispered. Relief flooded her gaze, and he knew he'd danced around the truth long enough.

"Your Majesty." Captain Andras pounded a fist to his chest, bowing, using the exact moment to seek Morozko out and interrupt them. "The mortal is healed. What would you have us do next?"

Morozko glanced at Eirah, who lifted her hands to her face, and fresh tears spilled down her cheeks. "Set up camp for the evening. We can inhabit some homes of villagers. Don't force your way in. If they refuse, we can sleep on the ground for a night." He shrugged. The last thing the villagers needed was another conflict—and this time with the royal guard. In the morning, they'd have to search the area. They hadn't come with a large party, and the villagers needed their resources. It would have to wait. *Those* bastards would have to wait. "We can assess the situation better come morning." He shifted his weight, hand on one hip, as he waited for the captain to excuse himself, but the male only lifted a brow.

"Are you all right, Your Majesty?"

Surely he didn't look as ruffled as he felt? Although, if his captain was inquiring, he must have. "Quite," Morozko spoke through gritted teeth and motioned for the captain to leave. "You're dismissed."

Eirah took two steps in Andras's direction before she paused, as if unsure if she should remain behind or check on her father. "I'm going to see my father now."

Morozko loosed a breath. "Go. I don't fault you for wanting to see for yourself." The last time she had seen her father was when she'd bid him farewell at the selection Vinti had hosted. Eirah had endured far more than her father would ever know in a short amount of time. Pushed her body to the breaking point, only to do it again. He frowned. *Because of me.*

"You will tell me everything when I'm done, then?" She continued to look over her shoulder at him.

He nodded. "You have my word."

Eirah darted around a bush, racing forward, leaving Morozko to his thoughts.

He would've preferred the knife biting into his throat than being left alone to mull over everything, but here he was. He reached above, snapping a branch off so he could crack it in several places. As if it would relieve his tension.

Tell her what you know. Tell her the truth. What you know and what you've seen.

I don't want to. Because if I do, it's acknowledging what will happen.

Morozko tossed the broken branch aside, and rather than pace a rut into the ground, he slid down the tree trunk, then sat.

What he knew was that Eirah didn't mean harm in his visions. She was there to help, and she cared for him in the images. That she could shift at will, communicate with her owl like he could with Nuka, and wield magic similar to his. But the remaining questions were, how would she aid Frosteria? Was it truly only in death that she could help?

Twigs snapped, then the sound of tree limbs creaking brought his attention toward the higher boughs. Nuka's yellow eyes homed in on him, his white brows furrowing in canine confusion.

Upset? Nuka didn't speak but conveyed images of discontent in Morozko's head, which he translated into *upset.*

"When am I not?" Morozko snatched up a leaf, shredding it before tossing it. The bits rained down onto his thigh, and rather than wait for Eirah to return, he stood again and took off down the road.

Not all the homes in Vinti had burned down. Smoke still spilled out of a handful of cottages, perfuming the air with its heavy scent. His guards aided the villagers, some carrying the bodies of the deceased, while others were extinguishing the last of the flames with their magic.

You're the king! Why did you let this happen?

Eirah's words played over in his mind. Morozko hadn't just *let* it happen. He wasn't keen on admitting he'd failed to protect Vinti. However, it wasn't all on *him.* Still, he loathed to admit that he hadn't prevented the massacre.

When he came to a cottage, still burning, Morozko called upon his magic. Snow dust kicked around him, rising as a cyclone, then, with his hand, he sliced downward. The burst of snow extinguished the fire without damaging the rest of the home too much.

Long before Eirah spoke, he could smell her on the breeze. The herbal soap clung to her, melding with a scent wholly her own. "Your Majesty," Eirah said, sidling up to his side.

Morozko turned on his heel, scrutinizing her features. Her eyes were red from crying, but there was less tension in her body than before.

"My father is resting now." She nodded, pressing her lips together. "Thank you for sending a healer."

Morozko remained quiet, his eyes shifting back to the burned home. He wasn't precisely relieved, but he was, he supposed, *glad* for Eirah.

"I heard the guard is staying in the village."

The weight of the massacre settled on his shoulders, threatening to send him to his knees. "For the rest of the night anyway, until we can better assess what we are facing. And to make certain that Vinti won't suffer another attack." He knew what the damage was by walking through—just not the death toll.

Eirah sucked her bottom lip in. "Will you stay in one of the vacant cottages?"

Because the inhabitants are dead.

He sighed. "I can sleep outside. It wouldn't be my first time." The cold didn't touch him, not like it did a human. In his youth, he'd run from the castle, angered by one of his mother's outbursts. Morozko had run as far from the palace as his legs would take him, and when he was too tired to continue running, he found a tall pine to sleep under. Nuka was only a pup then, not as large as he was now, and he'd curled his body around Morozko, protecting him. Eventually, the royal guard tracked him down, but after that, Morozko would often take to running away and sleeping beneath the stars.

Besides, the vacant homes could be used for tending to the wounded, like Eirah's father, or preparing the dead, like Petre, for a funeral ceremony.

"Don't be ridiculous. You can at least sleep under a roof." She paused, biting her bottom lip. "None of these homes can compare to the castle, but it's better than sleeping on the ground."

Perhaps he shouldn't have been surprised that she cared, yet here he was, carefully poring over her features. Kindness wasn't openly offered to him, king or not. "Very well, little bird. I'll lodge in one of the empty homes." He inclined his head, nodding. "Nuka can take watch with the guards throughout the night." He pointed to one of the towering trees nearby. "And your friend, too, if he feels so inclined." Morozko surveyed the sky, looking for the owl, but he was nowhere to be seen.

Eirah cleared her throat, and her voice trembled. "Nastya's home is empty... Follow me." She turned around and led the way to a small stone cottage. Several windows had been shattered, but the structure was intact.

Morozko peered down the road, noting he was only a few houses down from where Eirah's father, Fedir, rested. If need be, he could aid them quickly, especially with Nuka on guard.

Instead of entering, Eirah only stared at the home. Morozko figured she was recalling Nastya and whoever else once inhabited it before. "Come on, little bird," he offered and strode forward, pushing the door open.

With no hearth blazing, or candles lit, it was dark inside. Morozko snapped his fingers—flames leaped from candlesticks, and the hearth sparked to life. He walked deeper into the living space of the home and sat in a wooden chair next to the fire.

Eirah didn't sit right away. She gathered up some of the stacked wood and fed the fire. "You said you'd tell me everything."

"Everything," he echoed and leaned back. "That would take longer than a night, but I'll tell you what you want to know—need to know."

She moved to sit beside him in another chair, her dark eyes training on him in rapt attention. "What are these creatures that did this? And are they coming back?"

Morozko looked away from her and leaned his elbow on the chair's arm. His eyes watched the flames in the hearth lick and dance along the newly added logs. "When Frosteria rose against my mother, slaying her, she created a sinister creature known as a changeling. She cursed the land, ensuring that, even in death, she'd be honored in some way. By sacrificing a life willingly and speaking the ritualistic words, she received recognition because a wicked part of her lived on. This kept the seal in place, but should the sacrifice not occur, the seal would break, and her creations would run free."

His brow furrowed as he recounted his mother's treacherous ways. "I told Vinti of this, and they knew it would be the undoing of the land—of its ruler. It was a simple enough task, or so I thought. It's not my fault your people forgot." When he turned to look at Eirah, a complex array of emotions flickered across her face. Regret, sorrow, anger.

"I didn't know about any of this. If I had known, I would've sacrificed one of the animals myself," she whispered. "But we had a hard year—"

"I know," he ground out. "But in the broad scheme of things, it would have saved Vinti from its current heartache." Morozko shrugged a shoulder, not oblivious to their struggles. Yet there was a need for the sacrifice, for a fucking reason. "I didn't tell you because your people should have remembered such an important thing. And while foolish of me, I knew the immortals could handle what came their way, should the seal break."

A line formed between Eirah's brows. "Mortals age, our minds wither, and we die, in case you don't remember. So yes, things turn into tales or vanish all together. Sometimes reminders are necessary."

"It isn't your fault, but mortals have a way of keeping traditions, passing them down to one another. I thought this one would be no different." He sighed heavily, his frustration leaving him for the moment. "Before coming to the village, I had a vision."

Eirah's eyes widened, and she gaped at him. "You have visions?"

"I saw the ground cracking, changelings emerging, and you calling out my name, rushing toward me. At first, I didn't know your purpose, so when I came to the ceremony and saw your face in the crowd, I selected you. Your hatred for me was visceral, which only intrigued me more. You even tried to take my life. But why wouldn't you? With every reason to do just that." He laughed mirthlessly and combed his fingers through his hair before glancing at her again. There was no argument on her lips—no guilt, either.

"You *did* give me a reason for wanting to end your life," she admitted.

This time, when Morozko laughed, he meant it. "I suppose so." He leaned forward, elbows resting on his knees. "Over time, the vision became clearer. You had magic, and that's why I gave you my blood. It was supposed to bring forth what you possessed, but it's done *more*." He warred with revealing what he saw in her eyes, the sorrow, the worry, and how she rushed to him out of compassion. That wasn't essential to what she needed to know.

"So, why push me? Why test me?"

Morozko chewed on the inside of his cheek. "Because I don't know what you are." It hurt his pride to admit it, but he was here to tell her the truth.

Eirah's hands balled into fists, and she stared at the fire. "You don't know what I am?" she repeated, sounding incredulous.

He watched her closely, even as she refused to meet his gaze. Morozko couldn't blame her for being angry or frustrated. He'd done this to her, but it was part of a larger plan. "I know you have magic like mine and the ability to shift... That you're immortal now."

"But what am I?" Her voice came out in a whisper as though she were frightened.

"You are *Eirah of Vinti*. What does it matter *what* you are? As long as we know what you can do. *Who* you are is of more importance." He bowed his head, picked beneath his thumbnail, and sighed. "And I believe you will save Frosteria." At this, she finally turned to look at him.

Surprise lifted her brows, and she shook her head. "Are you jesting?"

"Not at all, little bird." He sat back in the chair and ran a thumb along his chin. "I don't tease when it comes to saving the land." Morozko paused, then cocked his head. "When my mother was slain, I was glad for it. As cruel as she may have been as a ruler, she was ten times worse as a mother. I was a means to keep her legacy alive, but other than that, I was a toy to pull out, to use or abuse however she saw fit." He tilted his head back, glancing up at the ceiling. Shadows stretched across the length of the room, disappearing into the darker crevices. "I saw her death before it happened, and she only knew this at the very end. She hated me more than the mortals at that moment."

Light danced across Eirah's face. She'd grown still and studied him far too closely. He didn't like it—he didn't want her to see deeper than his cool exterior. "Why not tell her?"

"Because she deserved to die. And Frosteria needed someone who actually sought to care for it. When I was crowned, I vowed to protect the land as I'd protect myself."

Eirah didn't argue with that. Although it'd happened long before she was born, Maranna's legacy lived on through the wicked tales the villagers and frost demons would spin. After a moment of silence, Eirah pressed on. "What about a sacrifice? Are you still planning to end my life?" she asked, her brow furrowed.

He mused over her question, carefully guarding his thoughts lest she hear him. Would a sacrifice aid their cause? Or would her death be for nothing? "I don't know. If there is another way, I'll find it, but I've tried an animal to see if it would buy us time. It didn't work. If there is to be a sacrifice, the vision is clear you are at the center of what is to come. No one else."

Eirah grew quiet again. "I think I should go check on my father," she murmured after a time. "Unless you want me to stay."

He flicked a hand in the air. "Go." *I don't want her to leave.*

Eirah hesitated for a moment, and he knew she'd heard his thoughts. But she waited for him to say something else, to ask her to stay. "Go," he repeated. This time she stood, glancing back one more time before leaving him. As soon as the door shut, he lashed out, kicking the chair beside him. This all stemmed back to his mother and her wretched reign. Now, Eirah knew, and it was up to her to process the information. Despite everything she'd endured, she seemed to handle it, and he commended her for that. A strength he'd not seen in many, and something akin to pride beat within his chest.

Morozko sat slumped in the chair, staring into the fire until sleep overtook him.

Eirah grabbed hold of his arm, stilling him. She motioned to a changeling as it leaped toward a child. Instead of colliding with the boy, the demon's body shimmered, stretched, and disappeared. At first, the boy convulsed, then, as he sat up, his eyes flashed yellow.

The mortal lifted his hands and glanced at them. An inhuman screech emitted from him before he ran off.

Morozko scowled. "They can possess mortal children."

"Then how do we know who is possessed and who isn't?" Eirah hissed.

"I don't know."

Morozko awoke with a start and pushed out from the chair. It took him a moment to look around and process that he was in Vinti, in someone else's home. When his nerves settled, he charged outside, and judging by the rising sun, he'd only been asleep for an hour.

Nuka roused, yawning, as he looked at Morozko.

"Your Majesty?" Andras stepped away from the tree he leaned against. "Is everything all right?"

Morozko smoothed his hand down his face. "No. We have a big problem."

"What is it?" the captain prompted, his shoulders tensing as he peered around.

"The creatures who did this... they can invade a child's body."

Which meant there was a distinct possibility that a handful of humans were already compromised. But how were they meant to eradicate them—by killing them all? Morozko curled his fingers into fists and growled. He wouldn't. There had to be another way.

16

EIRAH

Eirah peered up at the star-freckled sky. The torches around the village burned brightly through the darkness, not to give off light but protection from creatures that she now knew were created by Morozko's vicious mother. Changelings.

As for Eirah saving Frosteria? *Bah*! She couldn't bring a lick of magic to her fingertips at the moment, even though it churned within her. Could only will herself to shift into an owl, but what would that do? Get herself put into a cage and become a meal for someone? The one time magic had shot out of her previously may have just been a faulty occurrence.

A hoot echoed above her, and she glanced up at the sky once more, finding Adair circling her. "I didn't mean *you* would end up in a cage. *Me*."

He gave another hoot, following her as she hurried back to Saren's home, the snow crunching beneath her boots. Morozko was staying in an abandoned cottage alone, and he'd denied her offer to linger inside with him. The king had wanted her company, but he hadn't spoken the words aloud, only inside his head. He was a grown male, and she wouldn't treat him as a babe by asking him a second time.

Morozko had finally confessed the truth to her, making her understand why he'd chosen her as his sacrifice, given her his blood, and made her practice shifting. But it didn't make any of those things right. And she felt foolish, so incredibly foolish, and so should her village, even though it was their ancestors' fault for not passing the story down the generations. They had known *why* a sacrifice had needed to be performed... Yet they'd either forgotten or had chosen not to believe it anymore. If she had known, she would've been the first to bring a blade to one of the livestock, even if that would've meant less food on the village's table. It would've saved so many lives. But now, sacrificing an animal wouldn't do any good.

At some point, she may still need to sacrifice herself, but not yet, not until Morozko learned more from his visions... For her family, if it came down to it, she would still make the choice, just as she had chosen to go with Morozko when he'd first picked her at the ceremony.

Even then, a bit of anger boiled inside her, beating with each thump of her heart, that Morozko could've reminded her village why the ceremony needed to be carried out. If the village had known, they would've sacrificed a thousand horses.

"Eirah, we don't even have a thousand horses anymore," she muttered. "All right, that was a bit of an exaggeration, but we would've sacrificed one on the precise day." Because there was no sacrifice, the changelings had broken through their seal, her father had been wounded, her cottage destroyed, Petre was dead, and now Saren and the village had to suffer.

146

And yet, she blamed her village more than Morozko.

"I need what's left of my village to be saved," Eirah whispered. She still had a human heart even though she was immortal, while Morozko's heart was... It wasn't as cold as she'd first thought... but it wasn't warm and toasty, either.

Perhaps he's afraid...

"Bah!" Eirah trudged faster through the snow, past the fallen and broken cottages. She didn't want that side of her to come crawling back out, the side that may *understand*. After growing up with an evil demon of a mother who hadn't cared about him, who'd killed someone he cared about in front of him when he'd only been a boy...

"The bastard could've still been honest, Eirah," she hissed. He could have admitted he'd first brought her to his castle because he believed she was plotting to murder him. Which she had been, had *tried*. But that was after he'd chosen her.

Adair swooped down, lingering on Saren's roof, seeming to want to watch over them for the remainder of the night. She gave him a smile before pausing on Saren's porch, her hand gripping the door handle. Morozko didn't always admit everything in truth aloud—his words were covered in falseness at times. To protect himself, just as he would the land... He'd admitted that those were the two things he cared about.

As she opened the door she'd fixed earlier, something nagged her about his words. She needed to think harder—she wished she had a music box to work on while doing so.

When she stepped inside, her father peeled open his eyes. "Daughter?"

"It's me." Eirah tossed a log into the fire, then knelt in front of him, taking his hand in hers. He still appeared weak on the settee, but no blood bloomed on the bandages covering his wounds.

His broken glasses rested on the table, and his breaths came out steady.

"Has the king changed his mind about you?" Her father asked, hope filling his tired voice.

"No, Papa." Eirah's lips tugged up a little at the edges. "He has me as a pampered pet for now. But at least you and I have more time together." She would tell him about how the village had been partly at fault once his strength was up.

"This was like a gift, you coming here," he yawned when he spoke. "Even on this heinous night."

Eirah didn't want to give him hope that there was a possibility Morozko might allow her to live because she didn't even have hope herself. What was necessary would be what she needed to do. She had always told her father everything, but she didn't want anyone to know she held magic, that she was immortal, could shift into a bird. Her father and Saren wouldn't look at her differently, but the village would. They would believe she seduced the king to live, to gain magic. And so what if she had? Most would for their lives.

She thought about the kiss—that beautiful, awful kiss— where she could've pushed away but had only wanted to pull him closer. A kiss that she'd vowed would never happen again, but after the admission of his secrets—that it was all for Frosteria... and perhaps himself—nothing had changed because she could still die. But it would always be worth it to protect those she loved.

"I'm sorry about our home, your work, Mama's things." Eirah's voice came out on a choked sob as she squeezed his hand softly.

All of her things were now gone, too. But it wasn't her beloved romance tomes hidden beneath her bed, the macabre creations she'd made, or even the music boxes she'd worked on with her father that hurt her the most to lose. It was her mother's dresses that had been in Eirah's wardrobe. Sometimes she would open the wardrobe to inhale the fabric of one of the dresses because, even after all these years, her mother's light strawberry scent lingered. Now they were gone, and she would never have that part of her mother again.

"Everything is not gone. I have the ring she gave me." He held up his hand, showing the gold wedding band he continued to wear on his finger. Then he drew a silver chain from his pocket and placed the necklace into her palm. "And this is yours now. It was the only thing I had time to take."

Tears pricked her eyes as she held her mother's favorite locket. "Are you sure? You don't want to keep it?"

He shook his head, taking a breath, his eyes falling shut. "I have her memories."

As she fastened the chain around her neck, Eirah was tempted to check on Saren, but it was best to let her friend rest for the remainder of the night. She didn't want to wake her and have Saren remember everything that had happened, for her gaze to fall on Petre's still body. In the morning, Eirah would go to her.

For now, she cleared spools of thread and other scattered items from the floor, then settled on the fur rug in front of the fire. She didn't require the warmth, but it was a comfort as she cradled her mother's locket in one hand and held her other up to the flames.

Morozko's admission about his visions crept back into her thoughts. Before, she'd believed him to just be a bastard king who tumbled whomever he desired while wanting others to bend to his every command. All true, but there was more depth to him...

Eirah focused on the words he'd chosen to use. In his

vision, he'd seen the ground cracking, changelings, and Eirah calling for him, wanting to help him. When he'd spoken the words, there had been an emotion flickering in his eyes as he'd looked at her, something that he was keeping hidden from her. There was more to that moment, more between them, that he saw in that vision. But what was it?

Eirah wouldn't go back tonight, wouldn't allow herself to seduce or pamper him for answers. She studied the flames, repeating the prayer that her mother used to always tell her at bedtime, then asked her if she would watch over Petre in the afterlife.

With a sigh, she lay against the fur, watching the fire crackle until her eyes fell shut. Morozko's bright blue irises came to her. The anger in her heart had lessened to where she was starting to feel sorry for him. Anyone in the village would call her mad for feeling sorry for someone who had held so many secrets. She thought once more about the kiss he'd taken from her, the kiss she'd willingly given back to him. But he had told her the truth, while he could have continued to keep his secrets...

Eirah cracked open her eyes and gasped, hurrying to sit up, when she discovered Morozko standing above her, studying her.

"What are you doing?" she hissed, finding her father still asleep on the settee, light snores escaping his parted mouth.

"Nothing," Morozko said, folding his arms. "I came to wake you, little bird. We have matters to discuss."

SLAYING THE FROST KING

She scowled. "You weren't waking me. You were *staring* at me."

"So I was." He shrugged, motioning with a finger for her to follow him. "Come outside with me *now*."

With a frown, she pushed up from the floor and met him outside in the snow. "You need to learn manners. Not demand others to do as you wish the second you say the word."

"I am the king, and I can order whomever I want to do whatever I wish." He shrugged, offering a sharp-toothed grin. "Besides, we can't always get what we want."

"That includes you," she snapped. Something swirled in his gaze. A hint of worry? "What is it?"

Morozko lifted a brow, then took the blade of ice she'd left in the snow and pressed it into her hand. "Keep this on you at all times. We are to leave now. A few guards will remain behind."

"Now?" Eirah asked. "I'm not leaving what's left of my village after it was ravaged by creatures that *eat* people's organs. I haven't even helped Saren bury Petre. My father is still healing, exhausted, and his glasses are *broken*. He needs me."

Morozko stilled, eyeing her closely, but he didn't glare. "I had a vision," Morozko said it as if he was saying what color the sky was.

"And? What did you see?"

"Come with me."

He folded his hand around her arm, and she yanked away from him. "I will not."

Morozko's nostrils flared as he stood a hair's breadth from her. "This is not the time, Eirah. And so help me, I will carry you, as I did in my palace, out of this village."

"Oh yes, where you fed me your magical blood. Secretly, I

might add. And..." she trailed off. He hadn't called her little bird—he'd called her by her name. The smirk he usually wore was not there—the play in his stare didn't dance. "Something is truly wrong, isn't it? Please tell me. You confessed things to me last night that you've kept locked away. I may be nothing to you but a means to an end, yet don't I deserve honesty? Or am I to go back to being your bird in a cage, not knowing anything?"

You aren't a means to an end. You're a thorn in the bottom of my foot that makes me question everything I know.

Her eyebrows lifted, and she took a deep swallow as he sighed, knowing she had heard him.

"I will tell you now instead of back at the castle," he said. "But only because I believe you will save Frosteria. In my vision, these changelings... they aren't only here to kill. They can take over mortal children's bodies."

Her heart sped up. "Take over the bodies? I don't understand."

"There are children here who may have these creatures hidden beneath their flesh, so we must leave now until we can devise a plan. The only other option is to slaughter them, and I don't believe you or I want that."

Eirah looked at the remains of her home, the fire that had burned it down and had also helped to drive the changelings out. "You can show fire to everyone in the village. My father said the changelings are afraid of it."

"In their true form, they may be, but while in the shell of a mortal child, I'm not certain. Everyone surviving has been near the bonfire or had candles lit in their rooms."

A chill crawled up her spine. Innocent children she may have brought toys to could have these creatures inside them. Wicked creatures she had yet to *see*.

"We can't leave, Morozko. I can't leave my family again, as small as it may be. Put your blade to my throat now if you must because I won't go. If your guards return me to your castle, I'll shift and fly right back here."

He ran a hand down his face, the vein along his jaw ticking. "You are the most stubborn and insufferable maiden I've ever come to meet."

"And I'm glad we can both agree those are wonderful qualities," she drawled.

He arched a brow. "Tell me what your alternative is, then I'll decide if I will allow it."

Eirah thought about what they could do. She knew Morozko wouldn't let her remain in the village while he and his guards were back at the castle. And she also knew the king and his guards wouldn't stay here, either. An idea came to her then... "I know what will work for us both, and it gives us what we both want. We take the village survivors to your home."

Morozko scoffed. "No. Monsters inside them or not, you're not inviting an entire village into my home."

"You haven't heard what else I have to say on the matter."

"I've heard well enough. *No.*" His voice left no room for argument.

Eirah narrowed her eyes and continued anyway, "We bring the villagers to your home, *outside* the castle walls. In turn, we are not only protecting them from unknown attacks that may occur, but while they are there, we can discover who precisely may be taken over by changelings. As we wait, we will see if your visions continue, to possibly discover more about the future of things. Having them near your home is only temporary, Morozko. Not *eternally.*"

"That's twice you've called me Morozko now." His lips

curled up at the edges as he seemed to mull over what she'd said. "I suppose it's a better option than ending the lives of everyone here."

Eirah glowered. "That had better be a jest."

"It wasn't." He sighed. "These creatures are dangerous, born of evil, and a risk to the land."

"Perhaps you shouldn't only be concerned with the *land*, but the ones who live here, too."

His lips formed a thin line as he studied her. "The frost guards will leave now to form the ice housing in the forest near the castle. Fire will be lit in the center of each home to keep the mortals warm while we can also see if anyone appears frightened by the flames. I will tell the village to prepare their sleds and horses to leave tomorrow morning. You will speak of the underlying reason to no one, not your father, not Saren. And if you haven't already discussed your magic with them, it will be kept a secret for the time being. Do what you need to for now." With that, he turned on his heel and walked away from her.

Had he listened to her? Given in to her request? He had... Surprise washed over her, along with another feeling she couldn't quite name.

Eirah tucked the dagger at her waist and went back inside the cottage, finding her father still sleeping. She wouldn't disturb him just yet since he wouldn't have anything to pack anyway.

She entered the room where Saren slept in the chair with the fur blanket around her. Petre was still in the bed, his lips blue, his skin pale, and Eirah's chest tightened at seeing him this way. The wind blew through the broken window, and even though she couldn't feel it, she shivered.

Eirah lightly shook Saren awake. Her friend flicked open

her eyes, and her gaze drifted from Eirah to Petre. Saren's lower lip trembled, but she remained quiet.

"Let me help you bury your brother, then we need to pack your things. You and the rest of the village will be staying near the palace," Eirah said, wishing she didn't have to hurry her friend, but it was necessary.

She shook her head. "No. I'm not leaving Petre or our home."

Eirah knelt in front of Saren, placing a comforting hand on her knee. "It's only temporary, and I promise you will come back here. We can't leave Petre like this, either."

Tears rained down Saren's cheeks as she slowly nodded, standing up to pull the blankets back from her brother.

The rest of the day was spent burying Petre and packing Saren's things. Eirah's father was given a few pairs of clothing that had belonged to Petre, enough to get by. She'd seen her father's hands fidget as he remained on the settee as instructed by Andras. Eirah found a knife and a block of spare wood, then handed them to her father to occupy his mind.

Morozko didn't return to Saren's home, and as night fell again, she wondered where he was staying. Was he still in Nastya's cottage, or had he decided to go back to his palace?

But in the morning, Morozko was there, this time shaking her awake. Briefly, she wondered if he had studied her while she was sleeping again. Part of her believed he had.

"We leave now," he said.

Her father continued to sleep, and she tiptoed past him, grabbing two plums from a bowl on the supper table. She tossed one to Morozko, and he easily caught it. He turned it over in his hand, his brow furrowed as if he was confused about why she was giving him a piece of fruit.

"You need to eat, don't you?" she asked, biting into the sweet and juicy fruit. "Or have you already?"

"I'm not hungry. However, I find it interesting you're concerned if I eat or not," he said, bringing the plum between his plump lips.

"Who said I was?" She arched a brow.

He smirked. "Once we arrive near the palace, you will stay with me in *our* new home. So lucky for you, you'll be sleeping with me again."

Eirah tightened her fist on the plum as her father was now awake, staring between the two of them, blinking.

"Collect your father and Saren, then we leave." Morozko winked at her before shutting the door behind him.

"It isn't what you think." Eirah turned to her father. "He's a pest." She wanted to tell him the last time she'd slept in his bed, she'd been an owl, but Morozko had asked her to keep her magic a secret, and she wouldn't confess it now, not when the king agreed to bring her village to his home.

"As long as he hasn't hurt you, daughter." He sat up and his eyes widened as he lifted his glasses from the table. They were no longer broken, the glass perfectly smooth.

Her heart galloped, and she remembered her conversation where she'd hissed at Morozko that her father's glasses were broken. He hadn't responded, hadn't said a word, and yet he'd *fixed* them...

17

MOROZKO

Nuka waited just outside Saren's house, his eyes trained on the entrance, so the wolf was the first thing Morozko saw as he shut the door. Nuka's tongue lolled out of his mouth, and his plumed tail wagged furiously.

At least someone is gladdened to see me. Morozko sighed.

The king's lips twitched in a small smile as he crossed the distance to his familiar and rubbed beneath his chin. A bright spot amongst the wreckage of the village. More than a dozen mortals were dead, and a few homes had burned down, but what unsettled Morozko most was not knowing *who* could've been possessed. How many changelings had slipped through the seal, and how many inhabited the children of Vinti?

Before waking Eirah, he'd gathered his guards and scoured the village for any visible signs of changelings. Unfortunately, they had discovered none. Of course, doors were hanging from their hinges, windows shattered, and livestock pens were snapped, but *nothing* of those dreaded bastards.

How many? It was a question that plagued him. How many had escaped? If he went by his visions, he'd say nearly two dozen, but could he rely on those alone?

Morozko pinched the bridge of his nose, groaning. "If they'd listened, Nuka, none of this would be happening," he ground out. Yet, if they *had* listened, if the villagers hadn't forgotten as time passed, he'd never have met Eirah. Morozko did, in fact, regret not reminding them. Not because of the lives lost but because of what it meant for him now. Still, he always assumed he could handle it and thwart any issue that arose from it. But now? Doubt lapped at his conscience.

His fingers curled into Nuka's fur as he mulled over that notion. In a short time, Eirah had wheedled her way into his mind. Morozko didn't want to acknowledge it, but what was the use? If he'd never met Eirah, his life would've remained in the same dull, monotonous pattern.

Eirah was infuriating, but at the very least, she broke up his routine. Now that he thought about it, she had entirely disrupted his life. He hadn't taken a female to bed since he had left for the selection in Vinti. His lips quirked into a sardonic smile—not unless one counted having a fluttering bird slumbering next to them.

But Morozko would be lying to himself if he said he didn't want her bare body pressing against his, her breath against his neck and arms around him. And that was the least of it. Damn it to the deepest crevice. He wanted to taste her lips more. Let his fingers glide and explore what part made her sigh or moan. Whether she was a virgin didn't matter to him, but knowing he could teach her a plethora of things, including what pleasure was, sent his heart racing.

He blamed his visions for softening him toward her, but in truth, it was just Eirah. How, even when afraid, she fiercely braved what he—life—threw at her. And when he baited her, she rose to the occasion instead of cowering. As if, perhaps, she were an equal. She didn't deserve death, and the promise of her end stirred his ire.

Morozko couldn't spend too much time dwelling on that thought because Eirah's voice, chiming over the gathering throng of villagers, interrupted him.

He turned as she approached, her arm looping through her father's as he walked forward. Fedir's bespectacled gaze lingered on Morozko for too long, and, in turn, he lifted a brow. He'd fixed the man's glasses, not because he had any sentiment toward him but because of how distraught Eirah had been. It seemed a small token in the broad scheme of things.

As her father stared at him, Morozko wondered if the mortal still ruminated over the idea of Eirah in bed with him. Despite the melancholic mood, Morozko chuckled, and Eirah's eyes found his.

Hooves clopped onto the frozen ground, and one of Morozko's guards led a shaggy chestnut horse up to them. Behind the palfrey was a simple wooden sleigh that had seen better days. Deep gouges marred the side, and the cushions hardly seemed like cushions. Still, the runners were in decent condition.

"Your Majesty," Eirah's father said, bowing his head. When his gaze caught Morozko's, there seemed to be a question burning behind his eyes. "Thank you for taking care of my daughter."

Morozko's lips remained in a firm line. He contemplated a silver-tongued retort—one that wouldn't reassure the man at all—but at the last moment, he reconsidered. "It is the least I can do." Not long after, Saren emerged from around the house

CANDACE ROBINSON & ELLE BEAUMONT

with another horse in tow. Morozko assumed that one belonged to Saren.

Eirah crossed the distance and embraced Saren, then walked up to her father and hugged him. "Keep your eyes open, both of you." She looked between them, offering the smallest of smiles before she made her way to Morozko.

Although Morozko was surprised she wanted to ride with him, he didn't show it. He schooled his features into an impassive expression as he extended his hand to Eirah. "The guards at the palace have likely descended the mountain to meet us halfway. We need to keep a decent pace, but in the end, we're only as quick as our slowest traveler." He clucked his tongue, and Nuka, taking the cue, laid down.

As Eirah curled her fingers into Nuka's fur, he turned his head and nudged her with his nose ever so lightly, then licked her. She blinked, stunned by the act. With a smile, she climbed up into the saddle.

Morozko sighed. Even the wolf's affections were compromised. Before long, what remained of the village surrounded them. He surveyed the faces, trying to see if any struck him as odd. Could he see the glimmer of a demon in any of the children? Sadly, none scraped at their skin or hissed with bared teeth at him. It would've made it easier if they did.

Perhaps they'd have luck with the fires blazing inside the ice structures. If they were lucky, a few would scramble outside, afraid to draw near to the inferno within.

Nuka nudged him, sensing his inner turmoil, no doubt. But Morozko couldn't think on it too long as he needed to lead the villagers to the encampment. He truly didn't want to because he feared what lurked in the mortals—and in the woods, too. No part of him wanted to bring that so close to his home.

Yet, here they were.

Morozko climbed into the saddle, settling behind Eirah, which might not have been the most brilliant of ideas. She nestled between his thighs, and whether she was aware of it or not, she leaned into his chest. The scent of her invaded his senses. Warm, floral, and so very enticing.

The memory of her lips against his flashed in his mind, but he was careful to shield his thoughts, not wanting her privy to them. Still, the feeling of her body against his, melding with that moment against the tree... If he didn't distract himself, Eirah would know where his mind was soon enough.

Before he set off, he brushed a few strands of Eirah's hair to the side, exposing her skin. She shivered, but he knew it wasn't because of the cold. The urge to press his mouth to the spot just behind her ear grew more and more. Instead, he leaned against her back and kept his voice low as he said, "I hope I don't regret this." Even as he spoke, he wasn't certain whether it was regarding the camp or staying in one of the ice houses with Eirah.

In that moment, he wished he could hear her thoughts, yet nothing called to him.

With a cue, Nuka set off in a slow trot, allowing those in the sleighs to keep up without pushing their horses too hard. Morozko supposed, to a mortal, it was already cold enough. His breath billowed from his mouth in visible clouds, and judging by the thick fur coats or blankets the humans had wrapped around them, it was frigid.

The trees didn't tremble as Nuka trotted by. Their boughs remained frozen in place, unwilling to relinquish the ice encasing their branches. At least the wind was in their favor, for it didn't howl or push back.

Too many times, they had to stop their travels for a stumbling villager or one who had to relieve themselves, and the last time, Morozko ground his teeth together, a scowl on his face.

"What do you expect?" Eirah muttered, leaning against Nuka's shoulders as she stretched her legs. "They're not used to traveling like this. Especially up a mountain. It's cold. Have more patience with them. They're not—"

"Immortal," Morozko bit out. "I'm well aware. And it's the base of the mountain, not the top." He raked his hand through his hair and tilted his head back, glancing up at the purple-tinged sky. The sun was already losing its hold on the day. If they were lucky, they'd arrive by nightfall. However, at this rate, it'd take until morning if they kept stopping.

Morozko's stomach growled. Now he wished he'd eaten more than a plum that morning. Once they were settled, he'd enlist the guards to hunt down some deer.

"You should've eaten more." Eirah shrugged.

His eyes snapped to her face, and although his lips were in a tight smile, Morozko was more than bored and was inspired to poke the bear. So, he stalked forward, looming over Eirah, wondering if her inner grizzly would rise. "You know, little bird, I have a use for that tongue of yours."

She picked at her nails, only ceasing when he was inches away. "I think everyone is ready to finish the journey." Eirah turned around and climbed into the saddle. She stared down at him, eyebrow cocked, and head tilted expectantly.

Morozko's gaze lingered on her backside, and suddenly, he wasn't concerned about his rumbling stomach but the skin that awaited him beneath Eirah's trousers. Oh, he knew what it felt like from when he plucked her from the tub, but he was unfamiliar with the dips and curves.

"You're holding the group up, Morozko." Eirah motioned to the villagers, who were mostly already inside their sleighs or on their horses.

It was him shrugging this time. "Now they may know what it feels like to wait." Except, he didn't linger on the ground for long—he was too impatient, too over the slow journey.

Eventually, they came upon the royal guards. The frost demons sprung into action, helping those who openly struggled, and, unfortunately, aided a few dying horses into an eternal slumber. It wasn't pleasant, but a sword to the heart was effective.

Eventually, just before nightfall, they arrived at the encampment. Several ice houses dotted the clearing. Some were rectangular or square, and others rounded. The guards had done well to prepare the camp, for inside each one were also boughs of pine to create bedding and kindling ready to go for a fire.

"They need food." Morozko sighed and turned to Andras. "The water and food they brought won't last long. I am certain you're all exhausted, but hunt down some deer. They could use more blankets, too, I'm sure."

When everyone was settled inside their temporary lodging, Morozko dipped inside his house. It was tall enough, so he only had to crouch a little. A small fire illuminated the space, and a hole at the top allowed for the smoke to filter out. Eirah hadn't ventured inside yet—she was likely speaking with Fedir or Saren.

He pulled his cape off, then his sword, and set them aside his makeshift bed. His fingers loosened the ties of his shirt, and he lowered himself to the ground, crossing his legs.

A few moments later, Eirah poked her head in, and her dark eyes appeared bottomless in the firelight. "This is cozy."

Morozko's gaze shifted to the leaping flames, and he nodded, motioning to her bedding. "Come here," he mumbled. "I think it's time we practice some actual magic. No tests, no prodding." Now that he'd told her the truth about everything, he wasn't willing to play games.

Eirah sat next to him and rolled her sleeves up. She wiggled her fingers as she waited for instructions. "I don't know how effective this is going to be."

"That's why it's called practice. Besides, we need to be ready for anything. We can hope the fire will terrify the hiding bastards, but we don't know for certain." He reached out and took her hands in his, despising how his heart leaped on contact. Life buzzed beneath her skin, and he *felt* it. The warmth spread through his body, dizzying him as if he'd been deep in his cups moments ago. He dragged his fingers from her palms and down the underside of her forearms. "Call to your magic by closing your eyes. Imagine dunking a bucket into a well and slowly cranking it back up." He spoke in a soft, melodic tone.

She shot him a suspicious glance, then closed her eyes. Goosebumps formed on her arms, and he wasn't certain whether it was from him or her tapping into her magic.

He swallowed, trying to stop himself from studying her because the more he pored over the angles of her face and her full lips, the more he wanted to kiss them and taste her.

Eirah gasped, wrenching him from his thoughts. "I... feel it. It's hard to explain, like... a fire burning within."

He knew what his magic felt like, and in some ways, he'd compare it to the sensation of completion. A liquid burning within his chest until it erupted and bloomed into pure energy

—his magic. Morozko hadn't known she would experience anything like this, not until now.

He held his palms beneath hers. "Foster it. Keep feeding the fire, bucket after bucket of energy," he coaxed her, watching as thin strands of light streamed from her palms.

Eirah panted softly from the exertion but continued on, forming a brighter blue light. When it was the size of a snow-ball, Morozko gently turned her palms over, marveling at the sight. Outside of frost demons, he'd seen no other magic quite like it.

"Open your eyes."

She did, and awe filled them. Eirah squealed. "I did that. My magic... But what do I do with it?"

He cocked a brow. "Well, you could force someone into oblivion, but other than that... I'm not quite certain what or if you have specified magic. We can explore what you're capable of." If she was willing, or if Frosteria would allow for that. Who knew what lay ahead of the realm, for his visions were as much a blessing as they were a curse.

"How do I will it away?" Eirah closed her palms. The energy swirled at her knuckles, and when she opened her fist, it danced along her skin.

"Imagine lowering the bucket back into the well, returning bucket by bucket. Eventually, you'll learn to drop it at once, but for now, let's go slowly." As he spoke, she focused on her hands, and the flickering light diminished little by little until it snuffed out entirely.

Eirah was breathless and smiling with triumph. "That was... *incredible*." She leaned forward into his space, eyes brimming with excitement.

Morozko wished she would retreat, but she didn't, and his heart thudded wildly. He hated himself for it. For wanting what he shouldn't when Eirah was possibly the only way the changelings could be undone. By death or magic. Perhaps both, and he wished he knew which one it was.

"Let me try again." Eirah knelt before him, still too close for him to think clearly, but she offered him her hands.

His tongue grazed the tip of a sharp canine. This time, he didn't speak. He only took her hands, lifted them to his mouth, and brushed kisses along her digits.

I shouldn't want to kiss him as badly as I do now.

It took him a moment to realize Eirah's thought was blaring in his mind—he'd been thinking the same thing.

"Oh, little bird," he whispered, reaching out to nudge her chin with his finger. "But you do." Morozko nearly groaned the words as he closed the space between them. He allowed enough time for her to pull away, but when she didn't, his lips collided with hers.

At once, heat flared in his chest, igniting every nerve in his body. He tugged her onto his lap, and she nestled against him, as if she'd been crafted for him alone. His tongue dove into her mouth, drinking in the taste of her.

Eirah moaned, hardening his cock at once, and she shifted against him, winding her fingers into his hair. When her digits brushed his skin, the intoxicating feeling returned.

He withdrew his lips from hers, curious how *his* magic bumping against hers would feel. Morozko pinched his bottom lip with his canine and dragged his finger along Eirah's collarbone. Soft wisps of chilled air formed around them. "What do you feel?"

Eirah's breath hitched as she cupped his face. "You." She tipped her head back, and he snaked his finger down to the valley between her breasts.

Morozko leaned forward, pressing his lips against her

throat, and he moaned as she rolled her hips into his. "Little bird," he said, voice strained, "If you mean to stop, do so now because you're making it *very* hard for me." Oh, he wanted her, and he didn't bother to shield his thoughts. Let her hear how he wanted to taste every inch of her and trace every dip, every line of her body, until she quivered in ecstasy.

18

EIRAH

Eirah was making it hard for Morozko? No, he was making it hard for *her*. The way he held her as if she was the only woman he would ever want. Had all the other maidens felt this way? Yet she didn't want to stop, even though she knew she should, even though she knew she could still one day die by his blade. And that was precisely why she shouldn't stop, because she didn't know how much time she had left in this cold, beautiful, vengeful world.

As she rolled her hips again, feeling Morozko harden even more, Eirah wondered what would happen if she didn't have to die... What would happen between her and Morozko? Would he toss her back to the village with meaningless gifts? When he slid his hot tongue up her throat, she decided she didn't care—she desperately wanted him to teach her everything she'd ever read about in the romance tales she loved so much.

"Believe me," he purred in her ear as his hands cupped her

168

buttocks. "I can show you many, many things. Things you've never once read about, little bird."

"Do you have to hear my thoughts at the most inopportune times?" Yet her words didn't come out as haughty as she would've liked, and instead, it sounded more breathy, *needy*.

"Oh, but I rather enjoy these hidden thoughts of yours. How about we remove some of these thick layers between us now, shall we?"

"Your Majesty," a voice boomed from behind them.

Eirah startled, shoving herself off Morozko as if Andras might believe she'd never been there at all. Heat spread into her cheeks, and she looked away from the crimson-haired guard.

"Andras, what do you need?" Morozko narrowed his eyes, seeming to await an answer that had better be worth his while.

"I have an important matter to discuss with you." His gaze shifted to Eirah as if he didn't fully trust her.

"I'm going to check on my father and Saren," Eirah said to Morozko, not waiting for his response. "I'll come back soon." Even though she was curious to see what Andras had to say, she needed fresh air and to be away from Morozko, away from what almost happened between them. Something she wanted more of...

"What in the world did I just do?" Eirah scolded herself as she padded away from the ice house. "Was this a thank you for repairing my father's glasses?" But oh, did the king know how to touch and kiss. She wondered what else his deft fingers could do if they'd been without clothing.

At least a dozen ice homes spread across the small stretch of unwooded land, each housing several families. Her father and Saren were sharing one at the edge of the temporary village, close to Morozko's. He'd chosen a house close enough to keep an eye on the mortals while she and the king figured out whether the changelings had indeed taken over any of the children.

As Eirah trudged through the snow beneath the starry night, white wings caught her attention from above. A tug of magic pulled inside her as Adair swooped down, drifting nearer to her. He landed on her shoulder, surprising her. He'd done nothing of this nature before, and his talons pressed into her, but not painfully. As his bright orange eyes studied her, her cheeks grew hot again when she knew what he was thinking.

"Don't look at me like that," she whisper-shouted. "I wasn't doing anything but minding my business with the king." The owl slowly blinked as though he didn't believe her. "Oh, fine, I was about to let him ravish me in all the ways he wished. Not that you care to hear about any of this, but I seem to be no different from any of the other maidens." She would've confided in Saren, but her friend was grieving.

Adair cocked his head, his orange eyes glowing.

"Yes, there's something wrong with that! Most of the maidens wanted Morozko because he's the king, or to receive his gifts, become queen, get him to fall in love. I just want him because I'm possibly starting to care about him." Eirah covered her mouth to stop the stream of words lest she embarrass herself further. She narrowed her eyes, studying him as he watched her. "You see something good in him, don't you? Otherwise, you would warn me away, wouldn't you?"

Adair hooted and flapped his wings, taking flight once more. He didn't leave her, though, only guided her to her father's temporary home. It was a rounded shape like hers, with blocks of ice surrounding it. A black curtain covered a large hole in its center.

Eirah ducked as she peeled back the curtain and stepped inside. Her father sat by a crackling fire in the middle of the house, a fur blanket covering him while he carved a wooden figure. Most of the things Saren had brought must've remained in the sleigh because the space was bare except for two sacks, a basket of fruit and dried meat, canteens of water, and blankets. Saren lay fast asleep on one of the bedrolls, her back facing them.

"Hello, daughter. I was hoping you'd come by," Eirah's father said with a bright smile, looking up as he chipped away at the wood.

"I'm glad you're watching over her, Papa," Eirah murmured, sinking down beside him.

"She's like a second daughter to me."

"I wish I could talk to her, but I need to give her time." Saren had been quiet on their travels when they'd met during breaks. Her eyes hadn't been as puffy, but she'd continued to mostly stare at her hands.

"She'll come around. I didn't talk to anyone for a while after your mother passed." He wrapped his arm around Eirah, drawing her close.

"You don't talk to anyone now." Her lips tilted up at the edges as she rested her head on his shoulder.

"Like father, like daughter." Their village may consider her father different, but she wouldn't change him for anything in the world.

Eirah released him and peered at the basket of fruit and dried meat. "Did you have enough to eat? I can ask one of the guards to bring you something else."

"I'm fine. I already had my fill." He patted his stomach and expanded it, making her laugh softly.

Eirah chatted with her father for a long while, then went to Saren. She looked so young as she slept, her golden hair spread around her. Eirah knelt before her friend and kissed her on the forehead. "I'll check on you tomorrow and will send prayers tonight for Petre."

Saren cracked open her eyes, and she let out a small sigh. "Goodnight."

Eirah bid her father goodbye and ventured back toward her ice house. As she looked up into the trees, Adair released a loud hoot. She batted a hand in the air, pleading with him to hush.

When she approached the ice house, she was uncertain if she wished for Morozko to be asleep or awake. A part of her hoped he was waiting for her to finish where they'd left off. *Bah, Eirah! You can be so foolish.*

Drawing back the curtain, she slipped inside, finding Morozko alone, pacing back and forth as he sharpened his blade. She took a deep swallow, brushing her fingers against her throat. Had Andras's news meant her death should occur on this night?

"It's not for you, Eirah." He peered up, his face serious. "I don't want to harm you." A playful taunt wasn't there as she'd been expecting.

Eirah furrowed her brow and took a step closer to him. "Is everything all right?"

"No, it is not. My suspicions came to fruition. No child in the village is afraid of the fires. The guards brought food to everyone, and they were all near the flames, with no fear on their faces. My theory is that it's because they are inside the shell of a human. Perhaps the changelings believe they are protected this way, that no one will threaten them if they don't know who they are."

"Or perhaps they are all just fine. Perhaps they didn't go inside any of the children after all." She inched closer to him and pressed a hand to his chest, unexpectedly feeling his heart beat beneath her palm. "We'll find a way. Together."

Morozko looked down at her—a deep line settled between his brow as he studied her. "Besides guards, I've never had anyone offer to help me protect Frosteria. Much less a maiden."

"Perhaps because you never let anyone in," she teased with a smile. "But I suppose I don't either, so we're one and the same."

"I don't think you've done anything near as brutal as I have."

Eirah hadn't, but it didn't matter. As his heart continued to beat against her hand, she thought of their earlier moment together. "About what happened before. Between us. Do you think it was a mistake?"

Morozko arched a brow, tossing the blade to the ground as he backed her against the wall. "A mistake? I don't make mistakes, little bird. Not when it comes to pleasure." He lifted her chin, his thumb stroking across her skin. "If I'm touching you, it's because I choose to and because you want me to."

"Do you not find it strange that I hated you? That I wanted you dead and that you chose me as your sacrifice? That I may still have to die?"

He was quiet for a moment before shaking his head. "No, not at all. Because, in truth, I hated you, too, for what you represented. I still hate it. But I don't hate *you*." His finger trailed down her neck and across her collarbone, his expression unreadable. "Tell me you don't want my touch, that you'd rather me give it to someone else, and I'll leave you here alone if that's what you wish."

Eirah tightened her fists, frustrated at how he couldn't say things in a more delicate manner. "Then go. Pick another maiden, someone more beautiful, that you wish you could've chosen instead, you prick."

He smirked. "Is that jealousy I hear?"

"Yes!" she hissed. "You make me care one moment, and the next you make me furious!"

"And you just make me *feel*, little bird. Like no one ever has." He leaned in, his lips coasting across hers until he captured them. "You're the only one I think about kissing," Morozko murmured, his hands skimming down her waist, one drifting between her legs, pressing deliciously against the sensitive spot. She gasped in pleasure. "And touching. Do you want me to touch you thoroughly?"

Eirah's heart pounded in her chest, and her breaths grew ragged as she studied his hooded gaze, his plump, perfect lips. "Yes," she rasped.

"Then lay on the blankets," he uttered, pushing a lock of hair behind her ear.

"I've never—"

"I won't deflower you tonight, but I will teach you more than magic, make you feel pleasure like you've never felt before."

A heat spread through Eirah at his intoxicating words, and there wasn't a single part of her that was hesitant, that wanted to say no as he sauntered away from her, leaving her the decision.

Taking a swallow, she didn't only venture to the blanket— she slipped off her boots, then removed her clothing until she was bare before him, something that she'd shown no man before, and yet she didn't feel nervous. It was the second time he'd seen her this way, but this was different from when he'd saved her after nearly drowning in a bathtub.

As though she was his prey, his gaze never wavered from her when she sank down to the fur blankets. Morozko's eyes grew more hooded while he prowled toward her. Eirah's heart thrummed faster as he lowered himself in front of her, pressing his mouth to hers in a slow caress. He pried her lips open with his tongue and slipped it inside, tangling it deliciously with hers. His spicy smell overpowered her senses as he drew her closer to him, sending tingles of yearning throughout her body. Eirah ran her hands down his chest, reaching for the laces of his trousers.

He shook his head, pulling back, his lips swollen. "All in due time, but I'm pleasing you first. Now, lay down."

Eirah nodded, and his lips claimed hers once more before he gently lowered her to her back. In that moment, she didn't want to ever deny him anything. Then his hand came between her thighs as it had earlier, only this time there was no clothing to bar the way, nothing but flesh to flesh. She gasped, her back arching into his touch when his fingers moved in a circular pattern. Another needy sound elicited from her as his pace picked up, the rhythm luring her in further. She didn't know he could be so sensual, so thorough —she had assumed he took what he wanted, not gave like this.

"I'm going to taste you now," Morozko said in a gruff voice, "and if you want me to stop, you only have to say the word." He kissed down her neck, nipping and licking as he traveled to her breast. His tongue flicked over a peaked nipple before sucking it into his mouth while kneading her other breast. Morozko released his mouth from her nipple and continued his descent, kissing lower across her flesh, slowly, so slowly, until she couldn't hold back her pleas.

"Morozko, I need you."

"Keep saying my name like that, little bird, and I'll pleasure you for eternity. Now, part your legs for me."

A hint of nervousness finally crawled through her, not because she didn't want him, but because this would be the most vulnerable and intimate thing she'd ever done. Yet she wanted to be vulnerable with him after he'd opened up to her about himself in a way that he hadn't with anyone else. Biting her lip, she spread her legs for him.

Morozko lifted his head, his hungry gaze pinned to hers. "You're beautiful," he whispered, "All of you." He stroked his fingertips over her mound once more before replacing his lovely digits with his impish tongue. His fingers pressed into her thighs as he wickedly licked his tongue up her core.

"More?" Morozko asked, his lips pulled back in a devilish grin. He knew precisely what he was doing to her. "I need to hear it."

"More," she said, her voice desperate.

"Then that's indeed what you're going to receive." And then his mouth was on her sex, kissing her thoroughly, and she never wanted him to cease doing it. His tongue dipped inside of her as if he was making love to her, tasting all of her flavor. Her hands gripped his hair, pulling him even closer while he continued to feast on her.

A rapturous feeling like she'd never known, no matter how many times she'd touched herself, stormed through her. Her body quaked, and Morozko's name fell from her lips in a low moan. She wanted to scream it, but the entire village didn't need to hear her pleasure.

Morozko crawled up her body, his mouth taking ownership of hers, making her feel bold. She glided her hand down his chest, cupping his hardness through his trousers. "I think it may be your turn now."

"Mmm, I like this side of you." He grinned, nudging his nose against hers. "You can touch me *anywhere* you wish."

Eirah lifted his tunic, and he drew it over his head, tossing the fabric to the ground. "You lay on your back this time," she instructed.

"I'm at your command," Morozko growled, unlacing his trousers and pushing them off before laying on his back.

Eirah's eyes widened as she took in his long and thick length. She'd seen boys in Vinti, daring one another to sprint through the village bare, but of the few she'd seen naked, they didn't look as tempting as this.

"What do you want me to do?" she whispered. "I'm not sure how."

"Let me show you." Morozko licked his lower lip while gripping his length, slowly pumping. A glistening pearl bead rested at the tip, and she yearned to see what it tasted like, if his flavor was sweet or spicy. He gently grabbed her hand and guided it to his velvety hardness. She mirrored his movements, clumsy at first, but he didn't seem to mind as his lips parted, his gaze never leaving hers as she stroked him.

"Is it good?" she asked, her mouth coming closer to his.

He sucked in a breath, exhaling shakily. "It's glorious, little bird. Now, come here." Morozko sat up and lifted her into his lap, pulling her mouth to his. "Move against me. Just as you did earlier," he purred, his thumb rubbing her nipple. Eirah rolled her hips forward, her sensitive skin gliding along his heated flesh, and he groaned in pleasure. "Keep doing that, little bird." His lips came to the crook of her neck while his fingers tangled in her hair.

She rose up and down, gliding against his length, her eyelids fluttering when a new bliss coursed through her as her arousal blossomed.

Morozko's hands skimmed down to her backside, cupping it while urging her to move faster, *harder*. "Now come for me," he demanded. As if his words were magic, the pleasurable feeling she'd experienced earlier from his tongue crashed into her again, only this time stronger. Her own magic hummed and sang, blue light swirling around them as she gasped. Morozko released a deep growl, his body shaking beneath her, as he, too, reached his peak of pleasure.

He panted softly, sweat beading along his brow. "You're a fast learner." Morozko smiled. "Both in magic and in pleasure."

19

MOROZKO

Morozko tucked a few strands of Eirah's hair behind her ear and leaned in, pressing a lingering kiss to her jaw. His body still hummed from completion, and despite being content, a part of him wanted very much to claim Eirah in a way no one ever had.

He'd been surprised when she allowed the foreplay to continue. He had every intention of stopping and had even given her a way out. Morozko only wanted to show her the pleasures of his tongue, his touch, but when she regarded *him* and wanted to fulfill his needs, it took everything within him to *only* pull her onto his lap.

Eirah deserved more than a quick tupping. He wouldn't have lasted long inside of her, not with how pent up he was, and certainly not with her tightness wrapped around him.

Her taste still lingered on his tongue, and had they more time, he may have even drawn the moment out. But Andras's reports of no children shying away from the flames still troubled him. It meant this wouldn't be as easy as he'd thought.

What they needed—*he* needed—was another vision. A clearer picture of the horizon and what awaited them in the not-too-distant future.

Morozko's eyes lingered on Eirah's flushed face. He motioned toward his cape. "You can use that." It wasn't his imagination. Her eyes seemed brighter—like she was more aware of him than before. She ducked her head and used the discarded fabric to clean herself up.

When Eirah finished, her gaze caught his, and the elation that was there moments ago faded into something akin to doubt. "What now?" she whispered.

His brow furrowed, genuinely confused as to what she spoke of, but then it dawned on him. "What?" He schooled his features and took his cape from her, using it to wipe away the arousal from his thighs and abdomen, but kept his eyes trained on her.

"You know what I mean." She motioned between them, then pulled her layers of clothing back on.

Morozko remained silent, only watching as she covered her skin again. She may not have been conventionally beautiful like Saren, but she *still* possessed beauty. She was *more* beautiful to him now that he'd come to know her better. Eirah with her sharp angles to match her sharp tongue. Eirah with a tongue he wanted to feel more of. But what they'd become to one another now, even he was uncertain. He believed they were no longer enemies, and now he faced an even larger dilemma. If he did have a vision again, one that showed him sacrificing Eirah, would he go through with it?

No. No, he would not. And that answer alone presented another problem. What would he do to put right to wrongs? How would he drive the changelings back and undo what his mother had done?

He thought for a moment, carefully constructing his words so they didn't sound harsh. Something that could be difficult for him to do. "What do you want out of this?" Morozko couldn't say what he wanted because he didn't know, and voicing that there was one more thing he couldn't answer grated on him. He couldn't bear another uncertainty in his life. Between not knowing how to seal the changelings off, what or *if* sacrificing Eirah would do a damn thing, and not entirely understanding what she was, there were far too many unanswered questions for his liking.

Eirah spoke, her pinkened lips moving, but he couldn't hear her. His ears buzzed, sounding like a thousand flies swarming above his head. A moment later, his vision dimmed, and he tried blinking it away. He staggered forward, his knees buckling as he collapsed to the floor of the ice house, losing himself to a vision. In the distance, Eirah screamed for him, but he couldn't answer.

Morozko dragged his dagger along his fingertip and let the droplets fall onto Eirah's tongue. In turn, she did the same for him, and together they chanted. Snow kicked up around them, spiraling into a cyclone of green, purple, and blue. Morozko dragged his blade across his palm, spilling crimson onto the ivory snow, then watched it spread into a broad circle. The full moon's golden light reflected off the ground, but as a harsh wind blew, the light dimmed —or rather changed. Gone was the bright hue of the moon, and in its place was a dark cobalt orb.

Morozko swayed, clutching his side. "They'll be known as the krampi and will be our claws when we cannot reach the changelings."

The vision jumped forward in time to a grand battle, where Morozko and Eirah sat atop Nuka.

A battle raged before them, the krampi slaughtering the

changelings, hauling them to a grand, blazing fire, where they threw them in. Hungry flames lapped at their waxen flesh, and their wails rang out, piercing his ears. This time their bodies dissipated, but the gnawing feeling of them returning through the seal churned within his mind.

The vision leaped again.

Morozko's side no longer hurt, but his heart thundered away. Adrenaline coursed through him, urging him to rush into battle while his warriors raged, cutting down and chaining up the changelings as they scattered like mice.

Yet, here he and Eirah were, in the palace. It was the only way to ensure he wouldn't fall during the battle—that Frosteria remained safe.

Eirah opened her hand, and in it sat a brilliant blue stone. It pulsed like a heart. "This will aid the krampi in eradicating the changelings. After infusing the stones with their blood and your spell, the power within will help locate them."

Morozko sighed. "And this way, we can decipher who is possessed without needlessly whipping them."

Eirah shook her head. "I wish there was a better way to set the humans free."

Morozko drummed his fingers against his desk. "It seems so far away. A day without changelings..." He sighed, leaning forward to bury his face against Eirah's stomach, then wrapped his arms around her waist.

The vision dissipated, and when Morozko came to, Eirah was shaking him by the shoulders. She hovered above him, worry in her eyes.

"Morozko!" she shrieked.

"I saw," he stammered, struggling to steady himself to sit. "I saw what we must do. It's too late." His words jumbled together as he processed what he'd seen, savoring each detail. "Fuck." Morozko clumsily rolled onto his side and pushed himself onto his knees. He jammed his fingers through his damp hair and sucked in a breath. "It's too late to make a sacrifice. If I killed you now, it would be for nothing. The vision of you wasn't leading to your sacrifice at all, but something else..." Sweat trickled down his face and dripped onto the ground. He trembled not from exertion but from settling into the present.

"I don't need to die, then?" Eirah whispered, disbelief etched on her features. She brought her hands to her mouth and let out a quiet sob of relief.

"No, for you have more to give, little bird." Morozko blinked away the remnants of the vision and grabbed his discarded trousers, then yanked them on.

Eirah ran a hand over his shoulder, her cool fingers centering him. "What must we do?" she echoed. "What did you see?"

He swallowed roughly, trying to assemble his thoughts. "I know why you're here," he rasped. "As I've said, you're instrumental in all of this." He motioned with his hand to indicate their predicament. "You and I will create a demon to rival the changelings. An army of them will rise to keep them at bay. They're slain by fire, and it'll wipe them from our realm until they can regenerate beyond the seal. We need to whip the mortals to free them. And you are, indeed, the first witch."

Eirah placed the back of her hand against his cheek. If she was mortified by what he said, she hid it well. "You're feverish."

"I know what I saw! And I'm fine. It happens the closer I am to a pivotal moment." He grasped onto her wrist, his fingers gentle. Did she not believe him? He frowned, but then again—

"I believe you. Your visions haven't been wrong before, right?" When he said nothing, she nodded. "It explains their fear of fire. What else did you see?"

"A stone. You imbued a stone that could track them down, that removed the guesswork from it all." He shook his head, clearing his mind further, then grabbed his shirt and yanked it on. "And to expel the changeling from a child, we have to whip them."

Her eyes widened in horror. "*What?*"

"That's what I saw." While Morozko wasn't keen on the idea himself, he also didn't *see* another way. "Do you have another idea, then?"

Eirah sighed, shaking her head. "Do you know how much time we have left?"

"I don't." He chewed on his bottom lip, mulling over what he'd seen. "I never know when precisely things will take place. There are hints in the now, happenings that point toward the unfolding of it all, but never a precise moment." He paused, frowning, then paced back and forth.

"Wearing a hole in the ground won't put a stop to this. Sit down before you keel over." She closed the distance between them, took his hand, and led him to their bedrolls. "Tell me how we can plan for this. Tell me what we can do in the meantime."

She didn't say it, but she may as well have. *You're the king. You must lead us.* It wasn't her thoughts, only Morozko's inner turmoil rising, screaming at him to protect what was his.

With a sigh, he lowered himself to the fur blanket. "You know, I never wished to be a king." Why he felt compelled to tell her this now, he didn't know. Perhaps because she was the first person outside his servants to ever truly care for him. "I never wanted the responsibility or power. I wanted to remain hidden, far away from my mother's wickedness and the intrigue of court." He curled his fingers into his palms and sneered. "I hated it then, and I hate it now."

Eirah knelt beside him and settled a hand over one of his fists. Her eyes searched his face as if penetrating through all his hidden layers. "You are the king Frosteria needs, for you have a heart that isn't made of ice. That is what sets you apart from the queen, Morozko. Although, you do like to let us believe it is sometimes." Eirah's lips tilted up at the edges.

Her words ignited an inferno in his chest, blazing furiously to the point his breath hitched. She couldn't know what the words meant to him—to know that he wasn't as abominable as his mother eased an ounce of his torment.

When he didn't respond, Eirah used her finger to turn his face toward hers. "A thank you would suffice, *Your Majesty*."

Morozko lowered his gaze to her lips, which were still reddened by his kisses. A complex emotion he saw no use in defining blossomed inside of him, and he leaned in, his mouth skating over hers before he deepened the kiss.

His tongue glided along hers, slow and sensual as he savored the taste of her, the feel of Eirah as she moved into his arms. Morozko embraced her and withdrew his mouth from hers, then buried his face in the crook of her neck. "What we need to do is no straightforward task. I've done nothing like this before." He chuckled darkly, inhaling Eirah's floral scent. "It seems to me that is becoming a recurrence."

"Then, how do we go about creating a warrior who can rival a changeling?"

Morozko pulled his head back, eyes locking with hers. "Precisely how magic is carried on."

Eirah cocked her head, quirking a brow. She looked the part of an owl.

"With blood."

20

EIRAH

One of the things that horrified Eirah the most about Morozko's visions was the way a changeling would have to be removed from a mortal child—whipping them until the demon left.

"What are we waiting for?" Eirah said, hope igniting within her chest. "Let's perform the blood spell." Her gaze fell to Morozko, his brow slick with sweat and his body slightly swaying as if he would collapse again. Worry filled her at seeing him this way, not himself. "But first, you need to drink and eat something. We don't need you becoming any weaker."

"I'm fine," he growled, but it lacked the bite he usually possessed.

Eirah tilted her head to the side, watching him stumble as he shifted forward. "Take a moment to strengthen yourself, and don't be stubborn. Do you want to die before we can help Frosteria?"

He folded his arms and frowned. "That would end the changelings, wouldn't it?"

"Stop acting like a spoiled child." Eirah narrowed her eyes at him as she picked up a canteen filled with water and a peach from a wicker basket, resting on a desk made of ice that must have been created when she'd been visiting her father and Saren.

Morozko grunted while taking the water and fruit from her. He tipped the canteen to his lips and drank nearly half of the contents. As he bit into the peach, a trail of juice traveled down the side of the fruit, and he swiped his tongue up its length to catch it. It wasn't the right moment in the slightest, yet a heat pooled in her stomach, and all she could think about was how that impish tongue of his had not only slipped into her mouth but inside her depths.

"Your thoughts are growing loud, little bird." Morozko smirked, proving his cockiness had returned. He bit into the peach again, his gaze hooded as he studied her.

"Finish eating." Eirah's cheeks warmed, and she turned around to slip on her boots before he could catch sight of her pinkened skin. She was relieved he was coming back to himself, even if his words annoyed her.

As Eirah secured her cloak around her body, a thought trickled into her mind—she wasn't to be a sacrifice any longer. Where would that leave her and Morozko once she fulfilled her duty to Frosteria? When she'd thought her destiny was death, she'd wanted to feel pleasure, give pleasure, in a way she never had, and she'd chosen that with the king. But her impending death wasn't the only reason... So many feelings toward him resided inside of her that she couldn't untwine just yet—the knots were still too tight. However, she couldn't spend time mulling it over now—she needed to focus on what she now knew to truly be witch magic, what she'd been taught by Morozko. Together, they would somehow create a new demon race that could help save so many future lives that would be otherwise destroyed.

"Follow me to the back of the ice house," Morozko said, finishing the water before pushing the heavy fabric away from the entrance to venture outside.

The night still blanketed Frosteria, the stars flickering above, but Adair was nowhere in sight. Smoke continued to curl from the ice houses farther away, keeping the people of her village warm.

They came to a halt before layers of snow, ready for Morozko to bend to his will. "Let me see your hand." He drew a small ice blade from his hip, a smirk shaping his lips. "I suppose it's only fair that I taste your blood since you tasted mine."

Eirah scowled at him, remembering how she'd been tricked into drinking the wine with his hidden blood. She held her hand out to him, and he pricked the tip of her finger. A slight sting burned, but the pain no longer hummed when he flicked his tongue across it.

"Mmm, you taste of mint," he groaned.

Eirah's heart thrummed, singing in her chest. Somehow the king could even make tasting blood alluring. He then pressed the tip of his blade into his digit, and she avoided looking into his hungry gaze as she licked away the scarlet. It was heavenly, the spice, the frost, but she wouldn't dare ask for more, even though part of her craved it.

Morozko took the dagger and sliced a clean line across his palm, blood blooming to the surface.

A bright crimson droplet fell to the snow, and Morozko chanted words. It took her a moment to catch on, then she spoke the strange language alongside him. But nothing rose from the earth, no stir of unique, colorful magic.

"It isn't working." Morozko tightened his fist, squeezing more drops onto the snow, reddening the white. Still, nothing roused.

"Perhaps you need to use your magic to create the demon from snow first."

Morozko's lips formed a thin line, yet he held out his hand, letting glittery blue and white magic escape his fingertips. The snow and ice drifted into the air, collecting piece by piece, pressing into one another while shaping into a tall form with long, curling horns. Yet the demon's flesh remained snow and ice—no breath escaping its mouth.

"Try it with me," Morozko ground out, his voice strained.

Eirah was still discovering her magic—the possibilities—it wasn't only one ability, as most immortals held, but a combination of many. Gripping her mother's locket for support, she steadied herself, letting the caress of power unfurl within her, then allowed it to flow toward the figure. The glittery blue smoke wrapped around the snow form, and she smiled as it moved. She watched it lift a leg to balance on one foot, twirling and spinning in a slow and delicate manner just as the objects inside her music boxes would do. No song filled the air, only Morozko's sigh.

"Stop." He held a hand up, and the form ceased moving, crashing back into the snow to become a part of it. "This isn't working. My visions are never exact. They aren't step-by-step instructions on how everything plays out, but I know the krampi shouldn't be brought to life like this. It should've only taken our blood with the chanting." A struggle seemed to brew within him as he gritted his teeth.

Eirah wasn't certain what to do, but he needed comfort. So she did the one thing she could do and cupped his cheek, attempting to soothe him. "Ease your thinking. Go into the memory gently. Tell me precisely what happened, and I'll help you piece it together."

Morozko furrowed his brow, concentrating. "We were outside during the night in the forest near the palace. After we drank each other's blood, I spilled mine into the snow. The full moon changed to blue, then the—"

"That's it," Eirah gasped. "The moon isn't yet full."

Morozko glanced up at the half-moon, his teeth clenching harder. "That will be two weeks from now!"

Waiting wasn't ideal, and she didn't like the idea of what might happen between now and then, but they couldn't force the moon to become full, no matter how much magic they fed it. "We will have to wait and continue to keep a close eye on the village."

"Until then, we train more with your magic."

DAY AFTER DAY, Eirah trained alongside Morozko with her magic. Creating things. Elk that could race in the snow, birds that could fly in the air, beasts with sharp teeth that could fight. He didn't go easy on her, just as he hadn't when he'd had her shift into her owl form over and over again. Her spare time she spent with her father and Saren. Saren continued to stay quiet, keeping to herself while her father carved toys for the village children to try and help cheer them. Eirah offered to deliver the toys, seeing if she could seek out anything different about them. But the children all seemed the same to her, their eyes lighting up when she handed them a toy, not a flicker of yellow irises, no vicious snapping or anything wicked coming from them.

After her last delivery and praying to her mother to keep watch over the village, Eirah trudged through the snow to her ice house. She found Morozko pacing back and forth. The ground had worn thin from his boots, and she wondered how long he'd been doing it.

"You need to relax," Eirah said, lifting an apple to her lips. "And eat." She tossed one to him, and he didn't even try to catch it. "I shouldn't have to keep coddling you to take care of yourself."

He stopped pacing, his ice-blue eyes pinning to hers. "You need to be stronger."

Eirah inwardly flinched. "I can wield magic."

"Not enough. It needs to be more."

A pit formed in her stomach, and she set the apple on the desk. "Is that what I am to you now, your weapon? One that will never satisfy you? Before, it was a sacrifice. What will I be once this is done? A discarded piece of clothing? Another maiden you can pleasure and throw away?" Frustration ripped through her, erasing the concern she'd had for his well-being a moment before.

Morozko's face didn't soften as he tilted up her chin, even though his fingers were gentle. "You are a weapon, yes. Frosteria's weapon. But above all, you need to be at your strongest so nothing happens to *you*."

"Because then your destiny won't be fulfilled?" Eirah whispered, her frustration dissolving into something else.

Morozko laughed mirthlessly. "My destiny?" He shook his head. "No. I want you to be at your strongest so you won't die, little bird. For me."

Eirah blinked at his words, her chest swelling, and she didn't understand how he could always make her feel so many different emotions in such a short time. But before she could give a response, his mouth was on hers. She returned the kiss, her fingers interlacing in his hair. Days had passed since they'd pleasured one another, and she'd come to think that perhaps it had been a one-time thing because he'd believed her to be a sacrifice, that she wouldn't be permanent in his life. And when he discovered she was no longer needed in that way, it had changed.

As his lips coasted across hers, she lifted his tunic over his head and didn't miss a beat as she unlaced his trousers. "I want you to teach me more." Her voice came out breathy.

"What would you like to learn this time?" he purred, shoving his trousers away so that he was completely bare before her.

"I want to taste you." Eirah reached down and gripped his hard length, his head lolling back as heavy breaths escaped his plump lips. "Here."

"As you desire," Morozko cooed, unfastening the buttons along the back of her dress as he kissed the column of her neck while she stroked him. She released his length to let the fabric pool down her body to her feet. The king brought his mouth to hers again, claiming her, and his tongue plunged inside her as the kiss deepened. He gripped her buttocks, tugging her close so she could press against him more intimately. She could feel her arousal gathering between her thighs as he brought them down to his bedroll. His hard length strained against her, and she'd never wanted any male to sink into her as badly as she did Morozko.

He lay on his back with her on top of him. Eirah left his mouth, trailing kisses down his neck to his chest, and lower, and lower, and *lower*.

"I appreciate how fast you learn and even more how eager

you are to please." His voice came out deep, lust-filled, as she brought her hand to his hardness once more, then he hissed.

In her romance novels, Eirah had read about pleasuring a man's length with a woman's mouth, but she'd never seen it done before. Now she wanted to perform the act in a way that would make him plea for more. Not be the awkward village girl she'd always been seen as. "Tell me what to do next."

His ravenous gaze latched onto hers, enrapturing her without even a touch. "Lick me from base to tip, then take me into your mouth."

Eirah enjoyed learning things from scratch, whether it was creating a music box, working on a wooden doll, or even using her new magic. Leaning down, she first caught the glistening pearl from his tip with her tongue, something she'd been yearning to do since several nights ago. Morozko groaned deep, his hands tangling in her hair as she glided her tongue up his velvety skin, then took him fully into her mouth.

"Now," he rasped. "Would you prefer to suck me, or stroke me with your mouth? Do with me what you wish. Make me come, little bird. Make me come fucking hard." His words came between panted breaths.

Eirah's eyes fluttered at his naughty and delicious words, words she'd been waiting to hear all her life. As she moved her lips up and down him, she was unsure if she was doing it right, but her confidence grew as she worked him with precision, just as she would one of her crafts. Same as his blood, Morozko tasted of frost and spice, and she didn't want the flavor to fade. She stroked him, sucking, swirling her tongue along the tip.

Morozko's hips jerked, and that otherworldly growl left him as he spilled himself into her mouth. The taste of him became stronger while she drank his pleasure down, relishing it.

"Another lesson mastered," Morozko said, his chest heaving. He then brought her up to him, his mouth meeting hers, kissing her in a way that made it seem as if he never wanted to stop, in a way that made her not want it to end. His tongue sensually flicked hers.

Morozko looked down at her, his pupils dilated. "Do you want me inside of you tonight?" His voice was soft, almost gentle. Seeing this different side of him drew her to him even more.

"I do." Eirah ran her finger along his pointed ear. "I want you to be the one to take my maidenhead."

An unreadable expression flashed on his face, but then Morozko's eyes gleamed, and he smiled. "Give me a moment and your wish is my command, little bird." He rolled Eirah to her back, exquisitely caging her in with his hard body. "Tonight, I'll show you how generous I can be. And that, while I am cruel, I can be gentle, too." He trailed a line of heated kisses between the valley of her breasts, then down to her abdomen. "When we wake in the morning, I will offer something bolder, harder." He arched a brow, lips twisting into a confident smirk.

"Yes," she murmured, her heart pounding in anticipation. Before, she would never have let this king touch her, but now, she never wanted him to cease.

Seeming to read her thoughts, Morozko grinned wickedly, his mouth capturing hers again. His hand traveled to her mound, dipping two fingers inside her heat as the heel of his palm rubbed her bundle of nerves. Eirah moaned in delight, and his length hardened against her. The king's hand left her center to cradle her breast, his cock lining up at her soaked entrance. He didn't thrust within her right away. No, he rubbed against her until she thought she'd erupt with need.

With one enticing roll of his hips, he buried himself inside her. Only for a moment, a slight sting pierced her. As soon as it dissipated, Morozko's hips moved, his pace a lovely slow burn that gradually built.

Eirah dug her fingers into his back before skimming her hands down to grip his firm buttocks. Morozko lifted one of her legs to wrap around him, then did the same with the other, bringing him in even deeper.

He ground against the place she wanted him most, and each time he collided with her, the pleasure mounted. When she dared to look upon him, his features lacked their typical hard lines, and he watched her, truly watched her, as he undid her in the most intoxicating way.

A wonderful sensation traveled through her, nipping at all her nerve endings, becoming more euphoric. And then, as if an avalanche of pure bliss was falling inside of her, pressing harder on her nerve endings, she couldn't hold back Morozko's name from falling from her lips as her body shook with pleasure.

He kissed the crook of her neck while he thrust, his pace increasing until his body quaked, her name roaring from him as he came.

Both their breaths were ragged, and when he pulled out from her, Eirah was uncertain if she was to stay or return to her bedroll. But then he drew them onto their sides, so his chest was to her back, his arm wrapped around her middle. She wondered if he'd held all the past maidens he'd bedded like this once they were finished, but with how hard his heart thumped against her, she had an inkling that he never had.

No, little bird, I haven't.

Eirah smiled at his words, pleased that she could hear important things like this from him, things that he would never say aloud. Yet he continued to open up to her, and it was something that drew her in more and more. No longer an enemy, but something else, something she couldn't easily put in a box.

"Now we sleep," Morozko said in a gruff voice, "and in the morning, I'm going to have you grip the desk while I take you from behind."

21

MOROZKO

Morozko opened one eye. The embers from the fire flickered, but no light poured in from outside yet. If he was right in his assumption, it was just before dawn. He'd slept soundly, with no vision to disrupt his slumber.

Slowly, he sat up, reminding himself of where he was. He peered down, taking in the sight of Eirah curled up against where he had been, and everything came rushing back to him. The phantom touch of Eirah's fingers gripping him as he rode them into pleasure tripped his heart into a gallop, making the blood rush straight to his cock. In part, he wondered if having her beside him for the night relaxed him enough to rest.

It wasn't the first time he'd had her by his side while they slept, but it differed vastly from when Eirah fluttered around on his pillow. He'd bedded her, allowed her to remain by his side, and the thought of shoving her out of the ice house repulsed him. Whether she was a virgin or the village whore meant nothing to him. In fact, most he tumbled had been deflowered many moons ago. But in this instance, he could lay claim to Eirah. Branding her with his touch and ensuring she'd never forget him.

At that moment, Morozko didn't want her to *ever* forget him.

Eirah stirred next to him, rolled over and patted the bedroll, then looked around a moment later.

It was a simple gesture, but one that spoke loudly to him. No female ever looked for him, and if they did, it was only for another moment with the king. Not *him*. Yet somehow, Eirah, after everything, cared. Even though she could've been sacrificed, she still cared.

"You were snoring." Morozko shook his head as he stood.

Eirah's brow rumpled. "I was not."

He nodded, chuckling. "So loudly, in fact, it woke me up."

"You're still a prick." She laughed, tossing the fur blanket away to grab her linen shirt. As she rose to her feet, Morozko couldn't keep his gaze from drifting to the curve of her body, her milky skin, the way her rosebud nipples were peaked, as if demanding his touch.

Morozko tsked, reaching to grab her wrist. "Did you forget last night's promise?" His eyes fixated on hers, even as a blush crept up her neck and cheeks. Eirah didn't look away, but her confidence wavered a fraction as he leaned in. "Are you too sore?"

"No. I thought you might have changed your mind." She glanced up at him and lifted her hands to let her fingers drag along his bare chest before replacing them with her lush lips.

Goosebumps rose on his skin in the wake of her sensual movements, and warmth flooded his body. "I don't jest about such things," he said huskily.

Instead of speaking, Eirah only journeyed lower, her

mouth against his abdomen, in heated, reverent kisses. Her hands roamed along his thighs, to his backside as her tongue swiped along his length.

Morozko sucked in a breath the moment her lips circled his tip. For as inexperienced as she may have been, she certainly knew how to use her mouth.

Eirah dragged her lips to his tip, letting her tongue explore the dips and curves of his cock. Then, she descended on him, sucking hard as she drew back.

"What were you dreaming of last night? Was it me?" he whispered, threading his fingers in her hair. "Did you think about sucking my cock, little bird?" Morozko shuddered in delight as she took him deeper, and he groaned in appreciation.

He was hard before, but now? Morozko fought the urge to thrust his hips forward, but it was so damn hard. Her mouth worked on him, her tongue rolling against him. Every so often, her gaze would flick up to him, watching his reaction as she tried something new.

"That's enough," he rasped, gently tugging on her arms to raise her up. "I'll get my pleasure in a moment, but you... I want to hear you pant my name, understand?"

Eirah lifted her brows, her lips twitching into a smile. "We'll see."

Morozko closed the distance between them, his hips brushing hers. Eirah looked up at him, and he stepped forward, forcing her back, then he did it again until he pushed them over to the desk. "Spread your legs."

Eirah's eyes grew hooded as she obeyed, her nipples hardening even more. He bit his bottom lip, drinking in the vision of her as the scent of her arousal tickled his nose, begging him to devour her.

He dropped to his knees before her, glancing up at her, then slid his hands down her ass, tilting her hips at a better angle so he could access her delicious sex.

Morozko swept his tongue along her seam, then found the bundle of nerves, where he licked and sucked.

Eirah's hands knotted in his hair, and she writhed, gasping as he relentlessly worked her. "Oh, Morozko!"

His name on her lips both warmed and thrilled him. His cock leaped in anticipation, wanting nothing more than to bury deep within her until they were both sated. Yet, his mouth remained on her, his tongue circling her.

Eirah's fingers tightened in his hair, and her hips rocked against him. "Morozko!" she cried in between panted breaths.

He pulled his mouth from her, dipping a finger into her heat, working her through the waves of pleasure. "That's it, little bird," he murmured. And when she was nearly finished, he withdrew his finger and stood.

Eirah's dark eyes searched his, then she moved in, capturing his lips. Morozko opened his mouth, letting his tongue graze along hers. She pressed her hips into his, moaning, which nearly undid him.

He reluctantly drew back. "Turn around," he said roughly.

Eirah did as she was told, her ass brushing his length.

She was going to pay for that in the most delightful way. Morozko leaned in, nipping along the side of her neck as his arms stretched out, and he took hold of her wrists, guiding her palms down to the desk. He positioned her so she was leaning over the desk, bent over. Then he whispered silkily into her ear, "And feet apart. Wide enough to accept me." As she moved her legs apart, Morozko couldn't help himself and ran his hand down her wet core. He then rubbed his cock against her folds until her arousal slickened him, and with one thrust, he plunged into her depths.

Eirah learned this lesson just as exquisitely as the others. She pushed back with every thrust and kept her hands firmly planted on the desk, her nails scraping every so often. "Don't fight it," Morozko rasped out. "I want you to come for me, little bird." His thighs slapped against her backside every time he collided with her, his pace quickening. Morozko's pleasure was nearly at its peak, his cock threatening a release inside her.

"Don't... stop," she begged.

Such simple words. And how the fuck was he supposed to continue when she said such things? "I don't want to." He reached around, finding her bundle of nerves to circle as he continued to thrust within her.

Eirah's body trembled while she rippled around him, tightening and urging him to join her. Morozko groaned, taking it all in as he watched her pleasure unfold. He'd done this, and it was that thought alone that drove him to his own climax.

He shuddered shortly after, pouring himself into her. He had to catch himself, pressing his hands against the desk to keep from collapsing. Morozko sucked in the air, daring not to move as his legs felt useless, his muscles slack.

"If I'm to die," he exhaled, "I can think of no better way to go."

Eirah looked over her shoulder and shot him a half-hearted glare. "Would you cease talking about dying, at least for a moment?"

Morozko chuckled and eased himself from her. His body still hummed with spent pleasure. "As you wish." He padded toward his discarded cape, cleaned himself up, and then wiped the arousal from Eirah. "Still, a rather pleasant moment to wake up to, don't you agree?"

She grabbed the cape from him and tossed it aside, laughing. Not long ago, the laugh would've stirred Morozko's ire, but now, it was a lyrical sound that brought a smile to his face. "If not exhausting."

He cocked his head. "I don't hear an argument."

"You're incorrigible."

"Guilty." Morozko bent to grab his clothing, dressing before someone interrupted them. Eirah did the same, which was a good thing, too, for Andras bellowed outside.

It wasn't the captain who rushed through the makeshift door of the ice house but another guard, Qorlys. His black hair fell in several braids around his tan face. "Your Majesty, we need you at once. It's... a horde of creatures. Like from the village."

Morozko's good humor fled at once. His eyes widened, then narrowed. "A horde?" It meant the seal was that much weaker. "Fuck!" He crossed the expanse of the house, then turned on his heel to look back at Eirah. What he wanted to tell her was to stay put, to remain safe, and yet, he knew better. Eirah would no sooner remain behind than leave this wretched camp of villagers.

Why, of all times, did he have to become captivated by someone? Not just anyone, but Eirah of Vinti. An infuriating female who stirred emotions he had no right to possess.

"Your Majesty?" Qorlys prodded him.

Morozko shook his head. "Eirah, come with me."

She rushed forward, sparing not a second as she joined him and left the comfort of their temporary lodging.

"Guard the children! And build a blazing fire," Morozko bellowed.

Qorlys led Morozko forward to the edge of the clearing, and the distinct chittering noise he knew so well from his visions echoed off the trees. Like nails scraping down a stone. Morozko gritted his teeth, wanting to cover his ears to block out the atrocious sound, but as he joined Andras, his hand plunged into the snow at his feet instead.

Blue light burst from the ground, and as he drew his hand back, a long frozen blade appeared. "Captain?" He searched the area until he found Andras staring into the woods. A few frost demons paced back and forth.

Andras pounded a fist against his chest. "Your Majesty." He bowed his head, then glanced to Eirah. "They're circling us, waiting like a pack of wolves."

"Not wolves," Morozko hissed. "A wolf is a noble creature. These are no such things, for they are created in hatred." As if in reply, Nuka whined, towering over them as he padded forward.

"They're waiting for *us*." Eirah's voice remained steady as she spoke, but her eyes belied that steadiness, full of fear and anger. Morozko didn't blame her. She only knew what he'd told her, but he'd seen the creatures more in his mind than he wished to, heard their screams and chittering.

"Nuka, flush them out." His wolf leaped forward, and branches snapped from the wolf and the fleeing changelings. "Whatever comes this way, take them down with magic or a blade. You'll need to haul the bastards to the fire back at the camp!" he ordered the frost demons, then turned to Eirah, frowning. "And you need to tap into your magic, dig as deep as you can. They mean to kill us, and they won't stop until they do."

Eirah's eyes narrowed, and her jaw muscles leaped. "Then neither will I. They won't take anymore from us."

Morozko hoped she was right.

Nuka's growl echoed in the vicinity, and he emerged from the brush, snapping a small pine tree. A changeling dangled from his neck, growling and shrieking as it held on. The bastard's waxlike skin was even more sickly in the present as opposed to what he'd seen in his visions. Nuka thrashed while the changeling attempted to bite through his thick fur, to no avail. It was surreal seeing the creature now, and all Morozko wanted to do was kill it. One of the guards shot at the changeling with an arrow, and the creature tumbled to the ground, hissing. It crawled on all fours, intending to leap at Andras, but another frost demon unleashed a whip, and it curled around the lesser demon's throat. Ear-piercing wails sounded as the guard hauled the creature back to the camp.

A disturbing notion invaded Morozko's mind that this was part of the vision he'd seen. He glanced down, just for a moment, to consider his side. A wound wasn't there, and no blood oozed from his ribs, but as he looked up, Eirah screamed, reaching for him.

Blinding blue light bolted from her fingertips and shot over Morozko's shoulder, crashing into a changeling. He whirled on his heel and twisted his blade, sinking it deep into the creature's heart. Navy blood spilled on the ground, staining the white snow. This was the vision, but not. He wasn't wounded, at least not yet.

"Well done," he murmured.

Eirah stepped closer to him. "It almost got you." Her words were hardly above a whisper.

"Almost. But it'll take more than almost to kill me." When he looked up, a changeling was launching at her back. Morozko yanked free his blade and spun Eirah out of the way, so when the changeling launched at him, it landed on his sword.

How many *were* there? He ground his teeth together. "Drag these back to camp and send someone to take your place," Morozko ordered a nearby guard. He hadn't counted all the slain changelings, but little by little, he added them up. Eight. As far as he'd seen.

Morozko cut another down, slashing from shoulder to hip. "Burn the pieces!"

Eirah fought by his side, wielding her magic like invisible chains, coiling them around the changelings and thrashing them to the ground until they were lifeless, waiting to be burned.

By the time Nuka returned, he wasn't the only one who was breathless. "Are they all gone?" Morozko asked.

Nuka responded with a high-pitched yelp, which Morozko only assumed was a yes. Otherwise, the wolf would've leaped back into the brush and hunted more down.

"Are you hurt?" Eirah sidled up beside the king, frowning as she looked him over.

"No." He quietly assessed her, then took her chin in his hands, and seeing no grievous injuries on her, he relaxed. "You fought well." Morozko released her and turned to face the remaining frost demons. A few had fallen, and though it wasn't a significant loss, it was enough that should there be another attack, they might not fare as well.

They needed that damn moon to hurry up and change phases so they could perform the ritual.

"Qorlys!" Morozko bellowed. The frost demon scuttled forward. "Go back to the castle, alert everyone as to what is happening, and return with reinforcements. Ride with the wind at your back."

Qorlys bowed and dashed away in the snow.

Morozko looked to Eirah, who was staring up at the sky, more than likely thinking the same thing about the full moon. They couldn't *wait* that long for it, because if the changelings kept this up, they'd all be dead.

22

EIRAH

Morozko had sent Qorlys to retrieve more frost demons to help with the fight. There didn't seem to be many changelings left inside the encampment, but she didn't know how many were lingering elsewhere. These waxy creatures were worse than she could have imagined. Their yellow eyes held no pupils, and sinew partially sewed their mouths shut—a thing of true nightmares.

Eirah's magic had dwindled, her muscles ached from use, and sweat dripped down her forehead and neck. During the initial attack earlier, Eirah had helped warn villagers to remain hidden within their ice houses, behind their lit fires. There didn't need to be more casualties, and the king hadn't wanted them as a distraction that could risk more lives.

One of the frost guards grunted as a changeling shoved into him from behind. Morozko charged after the warrior to give aid as another changeling crept out from behind a tree toward her.

Eirah gathered what strength she had and dipped into her magic, her hands shaking as she formed a large lion out of snow. She thrust her hand forward, unleashing the snow creation. The lion leaped forward, slamming the changeling to the ground. But even as the lion opened its maw to bite off the changeling's head, it just passed through the vicious creature. Magic wouldn't work to kill the demon—they needed fire to wipe the creature from this world until it found a way to cross its barrier once more.

The lion continued to hold the changeling in place as the demon bucked and jerked its head around. Eirah was about to leave her position to find a torch to light when Qorlys returned with a flock of about three dozen guards behind him carrying torches.

"Over here!" Eirah called, waving him over as she strained to hold the lion's shape.

Just as Qorlys reached the changeling, Eirah lost hold of her magic, the snow of the lion collapsing to the ground. Qorlys didn't hesitate and shoved a blade clean through the changeling's stomach, blue blood blooming to the surface. As Qorlys pinned the creature in place with his weapon, another frost guard brought down his torch to the demon's waxy flesh. The flames licked away the loose skin while the changeling screeched an awful sound that pierced Eirah's ears and made her grit her teeth. The acrid odor of sulfur and decay it gave off invaded her nose. She held back expelling her stomach.

Two more changelings darted out from the trees—Eirah didn't have time to draw up her magic when a blade sliced straight through both necks, blood spraying.

Morozko held the sword, dripping with blood, in his hand as a frost demon set fire to both the changelings' remains.

"Cease, little bird," Morozko demanded, his chest heaving

as he stepped toward her. "You've done well. Andras scouted the area, and for the time being, there isn't a sign of any more, but I need to ask something else of you. Remember the stone in my vision that can locate the changelings? We need to create it now."

Eirah furrowed her brow, thinking of all the things she'd created in her life. Most were from wood or metal. "What kind of stone? I don't know much about them."

"The stones are just stones but are bound with your magic and a little of the changeling's blood. You cast a spell on them."

Eirah may be a witch, but she had yet to attempt to cast a spell alone. She'd been working more with Morozko on how to wield her magic or how to shift. "I can try. Bring me a few stones, and we can see what I can do."

He ordered one of the dark-haired guards to fetch a handful of stones from the river near the palace.

"Give me a moment," Eirah said to Morozko, then slipped into her father's ice house, where she found him inside with an arm protectively around Saren. The fire they sat behind crackled, and Eirah let out a breath that they'd remained safe.

"Thank you for staying here, Papa."

"You have magic, daughter," her father said, taking his arm from around Saren. When she'd helped warn the villagers, he'd fought her on it but then relented once she'd decided to show him her magic.

"I'm no longer mortal," Eirah whispered, worried her father would look at her differently.

Saren didn't say a word, only studied her hands, when her father spoke again, "Mortal or not, it doesn't matter. You're still my daughter."

Eirah smiled, her shoulders relaxing at his words. "I must

leave for now to help the king on another matter, but I'll return when I can. I promise I will tell you everything else soon."

"Stay safe, and call on me if you need my help."

"I will, Papa." Eirah wrapped her arms around her father, then turned to Saren. "Do you need anything? Another fur blanket?"

She shook her head. "No, I have all I need."

Eirah sighed, wishing she could spend more time with Saren, but she needed to make certain her friend remained safe.

She found Morozko walking through the encampment, scanning each of the ice houses, a scowl on his face.

"It still seems to be clear," the king said as he approached her, "but the bastards were drawn here for a reason. It was as if they knew we brought the villagers here. They had to have followed us somehow, or maybe they can feel one another, feel when one is in the shell of a mortal child."

Eirah's heart pounded at the thought that the villagers may not be able to truly hide from these demons. "Do you want me to scout around the forest in my owl form?"

Morozko brought a hand to her cheek, and the touch was comforting. "No, the guards are taking turns doing their rounds through the forest."

The dark-haired guard from earlier broke through the trees, carrying a handful of gray stones in his palm. "Here they are, Your Majesty. I can retrieve more if you need them."

Morozko took the stones, making a fist around them. "For now, keep watch. Make certain the villagers are fed, and tell them to remain in their homes. They are not to come out other than to be escorted to relieve themselves until we're in the clear."

"Yes, Your Majesty." The frost demon turned on his heel and rushed toward the other guards to relay the message.

Morozko's gaze fastened on Eirah, and he studied her for a long moment before finally saying, "Let's go back to our ice house so that you may work in private. Especially if another changeling comes lurking about."

Eirah nodded, and they walked side by side in comfortable silence. Morozko pushed the fabric away from the entrance, letting her slip inside first. The fire remained lit, not for warmth, but for added protection in case they needed it.

As the fabric fell behind Morozko, Eirah reached for the stones, and he batted her hand away. "I know it's dire, but you will not start this very second. You will drink and eat something to rebuild your strength. We cannot have you fainting."

Eirah sighed, knowing he was right. "Fine."

"Now, this is refreshing. I do enjoy arguing with you, but *this*, I could get used to." With a smirk, he handed her a canteen and a piece of dried meat from the desk.

She guzzled the water down as if she'd never drank a sip of anything in her life. Then she bit into the meat, the savory flavor waking her up a bit more. "Let me see a stone."

"I gathered changeling blood for you earlier as well." He dropped two stones in her hand, along with a glass vial filled with blue blood. She wrinkled her nose at the blood as she drew out the chair in front of the ice desk before lowering herself. Taking another bite of the meat, she set one stone on the desk and ran her thumb across the other's smooth surface. They looked like any normal gray stone, except somehow she was supposed to add magic to one.

First, she opened the vial and allowed the demon's blood to ooze a drop onto the stone. Then she homed in on her ability, letting it swirl inside her. A glittering white smoke curled out of her fingertips and brushed against the stone as if caressing it. Words naturally spun in her head, coming from somewhere inside her where they'd been hidden. She latched onto them, speaking the chant softly, her eyes shut. When she opened her lids, she gazed at the stone. It was still the color of charcoal. "What's it supposed to do?"

Morozko cocked his head, eyeing the stone. "Turn blue and light up when you need to locate a changeling."

She bit her lip, concentrating. "I can't get the color to change." But then she remembered something. When the time to save Frosteria was near, their blood would be needed to form the new demons and would change the color of the moon during the spell. But this, this was only her that was needed, and she now knew what else was necessary. "I need to add my blood."

"Allow me," Morozko purred, not hesitating to draw out a dagger from his waist.

"You enjoy pricking me too much," she huffed with a smile.

"No, I enjoy *touching* you, little bird." He gently grasped her hand, and her heart pounded at his soft caress. She couldn't help but remember their earlier encounter together. His hands everywhere on her, the way he expertly moved inside her, worshiping her.

Morozko pricked her finger, the slight sting interrupting her blissful thoughts. As the blood blossomed on her flesh, she pressed the crimson to the stone, repeating her chant one more time. And she came to a realization—she was performing a true spell, something no other immortal could do—only a witch.

A slight humming radiated from the stone, and she watched how the gray coloring changed to a light blue.

"You did it!" Morozko shouted, drawing her to her feet and pressing his mouth to hers so easily, seeming to become more comfortable with one another in a different way. As he was about to step away, she boldly tugged him back to her and captured his mouth with hers before releasing him to make another enchanted stone.

"Kiss me like that again and I may make you wait on enchanting another," Morozko said in a gruff voice.

"Perhaps once we finish helping Frosteria, I'll have you teach me much more." She smiled, heat creeping up her neck and into her cheeks.

"Oh, I have plenty to show you and will make you come in many ways," Morozko cooed. He took one of the stones and enfolded her hand over the other. "But for now, I'll start searching the cottages with the guards. Wait with your father and Saren until I need you. We need the element of surprise."

She nodded and left a moment after Morozko, wishing for him to remain safe. So much different than in the previous weeks when she'd wanted to end his life.

Eirah's father and Saren both rested inside their ice house, eating jerky. "Hungry?" Her father held up a slice toward her.

"No." A slight humming vibrated in her pocket, but her father and Saren didn't seem to hear the stone. With a frown, she slipped it out and stared at the flickering stone as it gave off a soft blue light.

"What's that?" her father asked, adjusting his glasses while casting his gaze upon it.

Eirah's heart lodged in her throat as she sat watching him. Changelings could slip into children—she knew this. But what if...

"Hold this for a moment," she whispered, placing the

stone in the palm of his hand. As he rolled it in between his fingers, the light vanished, not a single blue flicker.

Eirah took the stone from him, and it illuminated once more. A changeling couldn't be residing inside her, could it? But then her gaze flicked up to Saren, who was silently watching her. And Eirah knew. She needed to get Morozko.

"I'll be right back. I'm going to get us some fruit," Eirah said, keeping her voice steady while her heart thundered.

"We have fruit," Saren called from behind her, but Eirah hurried out of the cottage to locate the king.

When she stepped toward the next house, two hands shoved her from behind, knocking her to the snow.

"Morozko!" Eirah screamed, hoping he wasn't too far away.

Saren flipped Eirah to her back, holding her down by the shoulders, her fingers digging in sharply. She released a hiss, her blue eyes glowing a bright yellow.

As Eirah drew on her magic, trying to get Saren off her, the demon was yanked away. Eirah's father shouted at Saren to stop, but then she pushed him away from her. Saren lunged forward, darting in the opposite direction, yet Eirah caught up, tackling her to the snow. She grabbed Saren's arms and held them behind her while the demon jerked.

"Eirah!" Morozko bellowed, barreling toward her, his gaze wild until it settled on her.

"The changelings aren't only in the children!" Eirah shouted. Saren wriggled, her stare full of madness as she slipped from Eirah's fingers. "One is in her. Help me," she cried, tears pricking her eyes.

Morozko snatched Saren, yanking her to his chest. "You know what we have to do then," he said, his voice resigned. "You can leave, and, in fact, I wish you would." He turned toward the group of guards that were now there. "Qorlys, grab a whip from my ice house."

"Yes, Your Majesty." He bolted through the snow, only taking a few moments to collect one before returning with an ivory whip. Eirah knew what was to happen—she'd known from his vision, had been horrified by the sound of it, but more so now that Saren would have to be a victim of it. As Morozko held Saren, she spat and screeched louder, her eyes blazing brighter, seeming to know what was to come. In those eyes, there wasn't a single hint of Saren, only a monster. Eirah's chest tightened at the thought of Saren never returning to her.

Morozko glanced toward Eirah, his lips pursed. "This is your last chance to walk away, Eirah. I need to whip her."

"Whip?" her father asked, his eyes wide.

"No"—Eirah took the leather whip from the frost demon —"I will do it. She's my friend." Turning to her father, she said, "Trust me with this. It has to be done." She'd always wanted to protect Saren, and she'd failed in this sense, but now she could save her.

Morozko nodded, his expression neutral, becoming the king he was born to be. "As soon as I get her on the ground, strike."

"What if I kill her?" she said softly, tightening her hold on the whip.

"Then it would be much better than this. My visions speak truth. And I wholly believe the whip will save her."

"I believe in you, my king," she murmured. "I'm ready now." Even if Saren didn't survive, she would never want to live like this.

Morozko lowered a thrashing Saren to the snow more gently than he would've done anyone else, and Eirah knew he'd done it for her. As soon as he shoved himself backward, Eirah brought the whip down with an awful crack. A heinous screech tore through the air, and blue blood bathed the snow while yellow smoke wafted upward from Saren's back. Before Saren could crawl forward, Eirah slammed the whip against her flesh once more.

Hot tears stung her cheeks, every lash burning through the muscles of her arm, the sound of each strike making her heart jolt against her rib cage as she continued to try and release Saren from this monster's grip. With each strike, she told herself it was the demon she was hurting. Not Saren. Never Saren. And just as she was about to give up hope, a waxy form rolled out from Saren's body, causing Eirah to halt. The demon hissed through its barely-there mouth, curling its gnarled fingers, attempting to bolt away.

Morozko lunged forward with an ice sword in his hand at the ready as he dove for the changeling. He pierced it straight through the throat, then kicked its stomach with his boot. The demon collapsed to the ground, and Morozko buried the blade into its chest, blue blood staining the snow. The frost demons surrounded the changeling with lit torches, then set the creature's body on fire, its wretched screams piercing the air.

Eirah turned back around, dropping beside her father, who was already near Saren. Her friend's head was tilted to the side, her lips parted as she took shallow breaths. The changeling's wails echoed while Eirah pressed a hand to Saren's torn dress. But beneath the strips of fabric, no wounds or blood lingered. Eirah gasped—it was as if her friend hadn't been struck by a weapon at all.

"Saren," Eirah said softly, her fingers lightly pressing into her upper arm. "Saren, wake up."

A low moan escaped Saren's mouth as she peeled open her eyes, her teeth chattering. "Why is it so cold?"

"Do you feel any pain?" Eirah's father asked, removing his cloak and bundling Saren in it as she sat up.

Saren furrowed her brow and shook her head. "No, only cold."

"Do you remember a demon taking over your body?" Eirah asked, wrapping an arm around her friend's shoulders. "Or do you remember attacking me just now?"

"A demon in my body? Me attacking you? Are you jesting with me, or did you fall and hit your head?" Saren laughed softly. Then, when she looked around, finding no one laughing with her, her eyes widened.

Morozko stepped beside Eirah, a deep line settled between his brow. "She doesn't remember. It seems when the demon was exorcised, memories of her time as a changeling have been eradicated."

Saren paled, but she didn't curl in on herself. "Tell me precisely what happened. I can handle it."

Morozko nodded to Eirah. "Take Saren inside and explain it to her. I located a few more within the encampment, and I'm going to take care of them now."

Eirah handed him the whip, her fingers softly brushing his. "Be careful."

"Stay brave." He lifted his hand, tucking his knuckle beneath her chin. His brilliant blue eyes locked onto hers. "Remain here, and I *do* mean that." His gaze flicked to Saren and her father. "They need you, and I believe you need them, too."

As Morozko walked away, Eirah and her father helped Saren back into the ice house to warm herself by the fire.

"I'm waiting." Saren sat up straight, polishing off her tea

as though she hadn't been nearly beaten to death. Eirah explained everything that had happened, how a changeling had slipped inside her body at some point. Most likely, it had been back in the village on the night of the attack. Then she told her about Morozko, how she was no longer a sacrifice, and how she was now a witch and immortal.

"Now that is a tale." Saren blinked and blew out a slow breath.

"I'm going to be just outside the ice house, keeping watch," Eirah's father said, giving her time to talk with Saren alone.

"You seem more like yourself," Eirah murmured once the fabric of the entrance fell behind her father. "I thought the reason you were so quiet was because you were grieving."

"I am," Saren sniffed, "but I haven't lost you." She paused as if mulling over something. "I think you're keeping something from me, though. Why was Morozko touching your chin and being *ever* so gentle?"

Eirah was a bit embarrassed to admit what was budding between her and Morozko, but more so because she'd never felt this way about anyone. "I may have tumbled him and have feelings for him," she said under her breath.

"You gave him your *flower*?" Saren gasped, covering her mouth with her hand.

"After everything, that's what you're most surprised about?" Eirah laughed, her cheeks warming.

"Well, you *did* wish him dead the last time we truly talked about him," Saren pointed out, her eyebrow arched.

Before she could discuss any more about the Frost King's heart not being completely ice, a screech tore through the encampment. Another changeling had been found.

23

MOROZKO

Not everything Morozko had seen in his visions had come to fruition. For one, he wasn't swaying on his feet, bleeding from his side, and two, Eirah wasn't looking at him, panicked and fearful. However, that didn't mean it wouldn't come to pass. There was no way of knowing if that would take place tomorrow or two weeks from now.

But seeing Eirah's friend, Saren, in a state of possession, thrashing, and fighting against them, it was the sobering truth of the dangers they now faced. Not knowing fully who was no longer themselves but a prisoner to a changeling.

Morozko peered down at his hand, stained blue from battling rogue changelings. There had been half a dozen possessed villagers, far too many, in his opinion. He coiled the leather whip around his knuckles and lifted his gaze to Andras as the warrior approached him.

The captain of the guard grimaced and bowed his head. "Another small swarm is approaching."

Morozko's brow furrowed. They'd been burning the captured changelings, and the smell of charred flesh permeated the air. "Get ready, and protect the mortals." He glanced at the hilt of his ice blade, jutting from the scabbard at his hip. The stone Eirah gave him dangled from it, pulsing a vibrant blue. He blinked, his attention once more on the thick brush before him in search of where the demon was hiding.

A twig snapped, and low chittering filled the clearing.

Morozko's muscles tensed. "Steady—" The stone had been accurate, for a changeling leaped at him, shoving him to the ground hard enough that he saw stars. But Morozko was quick to lift his arm and knock his fist into the side of the changeling's head, sending it careening to the side.

The Frost King didn't wait for the creature to scamper away—Morozko unwound the whip, then coiled it around the creature's neck.

"You dare," he seethed, standing once again as he hauled the changeling to the fire to burn. The lesser being thrashed, clawed at its throat and bared its hideous mouth at Morozko.

The demon could buck, scrape at the ground, and wail until its throat bled, but it was useless. Morozko would not relinquish the bastard to anything but the waiting inferno.

He stalked to the fire, boots crunching snow and leaves beneath his weight. This changeling was just one of many that would be tossed into the flames, but they had to continue or face an infestation of them.

Morozko uncoiled the whip and gripped the changeling by the throat. "I wouldn't," he ground out, narrowing his eyes. He pried iron cuffs from his hip and secured them around the changeling's slender wrists. They were almost too thin for the manacles to hold the bastard. "I pray Maranna is in the depths you return to, and when you do, tell her she has failed. That I have wo—" The changeling swatted at him with its claws, scratching his face open. Blood trickled down his cheek, and he clucked his tongue, tossing the creature into the flames.

Embers jostled loose from the bonfire, and screams filled the air once more. The demon didn't thrash for long, the fire too hot, the bastard more willing to return to the depths of where it came than to stay behind and fight for the moment. *Pathetic.*

"Morozko!" Eirah called to him.

Panic lanced through him. Eirah, where was she? He spun around in search of her, noting the royal guards had done their part as well, and hauled the creatures toward the fire. But Eirah wasn't among them. She was *supposed* to be with her father, with Saren.

Something akin to distress—fear—no, *worry* plagued him. Morozko's gaze flicked from guard to guard, to villager, to ice house, until they settled on Eirah, hunkered down outside a nearby home. Her hair had come loose from its braid and whipped around her face as a breeze kicked up. When her gaze met his, Morozko saw the apprehension reflected in her eyes.

"Little bird," Morozko purred. "What are you doing?" He sounded deceptively calm for how quickly his heart hammered in his chest. Part of him had expected to find her with limbs shredded or a hideous, gaping wound on her side. Still, he wasn't necessarily at ease even with her crouched down beside a...

He squinted, cocking his head. A child sobbed, cradling its face. Boy? Girl? He couldn't tell at the moment, only that their hair was red. Morozko didn't know if it indeed was a child, so he unsheathed his sword, readying to use the butt of his blade to knock them unconscious if he had to.

"Are you mad? Put your sword down. It's only a *child*. I checked." Eirah shifted her hand, revealing a stone in her palm.

Morozko's shoulders eased downward, and he sheathed his sword. He sighed, wishing he could send her away from it all, yet knowing better than to think she'd just accept that sentence. Morozko jerked his chin toward her hand. "Can you make more of those? One for nearly all the frost demons?"

Eirah nodded. "I'm low on stones, though. I'll need to find more."

Morozko wasn't keen on the idea of her venturing off to the river by herself. "Go with a guard." The child shifted in Eirah's grasp. He stared up at Morozko but didn't speak at first.

Tears spilled from his vibrant green eyes. So, it was a boy. Freckles scattered along the bridge of his nose, onto his cheeks, and disappeared into his hairline. "They won't stop screaming," he whispered. "The monsters."

"Eventually, they will," Morozko offered as gently as he could. Not tonight or tomorrow, but eventually. "As for you, little bird. Was there a reason you called for me across the clearing?"

"I saw you fall, and didn't see you rise." Eirah brushed her hand down the boy's back, then pushed him toward the ice house's opening. He scampered away, leaving the two of them alone. She stood, sucking in a breath that sounded suspiciously like a gasp as she gave him a once-over.

Morozko shrugged a shoulder and turned his head. "The changeling is dead and, with any luck, sending my wretched mother a message." He lifted a brow, lips curling into a grin. "Does it diminish my—"

Eirah reached out, touching his face. Beneath her digits,

warmth spread, and Morozko squeezed her wrist gently. "Oh, stop, but it does add a certain rogue-like quality to you."

"Ah, does it now?" His lips spread further, and despite the discord erupting around them, he did so want to kiss her, embrace her even, until the madness faded away. "As much as I'd love to bask in the moment where you're complimenting me... Aside from stones, what more do you need?"

She nodded. "More blood. Before burning them, drain the changelings." Eirah glanced around.

He frowned. "I'll pass on the word."

"Your Majesty!" Andras bellowed from the distance.

Eirah shooed him. "I will be safe! Go see to your men."

Her dark eyes focused on him, and Morozko closed the distance, pressing a quick kiss to her lips before taking off toward the captain of the guard.

When he got to Andras, two frost demons lay bloodied on the ground, their necks torn open and crimson fountained from them.

"Fuck." Morozko gritted his teeth. There was nothing that could be done for his guards because the light had faded from their eyes already.

"There are a few changelings running through the brush," Andras rasped, lifting his hand to motion toward the direction they'd gone.

Morozko growled. "Not for long. We'll flush them out, send them back to the dark pit they came from." A low chittering rolled through the clearing, echoing off the trees. One was nearby, taunting him—his guards.

The king leaped into the bushes, bramble snagging at his leathers as he waded deeper. A branch snapped, and motion caught his attention just as a changeling lunged forward, swiping at his side. Claws bit through his leather tunic, tearing into his skin.

Morozko hissed. Fresh air lapped at his exposed flesh, and he didn't have to glance down to know that blood oozed down his side. *So much for the wound not coming to fruition.*

Unsheathing his sword, he waited until the creature launched at him again, and as it did, Morozko cut from the bastard's shoulder down to its waist. The two halves fell to the ground with a thud. He cleaned his sword off on his trouser leg, gingerly picking up the pieces of the changeling and hauling them to the fire at the encampment. Morozko was readying to join his guards again when a scream pierced the air, shrill and high. This time, it wasn't a changeling or a child.

This one he felt in his bones and in his mind.

Eirah!

There are two changelings, Morozko. I can't see them!

His heart leaped into his throat as he spun around, searching. *Where are you?*

Near the stream.

Did she bring a guard as he'd suggested? *Just hold on! I'll be right there.* Morozko charged forward. "Nuka!" His familiar was in the woods, sniffing out the lesser demons, but Morozko needed him now. So did Eirah.

Nuka ran into view, then darted down the pathway, sniffing the air in search of Eirah. Morozko only had the strange tug in the center of his chest, guiding him as to where she may have been. Similar to the time she had slipped beneath the water in the tub.

Leaves and twigs crunched beneath his boots as he approached the river. Every sound seemed amplified to him as he searched the area for Eirah, and although he was relieved to not find her strewn across the snow in pieces, he still hadn't found her whole, either.

Water splashed onto his boots as he stepped into the stream, then he jogged across it. She wasn't *here!* "Where are you?"

Here. Her voice was so weak in his mind, fading, but it stopped him from snapping at her, from berating her for the lack of description. She was weak... was she hurt?

Are you all right?

Nothing.

Where was here? Morozko jogged down the stream, glancing over the bank. She was nowhere to be found. But Nuka had trotted off upstream, and his deep woof alerted Morozko. He ran to where the wolf stood, pausing for a moment to take in the way Nuka's head bowed at the still body on the ground.

No. The word rolled around in his mind, gnawing at his heart.

Morozko's boots pounded on the ground, and as he approached Eirah, he fell to his knees, heedless of his own injuries. She lay on her back, sprawled, hair covering her face, but that wasn't what he focused on. It was the unsightly gash on her chest, exposing sinew, bone, and blood. So much blood.

This... wasn't at all how it was supposed to be, how it was to play out.

"Eirah!" He brushed her hair back. "Eirah, for once, listen to me. You are to live." Morozko ducked his head down, pressing his lips to her chilled forehead. She must have fought —he knew she would have.

Eirah wheezed, unable to talk with her lips. *As best as I could.*

"You did well, little bird." He dragged a finger down her cheek. "And now I command you to fight for your life," he whispered, voice breaking. "Because this isn't how it's supposed to end between us. This is where it begins." Morozko didn't think she'd heard him, for her head rolled to the side, and quiet echoed in his mind. "We were to rule side by side, infuriating one another."

Anger rushed through him, swift and fierce. He gingerly scooped Eirah's head up, placing it on his lap. "I vow they'll burn. All of them will burn and suffer for this."

He brushed his fingers over her pulse, weak but there. Morozko wasn't a healer, and his skills weren't enough to patch her up. Despite her immortality and inclination to heal, the wound was too great, and she was losing too much blood to heal on her own.

"Come on, Eirah." Small tendrils of blue skated across her throat, down to the gash, pouring into it and weaving flesh together. The act strained Morozko's magic, pulling it taut.

A moment later, Andras ran into the clearing, huffing. "Your Ma—" His gaze dropped to the body in Morozko's arms, and he didn't hesitate to move into action. "I will do everything I can, but we must bring her to the palace. Stitched together or not, her body suffered greatly." The frost demon removed his black cape and gently wiped away the excess blood from Eirah's chest.

"Are they dead?" Morozko's voice was void of emotion, even to his ears.

"All of them, Your Majesty." Andras's brow furrowed in concentration as magic spilled from his fingertips to Eirah's body. Little by little, the wound healed, tissue knitting together once more, staunching the blood flow.

Eirah sucked in a breath, but her eyes didn't flutter, nor

CANDACE ROBINSON & ELLE BEAUMONT

did she speak. However, her body shifted closer to Morozko in search of his comfort.

He loosed a breath, relief flooding him as some semblance of life returned to her. Morozko's gaze flicked to Andras, and he mulled over the words. The changelings were all dead. For now. *For now.* Until they rose again, and Morozko would ensure they died over and over. Horrifically at that.

"Eirah and I will return to the palace with a handful of guards, but the rest will remain behind with the villagers." Morozko shook his head ruefully. "This has only begun and will worsen as more changelings slip through the cracks."

Andras nodded. "I'll ready a sleigh for you two." The frost demon stood, bowed his head, then turned on his heel, leaving Morozko with Eirah.

He slid his hand to her throat, reassuring himself that she was, in fact, still alive. There, beneath his digits, her pulse thrummed stronger than before, but still too weak. She'd lost so much blood. Too much.

"You'll be cross with me for leaving everyone behind, but you're in need right now." Morozko slid the cape beneath her body, wrapping it around so it hid the split clothing. Her father would need to know, as would Saren, and they didn't need to see how grievous the injury had been.

When Andras returned with the sleigh, Saren and Eirah's father were with him. Morozko lifted Eirah into his arms and carried her to them.

"Oh, my stars, no." Her father leaped from the bench and cradled Eirah's cheek. Tears sprung to his eyes. "Is she..."

"She's alive," Morozko supplied.

Saren rushed forward, clutching onto Eirah's hand. "Not you, too. I can't lose you, too."

Morozko brushed past them, placing Eirah onto the cushioned seat. "Eirah isn't lost. She is resting and in dire need of it." He sighed heavily. The exertion of fighting, the weight of his emotions, his fear of losing Eirah, everything threatened to chain him into place. But he shook it off. Eirah needed him, so did the villagers, and now... Frosteria needed a king ready to fight for it.

"Take her away from here then," Fedir pleaded. "Hole her up in your palace!"

Morozko's lips thinned. "I aim to." He pulled a fur blanket up, tucking Eirah in with it, even if she couldn't feel the cold. "And, unfortunately, I'm bringing the both of you with me."

"What? Why?" Saren blanched and stared at him with wide, tear-filled eyes.

Morozko laughed mirthlessly. "Because if I leave you behind, she'll never forgive me." He motioned to the back of the sleigh. "Now get in. I don't plan to stop until we arrive at the palace."

The battle had been won for now, but that was it. Only one battle down while a war awaited them.

24

EIRAH

"Little bird," a deep voice whispered. "You have to wake up."

Eirah gasped for breath and flicked open her eyes, jolting forward. Her wild gaze met blue irises but not the ice-blue ones she was searching for.

"Easy now," Saren said gently, her hand at Eirah's shoulder, holding her back from— Where was she? She was no longer outside in the snow or in one of the ice houses. The feeling of fire no longer spread from her chest. The wound the changeling had given her must have healed.

As her gaze settled on a large wardrobe and a desk cluttered with her supplies, it took Eirah a moment to realize she was in her room inside Morozko's ice palace, not near the bank of the river in the snow.

"Saren?" Eirah finally croaked, her voice dry and thirsting for a drink. "What are you doing here? How did I get here?" She peered down, finding herself dressed in a lacy white nightgown, her skin smelling of lavender. Not a speck of dirt or blood anywhere. She'd been dressed and bathed.

"You've been here for *days*." Saren sighed, handing Eirah the glass of water from the bedside table that she desperately needed. "Ulva and I have been taking care of you. Your father is here, too."

"Days? *Days*? Did I miss the full moon?" The last thing she recalled had been her fetching the stones she'd needed from the river when two changelings had attacked her. One had slashed her through the chest as soon as she'd whirled around, but she'd held them off with her magic. Yet it hadn't been enough as she'd called for Morozko to help her, so she'd shifted, flying upward enough to make the changelings leave. Her strength had waned, and she was incapable of allowing her wings to carry her anywhere else. Yet she'd managed to land back into the snow without breaking her bones before shifting again. She couldn't remember much more than that.

"Relax, the full moon has yet to come. You deserved the rest after what you suffered." Saren moved a lock of hair out of Eirah's face.

"But you deserved rest after all *you've* been through."

"Oh, I think I've had about enough of that. If you've forgotten, I was resting while the changeling was inside me."

The memory of bringing down the whip to Saren's back haunted her and sent a shiver through her as she recalled the horrid sound. "Please don't tease about that. At least not until those bastards are truly gone." Eirah took a long swig of the water, the liquid quenching her thirst and moistening her dry throat. She couldn't stop herself and gulped the remainder down.

"You frightened me," Saren whispered, taking the empty glass from her.

231

"At least we have tales to spin, I suppose." Eirah shrugged and blew out a breath.

"Ones of nightmares." She paused, a wide smile spreading across her cheeks, her dimples showing. "Oh, and in case you were wondering, after saving you, the king has been in here watching over you, too. A *lot*."

Morozko... A fluttering sensation buzzed within Eirah's chest and stomach. For the days she'd been unconscious, he'd been with her, even as she'd dreamed. As if he'd heard his name spoken, the door opened to reveal the king. He hadn't bothered to knock or ask if he could come in—he did, as always—sauntered into the room. Only now, it didn't bother her. Relief washed over her at the sight of him, and her heart thrummed a little faster. His white hair was pushed behind one pointed ear, the sleeves of his black shirt rolled up. His pale gray skin shone as the fire crackled, its light highlighting his sharp features. Captivating.

"How did you know I was awake?" Eirah asked.

"I felt it," Morozko said, staring at her as if it was only the two of them in the room. "May I have a moment alone with her?" He didn't remove his gaze from Eirah while asking Saren the question.

"Of course, Your Majesty." Saren bowed her head, her blonde braid falling over one shoulder.

"Fedir is downstairs having breakfast with Andras." Morozko's gaze slid to Saren, then he smirked. "Perhaps you can have Andras go with you afterward to gather fruit for the village again."

"Andras? I'm certain he has more important duties." Saren's cheeks pinkened, and Eirah watched her friend smooth out the skirt of her dress.

"Doubtful," Morozko murmured.

"Why are you turning pink?" Eirah arched a brow at Saren. What had she missed while asleep? It very much seemed her friend found Andras more than handsome, which was surprising because Saren rarely blushed over anyone.

"Hush. And don't give me that look," Saren hissed, still flustered. "I'll see you in a little while."

Eirah grinned as Saren shut the door behind her. Her gaze then returned to Morozko, his hooded stare pinned on her. He wasn't saying a word, as though waiting for her to.

"Well, are you going to speak?" Eirah asked with a smile. "Or are you going to continue looking at me as if I almost died and came back to life?"

"As if that didn't happen." He sank beside her on the bed, and she breathed in his enticing spicy aroma. Comforting, soothing. A spark of playfulness ignited in his eyes, then faded. "I've seen many things in my lifetime, but finding you in such a state is the one I'd like to forget most."

"I should've been listening for danger more, the way you taught me," she whispered, hoping she would never find him the way he had her. "But thank you for saving me."

"If I had to destroy Frosteria to do it, I would have."

"Now, let's not be dramatic." Eirah laughed. But he remained serious, and the smile slipped from her face. She reached forward, taking his hand in hers. "I'm here, Morozko. I'm all right."

His throat bobbed, and he brushed his other hand across her cheek. "You're strong. Brave. Aggravating. Beautiful. Passionate. Caring. Everything I didn't know I could want. And *frightening*, so damn frightening. Me, the king, who never gets frightened. But I was. More than I ever have been, little bird."

Eirah's lips parted, and she was at a loss for words, unsure of what to say. Her hand left his to cradle his face. "As for you, I wouldn't change anything at all."

"Oh, I'm sure you would." He chuckled. "But I have another matter to discuss. A recent vision."

A pit formed in her stomach, nervousness crawling through her. "Oh? Is it something worse? Please tell me it isn't." The full moon wasn't far away, and she at least wanted peace to remain until then.

"No, in fact, I think it may please you." Morozko brought her knuckles to his lips and kissed them softly. "There's one more spell for you to cast before the full moon if you and the mortals wish. It's a way to protect them, to give them what we have."

Eirah's brow furrowed. "What is it?"

"You are the first witch, Eirah, and as such, we don't know what to expect. But in my vision, I saw the villagers become immortal, and it was because of you."

Eirah blinked, taking in what he'd said. The entire village could become immortal? It wasn't only a favorable thing that they could live forever if they chose—it would protect them more easily against the changelings. The lesser demons could still slaughter, but they wouldn't be able to sneak their way inside innocent mortal bodies and hide.

"So, Saren and my father may live forever?" she asked.

He nodded. "If they want to, then yes."

Giddiness swarmed through her as her heart swelled, but if they chose not to, she would accept it. She pushed up from the bed when Morozko drew her into his lap, her hands catching on his shoulders. "I think not, little bird," he whispered in her ear, his voice gruff.

She looked down at him with a grin. "And you truly believe you can still tell me what to do?"

"I am king, aren't I?" He smirked. "The mortals can wait a few moments. Let me be selfish a little longer."

Eirah relaxed in his arms and her fingers entwined in his hair. He closed his eyes at her touch, and she pressed her lips to his. "I want you so very much."

"I'll give into anything you damn well please," he purred. "That is if you aren't hurting."

"I'm more than fine. And clean."

"I would take you dirty." Morozko's lips fell to her neck, and he trailed open-mouth kisses along her jaw. His hands skimmed down her waist, gripping her buttocks and urging her closer. His length hardened against her, making her eyelids flutter. "So dirty."

The door opened, and Eirah froze, her gaze connecting with her father. Heat stormed up her neck and spilled into her cheeks.

"Oh, oh my. Does no one knock around here?" Her voice came out high-pitched as she crawled off of Morozko.

"I can— I can come back," her father stuttered, turning to leave.

"No need, Fedir," Morozko called, not a hint of embarrassment on the king's face. "I suppose you would like to see your daughter." He stood from the bed, kissing her knuckles once more. "I'll see you soon, little bird. We can finish *this* later."

Eirah narrowed her eyes at his back, then turned to her father, her cheeks still warm. "Don't mind him, Papa. It's nothing. He's just... he's..."

"That didn't look like nothing, daughter. It's truly none of my business, but I can see you care for him."

Her father had never tried to interfere with her romantic life. If she never chose a man at all and continued to only work on her toy-making, he wouldn't have minded, and if she had, he would only wish for her to be happy and for him to treat her well.

"It started with an unusual circumstance, did it not? I don't know what is to come next, though." The words Morozko had spoken earlier didn't mean he loved her. But that, that word, she now knew. That was the only word to express what she felt for him. Somehow along the way, through everything, through magic, through pleasure, she'd fallen in love with the demon king she'd once believed to be nothing but a prick. He could still be that, yet he was so much more.

"He's a good king, even if I haven't always agreed with his choices. But he saved you, and for that, I owe him my life," her father said.

Eirah nodded, taking a deep breath. "I have something to tell you, Papa. You know how I have magic, that I'm a witch?"

He slowly nodded. "Go on."

"I have the ability to grant immortality to humans. After what happened with the changelings, I believe it would be best to take it, to be protected in this cold world. But it's not my choice to make for you or the others."

Her father's eyebrows lifted as he pushed his glasses up the bridge of his nose. "Immortality? I don't know. Your mother..."

"You don't have to choose immortality for me, Papa. I know you miss Mama and want to reunite with her one day." Eirah's fingers brushed her mother's locket at her throat.

"How about this, daughter? I take it and live as long as I desire, and when I decide I want to reunite with Liabetta, then I will."

She smiled as tears pricked her eyes. "I think that's the perfect decision."

Ulva insisted on preparing Eirah in finer attire to meet with the village. Saren had been more than relieved to take immortality after what she'd been dealt. Eirah had chosen to assign Saren to speak with the villagers prior to the spell so she could tell them about her experience with the changelings. As not to persuade them but to see the true lurking danger.

Eirah's father and Saren had left a while ago to venture to the ice houses. Morozko now rode on his wolf as Eirah flew through the air in her owl form. Just as she was about to swoop downward, Adair slipped out from a tall pine tree, flapping his snowy-white wings toward her. They flew side by side for a few moments before she beat her wings toward the ground, shifting, finally not falling face down in the snow. Adair landed on her shoulder, his talons digging in slightly.

"Did you miss me?" She smiled, brushing his soft feathers, the wind circling them. "I know. I most likely put fear in you. If I were gone, then whose familiar would you be?"

He cocked his head, narrowing his eyes at her.

"I was only jesting." Eirah laughed softly. "But thank you. Saren told me you lingered outside my window, watching over me during the night."

She trudged just a little farther in the snow when she caught sight of Morozko's crimson cape.

He stepped away from Nuka, beckoning her closer with a finger. "You should've taken the wolf."

"Perhaps on the way back. I needed practice."

Adair darted back into the trees, leaving Eirah and Morozko to break through the forest, approaching the ice houses. Saren stood at the front of the crowd, wearing a light blue dress and a thick fur cloak that Ulva had made her. Xezu and Ulva stood at the edge of the crowd, believing this was the best choice they could make for one another as well as protecting their king.

"The village is unanimous," Saren said, turning to them with a smile. "After seeing the changelings, after hearing my story, they want to take immortality. They want to thrive in the cold, with the possibility of gaining magic, to protect their loved ones. They're more than ready for that and have their daggers prepared."

Eirah nodded, meeting the eyes of all the villagers who'd survived. Familiar faces like the chieftain and his son, then others she barely knew or not at all. It was strange seeing them look at her this way, not as if she was odd, but in awe, with respect. Or perhaps it was only Morozko they were looking at this way.

"This is your one chance before we begin," Eirah spoke to the crowd, hiding the nervous emotion brewing inside of her. "If anyone chooses differently, then leave now."

But every villager remained. She remembered what Morozko had told her before they'd left, how to perform the spell, but she would find the words as she had when she'd given magic to the stones.

Lifting her arms in front of her, Eirah closed her eyes and dug deep inside herself, locating the words she needed. Waiting and waiting until finally, they drifted to her mind, forming in a language she'd never heard before.

As she opened her eyes, she chanted them softly. Wispy blue and white magic curled out from her fingertips toward the crowd. Her power caressed their flesh, seeping inside their skin, burying itself until it rooted. And she could feel how this was a gift that she would be unable to give again.

The villagers remained silent, each of their expressions different. Some worried, others eager or unknowing. When the magic no longer surrounded them, Morozko spoke loudly, "Now prick your fingers and let a drop of blood fall to the snow. This will bind you to my land as an immortal for as long as you decide."

Daggers pricked fingers, and drops of crimson fell to the snow, one after another, speckling the white with ruby, the string pulling taut within Eirah.

And it was done.

25

MOROZKO

The full moon wasn't too far away, and it was apparent that the seal had broken entirely, for the changelings had crept their way up the mountain while Eirah was recovering, threatening to invade the castle. But the frost demons ended that, cutting down the threats and burning the bodies.

Amid the discord, there was one bright spot, and that was Eirah granting the villagers of Vinti immortality, and in one grand effort, there were no more mortals in Frosteria. There was some relief in knowing they were protected against the wretched bastards.

Morozko sighed, standing against the fireplace mantel in his study. Logs stirred in the brazier, tumbling and flicking embers up the chimney. He clenched his teeth, willing the buzzing thoughts to quiet in his mind, but it seemed impossible. Eirah had nearly died not long ago, and his kingdom was under attack by changelings. The fate of Frosteria seemed bleak, but his visions said otherwise.

There was a solution, but they had to *wait* for it. Wait for the full moon, when they could perform the ritual and bring forth the krampi. Morozko only hoped it wouldn't be too late for them.

A knock sounded, tearing him away from his thoughts. "Come in." He glanced toward the door as it swung open, revealing Xezu. His skin held a new glow to it, lending him a more youthful appearance, and it was all because of Eirah's gift to him and his wife.

Morozko had remained by Eirah's side until the end of the villagers' change, but when she was through, he gave her time with them, allowing her to explain what she knew. Any more questions he'd answer at a later time—he was in no mood to tutor anyone.

"Your Majesty." Xezu bowed his head. "The frost demons are keeping their lines of defense up regarding the changelings. So much has happened in so short of a time." His wise eyes studied Morozko a little too closely. "And I want to know, how are you faring?"

His steward's question was loaded far too heavily. Morozko drew in a breath, smoothing the lines on his brow. "Well enough," he responded tersely.

"With all due respect, I believe that's a lie."

A lie? Morozko scowled at Xezu, hating the mere fact that he was able to pick up on his state of being. Because, in truth, he wasn't well enough. Eirah had almost died in his arms, and while she was healing in her room, he'd had time to dissect what that meant to him. He'd grown attached to her, even realized it had bloomed into a deeper emotion. *Love?* He'd never loved a thing in his life, not even himself. So how could he love another?

Still, the idea of living a life without Eirah in it seemed dull and lackluster. He'd grown accustomed to her presence, and when he no longer had her near him, Morozko longed for it once more.

"I think you ought to tell her," Xezu prompted.

Morozko stopped himself from snapping at him, stopped the words—*tell her what?*—from spilling from his lips because it was pointless. If Xezu knew, it was rather obvious.

"What if—"

"She chooses not to stay with you and lives a life with the other immortals?" Xezu finished, then stroked his chin, a shrewdness glimmering in his eyes. "Then, I say she chose wisely, Your Majesty."

Heat flooded Morozko's cheeks as his temper flared to life. He stalked forward, finger raised, but wasn't able to get the words out in time.

"I must say, this is refreshing to see. King Morozko unsure of himself..." Xezu smiled warmly and continued, "Eirah has a choice, and it is hers to make, but she needs to know *everything*. And I mean how you *feel*, Your Majesty." He rapped his fingers against his chest, then dipped his head. "I think it's time I leave you to do just that. Oh... the last I saw her, she was in the foyer."

Before Morozko could open his mouth to chide his steward, the man left the room.

The last thing Morozko wanted to do was suss through his feelings, but he had to admit, he was fond of Eirah in a way that melted his icy layers. She saw through them to him. And that continuous pull drew him across the room and into the hall.

His brisk stride brought him down the corridor to the grand stairwell, and as he descended the steps, Morozko surveyed the foyer. He spotted two guards at their posts, standing rigidly, but no Eirah. He frowned.

Ulva walked by, took notice of him, and bobbed a curtsy. "Your Majesty."

"Eirah?" He narrowed his eyes, not glaring but in confusion. "She was down here."

"She's in her room. I just drew a bath for her. She said her body needed the numbing warmth after all her efforts." Ulva pressed her lips together to keep from smiling and glanced away from him.

Morozko didn't say another word as he turned on his heel and ascended the stairs once again. His heart raced, melding with his thoughts and the notion of a bare Eirah soaking in steaming water. His needs had no place here, not while he wished to speak on heavier matters, but it was undeniable. Morozko yearned for Eirah. His cock straining against his trousers was proof of that. But he could nearly taste her lips against his, only adding to his silent torment.

Once at her door, his eyes met with Kusav's, who bowed his head. Morozko thought about knocking, but it seemed foolish to begin doing so now. After he'd already ravished her, and all the times he'd just abruptly walked in. But this was different, a monumental occasion when the Frost King would admit how he felt.

Kusav visibly bit the inside of his cheek, likely to keep from blathering about Eirah being in the bath, which was all the push Morozko needed.

He opened the door—Eirah was not on her bed nor at her desk, fiddling with her tools, or rummaging through her wardrobe. Morozko used his heel to return the room to privacy. The scent of juniper spilled into the bedroom from the bathing chamber, courtesy of Ulva's soap-making. Gone were the remnants of his clove, and instead clung the floral fragrance. Clean and comforting.

Morozko removed his cape, folding and placing it at the bottom of her bed before padding into the next room. Eirah lounged in the bath, head tilted back as the steam rose around her. She appeared to be sleeping, but he knew better.

As he stepped forward, her lips twitched to keep from smiling. His cock hardened at once, imagining slipping into her welcoming depths and pulling moans of pleasure from her.

Morozko knelt behind the tub and leaned in toward Eirah's ear. She still didn't acknowledge him by speaking, however, her skin was covered in gooseflesh. "Hello, little bird," he cooed softly, dragging his nose down the smooth column of her neck to kiss and nip at her shoulder.

"Still haven't learned the art of knocking, I see." Her breath hitched as he bit down with a little more pressure.

"What's the point? It's my castle anyway," he murmured, dipping his hands into the water to take the cloth from her. Morozko brushed the fabric over her nipples, and the peaks hardened as he swiped over them again.

Eirah shifted in the tub, expelling a shaky breath. "Did you only come in here to tease me?"

Morozko skated his lips along her shoulder, then back up to her ear. "Mayhaps. It is what I'm best at."

"Do continue then," she groused in play.

He shifted the cloth into his opposite hand, using it to taunt her nipple once more. Eirah wasn't the only one affected by his ministrations. His length strained against his trousers, but he could wait until she was ready for him.

Morozko dropped the cloth off to the side, this time using

his fingers to circle around her hardened peaks until Eirah's back arched and she moaned.

"Do you want me in there with you?"

"You usually can read my mind, can't you?" She smiled, turning her head to look into his eyes, and a fire blazed in hers, the same inferno that churned away within him.

"Say it." He lifted his brows pointedly and slowly drew his thumb in a circle.

Her smile grew wider. "Morozko, I need you in this tub right now." *Or I'll drag you in here myself.*

"Ah, there's the fiery bird I know so well." Morozko stood, and his nimble fingers undid the buttons of his linen shirt before he carelessly discarded it on the floor, then removed the rest of his clothing.

His length twitched in anticipation of plunging into Eirah's wetness. But first things first...

Morozko stepped into the warm water, sitting down across from her. He took in her appearance, rosy cheeks, impossibly dark eyes wide from arousal. He chuckled, leaning forward to brush a soft kiss on her lips. "Let me finish bathing you." Although, he had little intention of cleaning her. No, Morozko wanted to pleasure her until she was crying his name out.

He dipped his hand into the water again, fishing around for the cloth and purposely skimming his fingers along the inside of her thigh. She drew in a shaky breath.

"You aren't intending to wash me." Eirah shifted her legs, opening herself to him. "Are you?"

Morozko glanced upward, his lips curling into a devious grin. "In part. At least, that's where I'll start." The fabric traveled along her abdomen to her thighs, and when it came to her legs, he lifted each one, tenderly wiping them clean.

But when he was done washing her, the cloth disappeared again and Morozko's fingers walked up her thigh to Eirah's center. While he'd come to confess how he felt, he also needed this moment to bolster him. He knew pleasure and what to expect from it—when he told Eirah how he felt... he didn't know *what* would happen. What words would tumble from her lips, or if she'd even accept what he was willing to offer her.

"Please," Eirah whispered, shifting forward.

Just one word, though simple, sent his pulse racing. "In a moment, little bird, but enjoy yourself first." His thumb brushed over her ball of nerves, circling it even as he slid a finger into her. As she accepted his digit, he pumped within her. Eirah's eyes closed, and she leaned against the tub, tilting her hips so he gained better access.

Morozko slid a second finger into her, crooking them to find her spot, and as Eirah's hips rocked, he knew when he'd struck it.

"*Oh,*" she breathed, arching her back. Using his free hand, he grazed her nipple with his fingers.

Morozko quickened his movements, watching Eirah's brow furrow and her breath hitch as her pleasure unfolded.

"Morozko!" she rasped, gripping the edge of the tub.

His fingers worked her through the waves of ecstasy, and when they subsided, he withdrew. Now, he wanted to bury himself in Eirah, pulling as many cries from her as possible.

She slipped forward until she straddled him. Her hair clung to her shoulders and her breasts. He brushed the wet locks back, drinking in the sight of her flushed body.

Morozko's cock leaped in response, and he grinned up at her, his hands squeezing her hips. She wriggled atop him, her sex gliding against his length. He groaned, leaning forward to press heated kisses along her abdomen.

"I want you closer." She ground herself against him, eliciting a hiss from not only him but herself. Eirah rocked her hips, bearing down against his tip.

Morozko shifted his hand from her hip to between them, positioning himself at her entrance. She rolled her hips once more, and this time, he thrust his upward. Eirah gasped, her hands settling on his shoulders as her core gripped his cock.

"You feel so good, little bird," he murmured while dragging his lips along her breast, then taking her nipple into his mouth, sucking and grazing it with his teeth. She tremored, then she began a steady rhythm of rising and falling.

Water splashed over the tub's rim, splattering the floor each time she collided with him. And he didn't give one single fuck. Morozko slid his palm along her thigh, to her backside, and guided her down with every upward thrust he made.

Eirah's nails scraped along his shoulders, stinging just enough to add to his pleasure. The ecstasy mounted, growing higher, then even higher. Eirah's inner muscles clamped around him, breathy moans escaping her, undoing everything within him. "Fuck!" he groaned, spilling himself into her as she rode them both into bliss.

After the last dreg of pleasure faded, he wrapped his arms around her, tugging her flush against him.

"I may sleep for days straight after this." Eirah laughed, moaning as she moved on top of him.

"Oh, little bird, stop moving." Every time she shifted, the sensation was nearly too much to bear. He chuckled, then eased her off of him.

Eirah glanced up at him, and he noted the exhaustion

beneath her eyes now that she wasn't full of adrenaline. "One of us needs to remain awake."

He nodded, smirking. "I am *quite* alert." He stood, leaning down to pick her up, and stepped out of the tub.

"What are you doing?" Eirah squeaked but didn't thrash in his arms.

"Putting you to bed." He lifted his brows pointedly, then carefully deposited her on the fur blankets.

"Did you forget something?" Eirah grinned, blinking innocently at him. "My robe."

Morozko rolled his eyes, sighing before he pushed away from the bed and strode into the bathing chamber to grab her robe and a towel to dry her hair. The robe he placed beside her, but the towel he used gently on her hair. An act he'd never done for anyone else. It was too intimate, too personal, and none had been so close to him.

She slid the robe on, eyeing him as he dried his hair. "What are you doing?"

"Drying myself?" he said coyly, but there was no use putting off what he came to her room for. "You make this difficult. You make *most* things difficult." Morozko slid beneath the blankets and stared at her for a long moment. His heart thumped wildly in his chest with love for Eirah of Vinti. For her resilience, bravery, and how quickly she'd adapted to her new life.

Eirah remained sitting atop the blankets, and confusion swept across her face. "Are you going to be a prick after *that*?" She jerked her head toward the bathing room.

"No," he whispered, pushing himself up. The blankets spilled around his waist, and he wished that he could speak the words as easily as they flitted around in his head. "You have a choice to make," he began, grimacing at how harsh the words sounded. "What I mean is... I wish for you to stay in the castle. If you stay, you have a place by my side, as my equal—as my queen—forever."

Morozko sucked in a breath, as if a weight had lifted from his chest, freeing him to speak with ease. "You've done the impossible, Eirah of Vinti, and captured my heart. An act I didn't think anyone capable of." He was quiet for a time, and she remained silent as well, peering at him with wide eyes.

The fireplace crackled, but that was the only sound in the room, making Morozko uneasy. Not knowing what Eirah was thinking, he wished in that moment she'd let her guard down, and allow him to hear her. If she rejected him, he'd let her go, but if Eirah chose to leave, would he recover?

He clamped down on his bottom lip, his sharp canine biting into it. "Is this how you wish to slay me—with suspense?" Morozko attempted to jest, but he didn't laugh or smile.

"Oh, you foolish king." Eirah closed the distance between them, cupping his cheeks. "Of course I'll stay. And in case that wasn't clear enough, I love you."

Relief flooded him and a warmth he'd never felt touched his being. Morozko leaned in, brushing his lips against Eirah's, then deepening it as he slid his tongue into her mouth. He withdrew, and she pressed her forehead to his.

"Against your better judgment, perhaps," he taunted her, then pulled Eirah into his arms and cradled her, tilting her backward before taking possession of her lips once again.

Eirah laughed against his mouth. "Perhaps." She dragged her fingers down the nape of his neck to his shoulders. "If I stay, if I become your queen, I do have a request."

Morozko lifted his head, squinting at her. "Oh?" What did

the little bird have up her sleeve? What could she possibly want?

She smiled slowly, tugging a strand of his hair. "Love me for the rest of your days, Morozko."

The words, while simple, held a vulnerability to them. Morozko lifted his hand, stroked her cheek with his knuckles and kissed her tenderly. "I vow to love you until my dying day, Eirah."

And a vow was never to be broken when spoken by the Frost King.

EPILOGUE
EIRAH

Morozko proved to be quite the lover, taking care of Eirah thoroughly again and again until she was a useless heap on his bed. She shouldn't have been surprised, not with all the lovers he'd had over the centuries. Envy didn't course through her because she'd drawn something new from the Frost King, something she hadn't known existed within him as his icy heart defrosted. Humanity.

Compassion still lingered within her, too, and she would teach it to their children if she and Morozko decided to bear them. Eirah still couldn't wrap her mind around the fact that he'd asked her to be his queen, and she just hoped she could become worthy of all the lives in Frosteria.

No longer did humans exist in Frosteria—it was now a world filled with immortals to live as long as they wished. That evening, she and Morozko would perform their duty, and she hoped his vision was true, that these new demons would help to keep the changelings at bay.

Eirah peered at Morozko beneath lowered lashes, the fur

blanket barely covering his thigh, exposing the curve of his buttocks. In this lighting, Morozko appeared younger, his expression serene, and she wanted to press her lips to his, then wake him with her mouth around his length. All in due time—she would save that for another day. For now, she had a different plan for him.

"I wouldn't mind you expressing your desire first," Morozko whispered, his lips tilting up at the edges as he slowly inched the blanket down even more.

"Bah!" she hissed, bringing the furs back up even though she was enticed to rip them away. "Don't ruin it!"

"I didn't hear the rest of what you were thinking. Only the part about your lips around my cock," he purred, his pale blue eyes cracking open. "I can be patient, though. Surprise me with your endless creativity. I'll be waiting."

With a smile, she pressed her lips to his in a kiss, one that was meant to be quick, until he pulled her atop him. Her heart craved him, his touch, his taste.

Eirah's hands traveled up his warm chest to cradle his face. "I promise I'll return before we have to leave tonight."

"I won't move from this position until then." He smirked, his fingers skimming down her back to her hips.

Eirah was tempted to stay, tempted to let his length fill her completely, to ride him again. But somehow, she tamped down her lust and slipped off of him to put on her silky robe. She glanced at him over her shoulder once more, as if she was going on a far journey and would never see him again. Would it always be this way? Filled with so many beautiful and fragile emotions? She hoped it would last for eternity. "See you soon, *Morozko*."

He grinned wickedly, daring her to come back in bed with

him, but she hurried out the door before she spent the remainder of the day bare with him.

With a light laugh, Eirah padded down the hallway and almost bumped into Ulva as she slipped from a room. The servant gave her a radiant smile, her immortal skin practically glowing beneath the candlelight.

"Good luck tonight," Ulva said, pulling a piece of fruit from her wicker basket and tossing it to her.

Eirah caught the peach as she said, "Continue your prayers." She would need all she could that night. Morozko was given a recent vision that not only would their world be affected by the changelings, but another realm filled with mortals would be as well. It made the situation more dire than ever since the lesser demons could take over those humans' bodies.

"All of us will be."

Eirah bid her goodbye and opened the door to her room. Morozko had told her she could move her workstation to anywhere in the palace she wished, but Eirah was quite fond of this room now. And she also enjoyed the balcony view, where she could easily venture out to speak to Adair if he chose to visit.

From her desk, Eirah lifted the music box she'd been working on, not realizing it had been meant for Morozko all this time. She took a seat and brought her tools closer to finish carving and painting.

Once the paint was dry, she pressed the pieces inside and adjusted the gears. It took longer than she'd expected, but it needed to be as close to perfect as she could make it. She then tucked the box into her robe pocket and went back to Morozko's bedroom.

Eirah didn't truly think the king would still be lingering

there. But he was, and her heart caught at the sight of him. Morozko sat against the headboard, a lock of hair hanging across his face that she wanted to tuck behind his pointed ear. His gaze was focused on the pages of a book as he took a bite from a plum.

"You waited." She grinned, shutting the door behind her.

"I told you I wouldn't leave the bed until you returned, little bird." Morozko snapped the book shut and watched her with a predator's heated gaze.

"Oh yes, a king who can get servants to bring him anything he wishes. I forgot," she teased.

"I didn't bother to get dressed, either." He leaned forward, the fur blankets dropping even lower.

Eirah's cheeks warmed as her eyes wandered to the outline of his length beneath the blankets, knowing he was ready to take her again.

"I wanted to give you something." Biting her lip, she fished out the small music box and hid it behind her back.

"Oh?" His brow furrowed in confusion, and he tilted his head to the side, trying to take a peek. "Is it something you made?"

"It is." She smiled and relaxed on the bed, placing the music box in his hand. "I know you might think of it as a silly thing, but I hope you like it anyway. If not, you can always give it back to me. I don't mind."

Morozko didn't say a word as he drew the box closer and lifted the lid. He wound the silver key at the back all the way around, then he watched the figure of him, holding her in owl form, spin to a slow and wistful song. His throat bobbed while continuing to study it, his eyes never leaving the figures.

"Perhaps I can carve something different to place inside or choose another song to use," she whispered when he remained quiet. "I'm sure you've been given grander gifts throughout the centuries."

"You will do no such thing," Morozko murmured, resting it on his night table, his gaze pinned to hers. "I have never received such a perfect gift." The king's lips curled up at the edges, and he drew her to him, bringing her into his lap, her legs cradling his strong thighs. "Now it's my turn to give you something. This is part one of your gift." He slowly drew open her robe and peeled it from her skin, sending a delicious shiver through her. Morozko flicked his tongue across her nipple as he pushed down the blankets from his hips. His fingers dug into her waist, her softness pressed against his hardness. "I'll start by tasting you here, then I'll savor every inch of you." He brought her nipple in between his lips, eliciting a moan from her.

As Eirah released more pleasurable sounds, she knew this was an exquisite gift that the Frost King would continue to give.

"It's time," Morozko said when night started to fall.

As Eirah slipped on the clothing Ulva had made for her, she smiled. Tight white trousers, a dark corset to go over an ivory tunic with alabaster feathers on the shoulders. It was impeccable. Morozko tied the laces of the corset for her in the back, and a nervous feeling soared through her. She supposed that half the weight of this action tonight depended on her. At least she wasn't alone in this, but what if her blood didn't truly help the king as was foretold it would? It had failed when they'd tried before, but the moon hadn't been full yet.

Together, side by side, they headed out of the palace into the night. The wind blew harshly, and the full moon shone high in the sky, the moon they'd been waiting for. Morozko lifted his hand and light blue orbs danced along his fingertips, then lifted, hovering above them and lighting the area. Adair flew across the velveteen sky, his wings beating against the wind as Nuka stepped out from between two trees. Everything was in the proper place.

"Where would you like me to draw your blood?" Morozko's finger drifted down the valley of her breasts. "You should've worn the robe out here." He leaned forward, whispering in her ear as his digits drifted between her legs to a tender spot on her inner thigh. "I could've done it right here."

Heat coursed through her and she laughed softly. "Do you have to make everything intimate?"

"With you, yes." Morozko lifted her hand, and he kissed the tip of her finger as the snow rose to form a dagger in his other palm. With the ice blade, he pressed it to her flesh, and she pulled in a sharp breath at the light sting. A bright pearl of crimson beaded to the surface, and he slowly licked his tongue across the blood as his hooded eyes held hers.

"You are delicious." Morozko grinned wolfishly at her. "Now, where do you want to taste me, little bird?"

"I don't think you want to know the answer to that question at the moment, Your Majesty." Eirah smiled, trailing her fingers across his. "I suppose this one will do for now, though."

"Don't tempt me," he groaned. "We have a task to complete, but I'm not above pleasuring you right here."

"Perhaps I'll let you after." Eirah arched a brow, taking the blade from him. She thought about the romance tales she'd kept beneath her bed in Vinti. Those males had worshiped their lovers in many places, many ways, and she wanted to become bold enough to eventually try them all with Morozko. She focused, piercing his finger and bringing it into her mouth, tongue swirling along his digit, lapping up the blood.

Morozko licked his lower lip as he watched her. He spun her around so her backside was flush with his chest. "Now, prick me again," he purred in her ear. "Let's create magic together."

They chanted the foreign words while blue, purple, and green rippled around them. This was it. This was the chance to see if their power could help save Frosteria. One of Morozko's arms encircled her waist, and she held up the other, then pierced his finger with the blade. A drop blossomed to the surface, and she turned over his hand, squeezing it so the blood fell to the snow.

Silence enveloped them as the crimson struck the ivory, but she swore it was the loudest thing she'd ever heard.

The red bled into the white, but just when she believed they'd failed once again, ruby spread across the snow, webbing throughout the area. Below their feet, the ground trembled, her teeth clacking together. Morozko drew them both backward, holding her close as though protecting her from the unknown.

Above them, high in the sky, the full moon's dark gray color changed to cobalt as a minty scent filled the air. Blood, snow, and ice rose from the ground, weaving and swirling together while a light blue glittering magic merged them all. A naked form of ice with red veins stood before them, layers of flesh crawling up from the toes to the skull to cover the new creation. Dark hair cascaded to his waist, and Eirah's gaze dipped down to his endowed length for a moment before flicking back up.

A male.

He was tall, muscular, built to destroy, to aid in the effort to put an end to the changelings. This immortal looked human, except curving obsidian horns protruded from his head, reaching toward the starlit sky.

And then he knelt before Morozko and Eirah, placing a fist to his chest. Adair flew down, landing on Eirah's shoulder as Nuka stood beside Morozko, watching as more demons rose. A female, her eyes a deep brown, another male with bright blue irises mirroring Morozko's, then more and more lifted and shaped from the snow, all beautifully sculpted, toned, and strong.

Once the magic was complete, a crowd of one hundred warriors knelt. Morozko placed his hand on the first male's shoulder. "Your name is Enox." He then touched the shoulders of the blue-eyed male and the brown-eyed female. "And you are Korreth and Orna."

One by one, he gifted names to the remainder of the new warriors before taking a step back. A group of frost demons came out from around the castle to prepare. The world was quiet, waiting for Morozko to speak.

"My faithful krampi, my sons and daughters, we have much to discuss as you prepare for your tasks. For now, the frost demons will get you dressed and fed, then lead you to your new villages. I will meet with you all tomorrow."

The krampi rose from their knelt positions—the blue-eyed male, Korreth, pressed his fist to his chest at Morozko and Eirah with honor—as the frost demons led them around the palace.

Eirah still couldn't believe she was to stay in Morozko's home, become a queen, help with the fight against the changelings. She'd been a toymaker before, something she would always be and would continue doing.

She whispered to Morozko, breathing out a sigh of relief. "You did it."

"It couldn't have been done without you, my queen. And I do think I owe you my second gift." He moistened his lower lip and arched a brow. "Now, we follow Adair."

"You plotted a secret with my familiar?" Eirah drawled, brushing her fingers across Adair's soft wing.

"I did." Morozko smirked as Nuka shook out his fur before lowering for the king to mount. He climbed atop the wolf, then held out his hand to her. With a swift tug, he lifted her behind him and she wrapped her arms around his waist.

"Can you give me a hint?"

"No, but with your arms holding me like that, you will receive a third gift once we arrive."

They'd done it. Together, she and her frost king, the male she'd once wished were dead. But now, he was more than she could put into words, and they would peel back more of their layers until the end of time.

THE END

Read on for a preview of *Slaying the Naga King* by Jessica M Butler—the next book in
Mortal Enemies to Monster Lovers!

SLAYING THE NAGA KING

PREVIEW

JESSICA M BUTLER

I

DESPERATE TIMES

Could you outrun a nightmare?

Or carry someone you loved out of its path?

Probably not. But you could always run toward it. Or try your best to prepare for its coming. Especially when it came every night to torment the people you loved.

Rhea noted the long slanting path of orange light that filtered through the oak branches over the windows of their tiny tree home.

Less than six hours before the next attack.

Unless the time changed.

Please, she prayed, don't let the time change. No extension or addition. If anything, it could just go away.

She adjusted the coarse sheet of paper on the low table and resumed sketching. Fatigue burned her eyes. What she wouldn't give for a night and day of peace. This breakneck pace had only intensified. It could not last forever.

But no one—not them, not the elders, not the Paras, not

the entirety of all the worlds' leaders combined—seemed any closer to finding an answer.

She rubbed her forehead and stared down at the dark lines on the page. They wavered a little, some of the markings less strong than others.

Usually drawing comforted her. Now though she felt only the desire to finish her illustrations so she could turn them in to her clients and get paid. She shook her head. Pity purchases. No doubt about that. But pity purchases purchased food as well as any other money.

It seemed like such a small thing. Like she was just staking out space for them to survive. To get through. To give Tiehro and Salanca, her spirit family, time to rest and hopefully to fight off this psychic plague or curse.

The pencil slipped between her fingers.

Fight it off...for how long?

The rest of the month?

The rest of the year?

The rest of their lives?

She set her jaw, tightening her grip over the pale wood. The lead scraped over the page with uneven pressure as she willed herself to sketch faster. There was no way to know for certain. And she needed to do something—to find some way to hope. She had to do something, or she was going to go mad herself. And then what good would she be?

A large firm hand grasped her shoulder. "You should be resting right now," Tiehro said, his gravelly voice hoarser than usual.

She kept her focus on the page, though she knew what she'd see if she glanced up. His straight purple-black hair tangled and mussed over his filed-down horns, his amethyst eyes bloodshot and watery, and his jet-black eagle wings tucked firmly against his back and yet showing traces of molting. She pushed the anger at their situation down. It wouldn't accomplish anything good. "I don't think you slept long enough."

"Funny thing about sleep. When you want it, it never comes." He nudged her again, then stepped back. "You should at least close your eyes for a bit."

"If I rest now, I won't get these done. If I don't get these done, I can't deliver them to my clients. If I don't deliver them to my clients, we don't get paid. If we don't get paid, we can't afford food. If we can't afford food, we have to hunt or gather. In which case, none of us will be sleeping then either. And as drawing is significantly safer than hunting, I think this is the best choice."

He staggered and caught himself on the coarse wall.

Her focus snapped to him at once. "It's getting worse?"

He held his hand over his eyes; his mouth twitched. "Just clumsy."

She set her jaw. He'd not only had to battle the nightmares but aura migraines and double vision. It had gotten so bad that as of last week, he couldn't fly. Setting the pencil and paper aside, she stood. "If you aren't careful, you're going to drop out of this tree. And then where will you be?"

"On the ground most likely," he said dryly. "A fall from this height wouldn't kill anyone though. Not unless they landed on a knife. Or a besred. You don't still keep that little blade in your shirt, do you? You might want to take that out in case you fall."

Of course she did. She always kept that little blade for sharpening her pencils. It was wrapped in rubber and stuck between her breasts. But it was never at risk for stabbing her. Even if it did, it wouldn't do much damage.

"At least we don't live on Ecekom where even the rocks want to eat you." She tried to smile, but it wavered. "I think we need to talk about moving, Tiehro."

They'd spent what remained of their savings to move to this little hut situated in the trees, over an hour's walk from Dohahtee and any other place with people and commerce. All in the desperate hope that distance from others in the psychic races would protect them. It hadn't.

And if Tiehro and Salanca followed the path of so many others of their races before them, there would come a point when they would not wake from the nightmares. When they would simply be—trapped. To her knowledge, no one had woken up from those comas yet. Perhaps they never would. If one fell, she might be able to manage to keep that one alive. But if both fell?

He didn't look up at her.

She forced her voice to be stronger. "I think we need to move back to where there are people who can help us. We won't be able to do this alone."

Tiehro stiffened. He straightened his shoulders and then gave her the most casual smile he could manage, the tightness in his expression wavering with his pain. "It'll be fine, Bunny. We'll find a way. Not planning on collapsing any time soon. This house is for you. To make sure you aren't without something."

The floorboards creaked beneath her feet. All for her. Part of her hated this little house, even though she knew they wanted her to have it with good intentions. "I know you're concerned about—"

He scoffed. "No. It isn't that." His eyes darted toward her, his expression slightly guilty as if he were trying to construct a poor half-truth. "I will not enter that place until I have no choice. I will not be near it until there is no choice. I might even rather die. If I fall here, I fall. You owe me nothing. I don't expect you to drag my comatose husk to their door." As his words sharpened, he winced. "I'm sorry," he said, softer this time. "Just the paranoia."

Rubbing the back of her neck, she tried to seem as calm and confident as before. He'd never been paranoid or suspicious before, but, even so, she wouldn't blame him for fearing Dohahtee. The psychic quarantine quarters were unpleasant for anyone to consider. Her own pulse quickened in fear at the thought of going that far underground with so many. But she was certain that it was largely because he didn't want this house to be taken from her. Moving to Dohahtee and paying for lodgings would likely require losing this house, small as it was. And then she would be homeless and without prospects once Tiehro and Salanca left on their own important journeys. Both off on their way to grand purposes and plans while she was left to putter around this place.

"If you want to go stay in Dohahtee, that isn't a bad idea," he continued. He crossed to the cracked basin on the far side of the room. The little cooking area was small enough that if he spread out his wings, he would easily fill it. "I can take care of this house. You could see about taking out credit against my name. If they'll give it."

"I'm not leaving either of you unless it's to do something that helps. But they do have medicines there and physicians who might be able to give you relief."

"The relief isn't worth the risk," he said. "Mark my words. Go in there. Only some of us come out. The rest—chopped up probably."

"They wouldn't do that—"

"None of us know what they would do. There are stories. Some of which are true. And it only takes one or two." He dragged his hand over his face, then blinked slowly. With a shuddering sigh, he picked up the squat stone kettle and checked the water within. "We wouldn't know until it's too late. We just—we have to find another solution. And we will, Bunny. But it won't involve selling this house. This house belongs to us—to you."

If she hadn't been worried before, she'd be worried now. He only used their childhood nicknames when he was deeply troubled. She hugged her arms around her middle, her fingers curling against her coral tunic. "Is there anything we could do to make Dohahtee feel safe and keep this house?"

He laughed ruefully. "If only it were that simple."

A weak smile pulled at his mouth. It didn't even come close to reaching his eyes. "It'll be fine. I promise. We're going to find a solution for this. The Paras and the council and everyone will figure out something. It's been a few weeks anyway. They're probably this close to finding the answer. Just wait and see, Bunny. Everything is good."

Her heart broke. "All right, Chickadee."

His smile pulled a little higher as he set the kettle on the stove.

Tears stung the backs of her eyes, and she released a slow breath, trying to regain control of herself. "They probably won't call you that when you join your new sodiwa."

"If—"

"There are no ifs." Sniffing, she rubbed her hand over her eyes, then crossed to the cupboard. Inside the deep shelves sat a variety of clay pots, covered baskets, and slim tins. "We both could use some tea. Salanca too once she gets back."

He peered out past the fur curtains that had been wedged up over the window frame to let the air in. "She's been gone too long. Should have been back over an hour ago."

"She said that was the earliest she'd be back. She's probably just following her lead."

Shaking his head, he kept his hand tight over the handle of the kettle. "Still...if she isn't back in the hour, we should go find her."

"Stop worrying." Salanca pushed through the door, her gait uneven for two steps and her Neyeb betrothal necklace twisted about. She shot him an almost playful glare, though her face was pale and beaded with sweat. Her long brown-black braid was damp, and her cheeks had heavy red streaks. "If I was going to die, I'd do it with far more dignity or dramatics."

"Or both." Rhea hurried to her. These two both struggling to stay on their feet and battling bouts of dizziness made her even less enthused with staying in a house thirty feet above the ground.

Salanca shook her head as she shooed her back, her heavy grey cloak swung with the movement, flashing the embroidered and beaded designs within. "No need for dying today, my loves. I have what we need. Everything is going to be fine now."

She set her lips in a tight line, not certain she believed this. Salanca was always coming up with crazy plans and strange schemes of one sort or another.

"How?" Tiehro demanded, hand still on the kettle.

Salanca gripped Rhea's shoulder, her eyes so bloodshot they looked almost fully red. "The Paras—the council—the elders—none of them are doing a damn thing that works. Only a matter of time before this takes everyone, including them. They're evacuating the cities even now, and all of the shifter cadres have been asked to go out and start searching for the fallen and get them to care facilities."

"I didn't ask why we needed to do something," Tiehro grumbled.

Rhea tried to tug her to the sleeping pelts on the opposite side of the little house. The thin patchwork curtains that provided a little privacy had been pushed almost entirely out of the way. "Let's get a little rest before tonight, all right?"

Salanca's grip tightened as she dug her feet into the wood floor.

Tiehro strode over and lifted her up, his arm around her waist. "You aren't going to fix anything by getting sicker."

"Don't pick me up, you big crow." She smacked his arm. "Don't you understand? I actually have the solution. We need to dream walk and thought project. It's going to take all three of us though. You both have to help me."

Frowning, he set her down in the center of the room on the edge of the woven red rug. "What? Where did you go exactly?"

"Ah ah. I have my secrets for a reason." Salanca wagged her finger at him, but she smiled nonetheless. Reaching into her cloak, she removed two items from the deep pocket on her right. A squat bottle with dark-purple liquid and a black glass bowl with a series of strange marks etched into it. "I found an incantation to apply in conjunction with dream walking and thought projection. We will ask to be shown either the source or solution to the problem."

"Either? Why not just one?" Tiehro asked, his frown deepening. "Doesn't this open us up to confusion?"

"Because we don't know what is or isn't connected to another person. There has to be someone that we reach for this. Besides, how hard would it be to sort out which one it is? It's safer this way. Trust me. I've worked it all out. You just need to do what I say."

Rhea hugged herself, uneasy. Salanca never needed help with mindreading. Her dream walking and dream weaving abilities were at such a profound level even as a child that it was a Neyeb elder who lovingly referred to her as the Tapir when he brought her to the home. In the past months, she had been expanding those skills into more arcane pursuits. A prickle of unease curled up her spine. "What exactly would we be doing?"

"Excellent question." Salanca pushed the table to the back of the room and kicked the rug aside. "It's very simple. We make the preparations and drink this special serum that will intensify our abilities. I will make the connection and send us forward to the source or solution, Tiehro will bolster it, ground it, and project it into Rhea's mind, and Rhea will interact with whoever it is and bring back the report."

"Salanca, we have no idea where this person is or if they even exist," Tiehro responded. "And if it is so simple, why wouldn't the Paras have done it or even the Council of Elders?"

"Because they didn't have this." She tapped her fingers on the black glass bowl. "Trust me. All right? Besides, it would take time to get it to them, and then you know how much time it would take for them to determine what could be done and how and whether it would be wise. And I don't know about you, Tiehro, but I don't want to go back into those dreams."

"I don't either," he said tightly. "But I don't want either of you hurt. This puts Rhea at tremendous risk. She is the one whose mind will be connected to this person."

"If there's a problem, she can end the connection, and we will pull her back. We'll pull her back regardless if it takes too long." She placed her hand on his arm, her fingers curling over his dark-green sleeve. "The only reason this is not dangerous is because it is the combination of our specific abilities. Because of you, we have far stronger power and focus. That is what your new sodiwa wants from you, yes? Because of me, that power and focus can be focused in the right place. And because of Rhea, we will see beyond the veil and understand what is happening without having to diminish either of our focuses. This is so perfect, it is as if we were destined to do this."

Rhea tightened her arms over her chest. "This isn't part of the Forbidden Arts, right?"

"Dream walking and thought projection form the foundation for so much of the Neyeb and Tiablo tradition," Salanca responded. "Without them, we would lack most of our abilities. There's nothing forbidden in using them."

"But what happens if Rhea is exposed and bound to someone evil?" Tiehro snapped. "You and I will be safe. She's the one who will be seen. There's too much we don't know. My strength and focus have been waning."

"It's better than nothing," Salanca responded.

"It could damage or kill you! Either of you. What if the answer is beyond our reach? What if it takes us beyond my ability to ground and yours to channel? I would rather die than see either of you harmed."

"Tiehro..." Salanca started, pinching the bridge of her nose as if she didn't know where to begin.

If this remained unchecked, one day her family would collapse and never wake again. Rhea hugged herself tighter. "I'll do it."

"See!" Salanca gestured toward her, her face brightening though her expression seemed rather crazed with her blood-shot eyes. She scooted the low table back and then grabbed for the seat cushions. "Now you have to help, Tiehro. It'll be far more dangerous if it's just Rhea and me."

A muscle jumped in his jaw as he looked between them, arms folded tight over his chest. "All right. But no unnecessary risks."

Salanca scoffed as if such a thing was unimaginable. She then instructed them to help her finish moving the furniture back to give them plenty of space in the center of the room. After that, they put the sitting cushions in a triangle on the floor, and each sat. She uncorked the vial with the purple liquid and offered it to Rhea. "Each of us needs to drink this. It enhances our abilities."

The glass bottle weighed heavy in Rhea's hand. She turned it over, watching the dark liquid slosh within. It smelled like tart raspberries.

"You remember how to cut the connection in dream walking and thought project, yes?" Tiehro asked softly, his gaze fixed on her. "Always look for the walls."

She nodded. One of the advantages of having a Neyeb spirit sister and Tiablo spirit brother. "I remember." Drawing in a full breath, she took a mouthful. At first, it tasted only like raspberries, then it became muddy, then once again it became like raspberries, the final note turning to something far more acidic and similar to a bitter red wine. She grimaced. Already her mouth was uncomfortably dry. "I don't suppose we can drink anything else?" She passed it to Tiehro as she wiped her mouth.

"Afraid not." Salanca held out her hand as Tiehro took his

swig and pulled a dramatically perturbed expression. "Don't be such a child about it."

"That's disgusting." He handed it to her anyway.

Salanca lifted the bottle up as if toasting them and then tipped a mouthful past her lips. Shaking her head, she then poured the remnant into the black glass bowl. That bright sweet scent filled the air. "It isn't really when you consider what this could require." Carefully, she placed the bowl between them and then removed a knife from the sheath on her sash.

Rhea opened her mouth to say something, but the words died on her tongue.

Was she—was she doing what she thought?

Salanca slit a line across her palm, then dripped the dark blood into the bowl. After setting the knife aside, she removed small pouches from the pocket of her dark-blue skirt. She emptied those contents into the bowl as well. Herbs. Hair. Chopped bark.

"What are you doing?" Tiehro's eyes widened. He lifted his hand. "You said this wasn't from the Forbidden Arts."

"Not all of it." Salanca bit her lower lip as she wrung more blood out into the bowl. "Most of it isn't at all. So don't even worry about it. The only reason this little tiny part is forbidden is because of the pain and harm to me, but I'm more than willing to pay it. It isn't nearly as bad as you might think."

Rhea opened her mouth to speak, the hair on the back of her neck prickling up. The Forbidden Arts were forbidden because of how dangerous they were and because they relied on the pain and suffering of others. "Whose suffering is this drawing on?" she said, struggling to form the words.

"Only mine. I know what I'm doing. But do not waste my

time with more questions. This is our only opportunity. I'm paying the price regardless. Let's at least have a chance at solving this problem, all right? If you don't do what you're told though, you make it dangerous for all of us."

Tiehro's eyes flashed with confusion, anger, and fear. Reaching over, he gripped Rhea's hand and squeezed it tight.

The edges of her vision had already started to blur, and an intense humming filled her ears, strong enough it was as if it wanted to drag her into the floor and down into the earth below.

Vaguely she heard him say something. The words danced around her consciousness. The dryness of her mouth and the cotton sensation in her ears absorbed so much of her focus, she scarcely felt Salanca take her hand. A vague panic rose within her. The colors intensified around her, bleeding out into a pool of inky black that absorbed the entirety of her vision.

Strings danced in front of her face, plucking and going taut. Wind stirred, then swept faster around her. It tugged at her hair, nearly pulling it free from its clasp.

She was floating in darkness, but those strings plucked. They sang with little cries and muted whispers. Water surged and trickled and splashed somewhere in the distance, at once as loud as if she stood in the tidal path of the ocean and then somehow as quiet as if a small creek chuckled beyond the forest and over a hill.

Nothing held her hands now. She floated freely through the air, blinking and trying to focus. Though she could not see, she knew she was moving. Somehow. Somewhere.

Glass shattered somewhere to her right. Rocks snapped and cracked. She spun around, her hair whipping into her face. Energy sparked, and thunder boomed. Something like lightning tore through the air, lighting up an enormous cave.

The air changed, turning cold for a breath.

Purple light shimmered around her, brilliant and undulating. A more intense shade as the puffs of fog that appeared over Tiehro and Salanca when the nightmares trapped them.

Something pulled her away, out from the open air and onto black stone. Veins of the same purple light branched out across the walls and ceiling, brimming and pulsing with jagged energy.

Was this what had caused the attacks? The plague? The curse?

As she moved farther away from it, it looked like an actual tear in the air itself. Purple light enflamed with blue and silver veins that arced and stretched at intervals like a dying heartbeat and a raging lightning storm at once. Beneath it was a mass of purple light with amethyst and silver streaks bubbling and churning.

Where even was this? What defining features were within this cave that she could even recall?

She stretched her hand out and opened her mouth to call Tiehro and Salanca. But her voice stuck in her throat. They were close, but she had moved beyond them somehow. The veil they'd mentioned—whatever that was—it was thick. The air had gone thicker too, all the sound and energy fuzzing in her ears as if there were thousands of bees clustered around her head.

But she wasn't alone. The air clung to her, crackling with energy and tension.

This had to be the source. Was there also a solution?

A perpetrator—she fell back.

Wait. No.

He stood—well, not exactly. He was half snake. Really more than half by the length of those coils. From the waist up, he looked like a man. He held a long-handled weapon of some sort as he swayed back and forth, his features blurred in a mass of indigo, turquoise, green, and cerulean. A naga? He lunged at something in the shadows with a snarl.

Then everything went black.

2

IN HIS MIND

Rhea looked around slowly as the darkness receded, blinking to moisten her dry eyes. They burned a little even now. But wherever she was, she had arrived. Whether at the source or the person who could help them fix it.

The hazy heaviness still filled her ears, not so intense as before yet more compelling. The more she listened to it, the more it droned, lulling her into a peaceful state, willing her to forget and simply exist in this place.

Wherever it was.

She pressed her eyes shut for a moment. No. No lulling away. Time to figure out what was going on. She could do this.

She was here to find the source or the solution. Salanca had formed the connection. Tiehro was strengthening it. She just had to observe and return. She cracked her eyelids open and tried to take everything in.

Hmm.

Not quite what she'd expected.

278

No longer did she hover above a cavern floor. No, now she was in a relatively small but luxurious chamber. Thick shiny satin turquoise cushions sat on striped rugs. Small carvings rested in shelves carved directly in the wall. But each time she tried to focus on the little carvings, they seemed to dissolve or move. The dark stone of the walls seemed more purple at some points, then more a deep grey, then charcoal. Sometimes indigo if she didn't focus on them at all.

A wardrobe with serpents, dragons, and other creatures carved into its frame in brilliant detail filled another cubby directly carved into the wall. The floor itself was smoothed dark stone.

As she turned, she observed a large bed pressed up against the wall, rich with bright silk sheets, padded blankets, and thick pillows.

All right. So this was a bedroom. What next? She squinted. Was anyone even here?

The covers on the bed stirred. Then a man sat up, frowning as he looked at her. "Hello?"

Oh.

Hello indeed. Her mouth went dry as she struggled to find words. It wasn't that she had never seen a man without his shirt or a handsome man half-naked, but he stole her breath just by sitting there. His powerfully-sculpted shoulders and ridged abdominals left no doubt regarding his strength. Yet the striking planes of his face outdid those, his bold features highlighted all the more by tapered lines that curled at his forehead and cheeks as well as over his biceps and shoulders like inky tiger stripes. His hair was a deep, rich-blue, some-where between cobalt, indigo, and black. Most of it had been bundled back into a series of braids with the odd silver bead and large blue and turquoise feathers worked in.

His eyes though—those stole her breath. Deep jade-green with a hint of gold around the pupils and scattered throughout. Highlighted with speckles of indigo and spots of light-peridot. A complex mixture of caution, sadness, grief, and loneliness overshadowed by a heavy brow. Over the years, she had sketched, painted, and drawn many portraits and often delighted in the depiction of eyes. Capturing personality and nature in a single still image. His would have challenged a master artist.

The man pulled a hunting knife out from under his pillow, pushed the thick shining blankets off, and stepped out of the bed, scowling. His long flowing turquoise trousers hitched up on his right leg, revealing additional stripes along his ankle and calf. "What are you?"

"Can you see me?" She folded her arms over herself, suddenly self-conscious. She hadn't really thought about whether anyone could see her. "Can you hear me? I'm here to help, not harm."

"Yes," he said slowly. He lowered the knife, and his expression became less hostile. "Somewhat. You're like a diamond of light. What are you?"

Salanca had said it would be obvious whether someone was the source or the solution. What was she missing? Was it possible that he was something else? She pressed her hands over her heart, a thought flowing to her lips before she even processed it. "I think you're in great trouble."

He scoffed, but the faintest of smiles appeared over his full lips. "You think?"

"Well, many are. There's some sort of plague or curse or attack that keeps happening. It's pouring out through the worlds. And something started it. My family and I used an— something to try to find the source or the solution of this, and before it brought me here, it showed me a naga." A terrifying naga. She'd read about them in stories. A shiver coursed through her. "Then it brought me here. So you're connected somehow. And my gut tells me you're in trouble too."

"Your gut." He blinked slowly, then sat on the foot of the bed. Its black frame rested almost on the floor, low enough she couldn't slip a shoe under it. "This is...rather confusing. I am struggling to keep up. I hate nagas. And snakes. Let's move this conversation back." He pressed his hands together and gestured toward her. "What are you exactly?"

She slipped closer to him, her pulse throbbing faster. "Just an Awdawm. An artist. An Awdawm artist."

His smile returned, broader this time. Oh. It made her heart stutter, and as it reached his eyes, they shone with rich-green depths that she could get lost in if she didn't pay attention. Thank Elonumato he couldn't actually see her expression. "Awdawms can't do this," he said, his tone now far more amiable. "Not unless something has changed."

"Usually not. But my family includes a gifted Neyeb and Tiablo." One of whom got access to something arcane and was probably among the Forbidden Arts and was probably going to cause a lot of problems for all of them. "So that does change things a little."

"And you came here..."

"To get answers."

He brushed the back of his knuckle against his cheek. "I don't have any to give. I am as confused as you."

"Let's start with your name and where you live? Your world's name? Where are we?"

He scowled once more, then shook his head. "No. Even if this is only a dream, some things are too dangerous. There is power in names, and I cannot guarantee we would not be overheard."

She sat at the other end of the bed. "All right then. But we'll still need something to call one another. What should I call you?"

He scoffed again, a slightly more mirthful tone in his voice. "I don't even know. Bitter. Or Sour perhaps."

"What about Chicory?"

He laughed. "Why that?"

Because his eyes were the color of jade chicory. She shrugged, then realized he might not be able to see the movement. "Because chicory can be bitter, but it is still important."

The left side of his mouth tweaked up. "Well...I suppose that is not so bad. Other than your name, which you should not tell me in a place like this, what should I call you? Sweet, perhaps?"

She wrinkled her nose. "No. I'm not really that Sweet. And not Sugar either. Or Honey." The only reason she tolerated Bunny from her family was because they had called her that when they were children. Or they were Killoth who just managed to make it seem charming rather than insulting.

"That's all right. I prefer salty to sweet anyway. Or salty sweet."

"Then Salt works." It really didn't fit. But the fact that he liked it suddenly made it more palatable. "Or Salt-Sweet." Heat warmed her cheeks. Were they flirting? She really shouldn't be flirting.

No. Wait.

This wasn't flirting. She was gaining information. Yes. That's what it was. She straightened her shoulders.

"Well, Salt-Sweet. I should warn you that I don't know how long I can make this haven last. I don't know how safe it is for you here. I don't even know that I'll remember this conversation when I wake."

"You're dreaming now?" It did feel rather like a dream.

"I don't really know. Perhaps? Most of me, anyway." His gaze drifted to the door as he tapped the back of his knuckle to his cheek. "Part of me is out there...fighting."

"Fighting what?" Her throat tightened as her fingers bunched into fists. "Is it the nagas?"

"Everything," he sighed. His eyelids slid shut. He rubbed his palm over his eye. "Everything all at once. It's bad here. And getting worse by the day. The fighting never ends. Eventually we will lose. Unless we find answers." His gaze grew distant as if he struggled to speak. "I don't—I don't think there are any real answers left."

She edged closer. "Where is here? Can you at least tell me that?"

"Beneath..." He drew his hand over his brow and then tilted his head. "Wait. You said that your friends—they aren't here with me. With my people. They're in other worlds? This has reached other worlds too? This cursed plague?"

"Yes. And eventually they're trapped in comas. Once they're in the coma, they don't wake up. Some of them are dying. Can you help us?"

"I did not know. This—this wasn't—" He stared off at the wall. "You should be careful, Salt-Sweet. This isn't—I don't even understand all that is happening here. I am so sorry that it has spilled into the other worlds. My people— we've done all we can to prevent that. But it is getting out of hand. I have to protect them. If that means I must sacrifice myself, then..."

"Sacrifice yourself?" She moved in front of him. "Chicory, tell me how to help you. I can take whatever message you want taken to anyone who will listen. I will find a way to speak to the Paras if you want."

"The Paras?" He blinked, his brow furrowing more as he avoided looking directly at her.

"Do you not know what they are? They're the leaders who oversee all use of the Tue-Rah and the worlds but not the leaders of individual nations. They are trying to find a solution to this problem with world and national leaders. If you can give me something to tell them, I'll take the message to them right away—"

He grimaced, doubling forward. "You need to go. Please. Go. I don't want you to see this, Salt-Sweet. No one—no one should see this." Heavy thuds sounded outside. As if a great force lashed at the door with heavy blows.

"Wait. See what?" She moved in front of him. Energy shimmered around him, blurring her vision. "Chicory, what's wrong? Please. Tell me! I'm going to get help, but you have to tell me what's going on here."

Something cracked. A loud crackling series of pops followed as if glass were exploding. Something wet struck her face.

She pulled back, holding up her hands to shield her face.

The world tumbled, spun, and burned. She struck something flat and hard, and the wind was driven from her lungs.

"Rhea?" Tiehro's voice sounded far away and muffled, but it grew steadily closer. The spinning sensation continued as strong hands seized her at the shoulders. "Rhea, follow my voice back."

It didn't even take conscious thought. It was as if someone had just swept her into a current and now pulled her along.

The air turned cold and thin, the intense scent of blood,

berries, and smoke singeing her nostrils. Gasping, she started, her fingers digging into the wooden floor.

Tiehro and Salanca loomed over her, staring, concern in their faces. Tiehro's shoulders slumped with relief. He covered his face, releasing a jagged sigh.

Salanca's face brightened. "You made it back, I knew you would!" she cried, dragging her up into a hug. "Tiehro, make the tea now. Rhea, deep breaths. Collect your thoughts. Then tell me everything. Don't try to talk just yet though. You probably won't be able to for a little while longer. Just a side effect. Nothing permanent."

Rhea blinked slowly, her mind still spinning. She'd made it back. Somehow.

Her hands hung heavy at her sides, her movements clumsy.

Tiehro shifted her up onto one of the cushions and gave her water to drink. Her chest ached as if hollow though. Chicory's face filled her mind. Poor Chicory. Sweet Chicory. Trapped in a cavern and battling the nagas. The thoughts tumbled and tangled in her mind, but one thing that remained clear was how much he needed her and how much she needed to get back to him.

Continue Rhea's story in *Slaying the Naga King*.

COLLECT THE ENTIRE MORTAL ENEMIES TO MONSTER LOVERS SERIES!

Read these scorching hot romances in any order for monstrous romance, morally grey leads, and guaranteed happily-ever-afters!

Discover them at www.mortalenemiestomonsterlovers.com

THE OFFICIAL PLAYLIST

Want to listen along while you read and immerse yourself into the world? Listen to the playlist below!

1. If I Had A Heart by Rachel Hardy
2. Wolves Without Teeth by Of Monsters and Men
3. Ice Queen by Within Temptation
4. No Light, No Light by Florence + The Machine
5. Lullaby of Silence by Jenia Lubich
6. Hands by Jewel
7. Every Breath You Take by The Police
8. Stand My Ground by Within Temptation
9. To Be Human by Marina
10. Nemo by Nightwish

ACKNOWLEDGMENTS

Morozko and Eirah want to thank you so much for reading their story! We absolutely love these characters and we hope you enjoyed it. If it doesn't snow where you are, we're sending you snow magic vibes now!

Our first thank you is to our families, who inspire us each day to continue to make stories. To the other Mortal Enemies to Monster Lovers authors, Carissa, Clare, Jessica, and Helen, thank you for allowing us to be a part of this wonderful series! And to Miranda for being kind enough to invite this book to be part of the series.

The book wouldn't be what it is without these wonderful people! Amber H., Jerica, Lou, Jackie, Ann, and Hayley. You guys are our very own real magic.

And a big shout out to our lovely readers! You are why we write and what drives us to continue. So thank you! Now, if only we could find a way to truly visit Frosteria and meet these characters, but for now, we'll use our imaginations.

MORE FROM CANDACE

Demons of Frosteria Series

Frost Mate (Prequel Novella)

Frost Claim

Faeries of Oz Series

Lion (Short Story Prequel)

Tin

Crow

Ozma

Tik-Tok

Vampires in Wonderland Series

Rav (Short Story Prequel)

Maddie

Chess

Knave

Wicked Souls Duology

Vault of Glass

Bride of Glass

Marked by Magic

The Bone Valley

Merciless Stars

Cruel Curses Trilogy

Clouded By Envy

Veiled By Desire

Shadowed By Despair

Cursed Hearts Duology

Lyrics & Curses

Music & Mirrors

Immortal Letters Duology

Dearest Clementine: Dark and Romantic Monstrous Tales

Dearest Dorin: A Romantic Ghostly Tale

Campfire Fantasy Tales Series

Lullaby of Flames

A Layer Hidden

The Celebration Game

Mirror, Mirror

Standalones

These Vicious Thorns: Tales of the Lovely Grim

Between the Quiet

Hearts Are Like Balloons

Bacon Pie

Avocado Bliss

MORE FROM ELLE

Demons of Frosteria

Frost Mate

Frost Claim

Immortal Realms Trilogy

Seeds of Sorrow

Tides of Torment

Wages of War (Feb '24)

The Hunter Series

Hunter's Truce

Royal's Vow

Assassin's Gambit

Queen's Edge

Secrets of Galathea

Brotherhood of the Sea

Bindings of the Sea

Voice of the Sea

King of the Sea

Standalones

The Dragon's Bride

The Castle of Thorns

About Candace Robinson

 Candace Robinson spends her days consumed by words and hoping to one day find her own DeLorean time machine. Her life consists of avoiding migraines, admiring Bonsai trees, watching classic movies, and living with her husband and daughter in Texas—where it can be forty degrees one day and eighty the next.

Stay up to date by signing up for Candace's newsletter! http://eepurl.com/dhV0yv

Join Candace's Facebook group and hang out with her
facebook.com/groups/candacesprettymonsters

Follow Candace on social media!

 facebook.com/literarydust
instagram.com/candacerobinsonbooks

ABOUT ELLE BEAUMONT

Elle Beaumont loves creating vivid and fantastical worlds. She lives in South-eastern, Massachusetts with her husband and two children. When not writing, she enjoys candle-making, crocheting, and taking care of her menagerie of animals. More than once, she has proclaimed that coffee is the lifeblood, and it is how she refrains from becoming a zombie.

Stay up to date and receive some free books by signing up for her newsletter! ellebeaumontbooks.com/newsletter

Join Elle's Facebook group and hang out with her
facebook.com/groups/ElleBeaumontStreetTeam

For more information visit
www.ellebeaumontbooks.com
Follow Elle on social media!

f facebook.com/ellebeaumontbooks
⊙ instagram.com/ellebeaumontbooks